NEW STORIES
FROM THE SOUTH

The Year's Best, 1989

edited by
Shannon Ravenel

NEW STORIES
FROM THE SOUTH

The Year's Best, 1989

Algonquin Books of Chapel Hill

published by
Algonquin Books of Chapel Hill
Post Office Box 2225, Chapel Hill, North Carolina 27515-2225
a division of Workman Publishing Company, Inc.
708 Broadway, New York, New York 10003

ISBN 0-945575-27-0

CONTENTS

PREFACE

"I always look forward to Ravenel's Preface to see if she's figured out how to define 'South'. She hasn't."

JAY PAUL, *Daily Press*, Newport News, Va.
in a review of *New Stories from the South, 1988*

The fifteen short stories in this fourth volume of *New Stories from the South*—culled from the 175 American magazines and literary journals I read over the course of the year—were first published in 1988. Thus all the stories here are certainly "new," as advertised. What's more, all fifteen authors claim Southern places of birth and raising. So, map-wise at least, the "From the South" part of the title's promise is also met. So much for the easy part. The tougher questions have to do with what it is about these writers' work that reflects their Southernness and whether it is sensible or useful to select and collect stories on the basis of geographical location.

Without my ever meaning it to, this Preface has become for me something of an annual inquisition: "So, how do you define The South *this* year?" (The voice I imagine asking this question has an intimidating Northeast accent.) I offer up the phrases and images that always seem to work so well in those travel pieces on the South —things like Mason-Dixon Line, the Old Confederacy, magnolias. "That's not what I mean," my inquisitor sneers. "And you know it." This is when the cold sweat breaks out and the longer I try, the harder it gets to describe exactly what the South means in literary terms (and, remember, it was hard for Quentin Compson, too). Calling it "a state of mind" sounds like a cop-out as well as a cliché and it may be as close as I ever come to a definition.

But whether or not I can define either the South or Southern literature, conventional wisdom has it that both exist. And when the term "regional" is used in literary discussion, it is most often used to indicate writing from and/or about the South, as if it went without saying that the South is the only region of this country that has produced a geographically identifiable literature. The *Village Voice*'s review of last year's volume opened with this question to the reader: "Can you imagine a book called *New Stories from the North*?"

Maybe it's a habit and we've all just gotten used to meaning Southern when we say "regionalism" and to expecting certain things of literature from the South. For new writers who happen to have been born and/or raised in the South, this habit is, in some respects, advantageous. It's hard and lonely trying to break into the American literary scene and a ready-made identity helps in getting noticed. On the other hand, having one's work directed by a set of expectations based on characteristics of past Southern writing is not an advantage.

Back in the 1950s, in high school, I took an after-school-hours, non-credit class in something new called Creative Writing. The teacher, who sold her own Southern short stories to *McCall's* and *The Ladies Home Journal*, gave everyone in our class of five teenaged girls a sheet that outlined, in mimeograph purple, the elements of fiction: Characterization, Plot, Setting. Under Setting, there was the phrase "local color." Remember local color? For a seventeen-year-old would-be writer living in Charleston, South Carolina, it was the obvious sub-element of fiction to employ and so, for me, meeting the requirements of Setting resulted in stories fairly dripping with honeysuckle and Confederate jessamine. Those stories did not manage to transcend the trap of local color—I was a young perpetrator of regionalism gone wrong.

For Southern writers, regionalism is a two-way street. Headed in the wrong direction it creates "Hee Haw." (Pat Conroy says that his mother once told him all Southern literature is a variation on one story: "On the night the hogs ate Willie, Mama died when she heard what Papa did with Sister.") Headed in the right direction —that is, allowed to take its natural course—it can nurture writers who have ties to the South and who write "what they know." And, in this day and age, the result of that combination fits no expected patterns. The fifteen stories gathered here are testimony. As far as Plot and Character go, what happens in these stories and to whom it happens could happen anywhere to anybody. It's the way what happens is perceived and related that unites this fiction in Southernness. Exactly why that is so is where the difficulty of definition comes in and the point at which I fall back on "the South as a State of Mind."

The real business of this anthology is not my struggle with definitions. Its real business is to celebrate the vivid diversity of that Southernness in new fiction writers from the South. These fifteen short stories are as different from each other as their authors' home towns are, as different as Oxford, Mississippi, is from Atlanta, Georgia, or as Charlottesville, Virginia, is from Browns, Alabama. But besides being from the South, the stories do all have one other thing in common: they are unexpected. See if you don't agree.

Shannon Ravenel

PUBLISHER'S NOTE

The stories reprinted in *New Stories from the South, The Year's Best, 1989* were selected from American short stories published in magazines issued between January and December 1988. Shannon Ravenel annually consults a list of more than 175 nationally-distributed American periodicals and makes her choices for this anthology based on criteria that include original publication first-serially in magazine form and publication as short stories. Direct submissions are not considered.

NEW STORIES
FROM THE SOUTH

The Year's Best, 1989

Lewis Nordan

A HANK OF HAIR,
A PIECE OF BONE

(from *The Southern Review*)

The summer I turned ten years old, I had a secret—it was a small collapsible military shovel, an entrenching tool, it was called.

I saw it in a junk store in Arrow-Catcher, my little hometown in Mississippi, and something about the fold-up-and-tuck-away nature of the implement made it attractive to me. At the same time I almost bought a metal canteen with a canvas cover—the metal dented and scratched, the canvas sun-faded and water-stained, ripe with authenticity. I envisioned filling it with Coca-Cola and, at night, secretly removing the cap and drinking lustily and privately in the dark. But when I unscrewed the lid and smelled inside, there was a hint of something that may have been urine, and so I passed on the canteen and paid my dollar for what was the real treasure anyway, the secret shovel.

There was no reason to hide the shovel; no one would have cared that I had it. And yet it was an instrument that begged to be hidden.

My bedroom was in the upstairs of my parents' home. It was small and interesting, with drawers and bookcases built into the walls to conserve space. In one wall there was also a desk, with pigeonholes and an inkwell, that could be revealed by unhooking a metal hook and dropping the desktop into place. There was a nice privacy in the hidden quality of the furniture in the walls.

And as long as I'm describing the room, I might as well tell that

I

on the ceiling above my bed my mother had pasted luminous decals of stars and a moon and the planets—Saturn was prominent with its rings—and a comet with a tail. For a while after I turned off the lights at night, the little lunar system above me glowed with whatever sweet magic there is in such novelties. Outside my window the vastness of the Delta sky and its bright million stars and peach-basket-sized moon could not compete with the galaxies inside my tiny bedroom and all its hidden geographies.

What I'm really getting at, though, is that in the back of my clothes closet—behind the hangers with trousers and shirts, behind the winter coats in plastic bags—there was a panel that could be removed to allow entrance into an even more secret spot, a crawl space in the rafters.

On the day I bought the shovel, I removed the panel in the back of the closet and slipped inside the crawl space to sit.

I had a stash of kitchen matches, from which I chose one and struck it and lighted a stub of a candle and then, careful not to set a fire, extinguished the match and spit on the tip. I sat cross-legged and sweaty in my hideout, inhaling the bad air of insulation and candle smoke, and thrilled at the invisibility of things.

And that was how I lived with my shovel for a while, I'm not sure how long, a couple of weeks I think.

Every day, when there was time, I crept into the crawl space and found the wooden matches and lighted the candle stub and extended the collapsed handle of the shovel and heard the extension snap into place. And then, in the broiling Mississippi afternoon, or mornings if I woke early enough, or sometimes at night when I should have been in my bed beneath the fake stars, my life was filled with the joy of secret things in secret places.

Soldier, miner, escaping prisoner—these were the games I played with the entrenching tool.

I had not yet used the shovel out-of-doors.

The summer inched through its humid hours. The figs on the trees along the chicken-yard fence swelled up ("swole up," we said) and ripened and turned purple and fat. I played barefoot and barebacked in the shade of the broad fig leaves and sometimes picked the fruit from the limbs and watched the ooze of fig milk from the stem as it covered my fingers. The figs were like soft wood on my tongue, and a sweet residue of poison hung in the Delta air, where the ditches had been sprayed for mosquitoes.

Some days my father brought home a watermelon, green-striped and big as a washtub, and the three of us, mother, father, and myself, cut it beneath the walnut tree and ate big seedy red wedges of melon in the metal lawn chairs.

Evenings my father fed the chickens—the Plymouth Rocks, the Rhode Island Reds, slow and fat and powdered with dust—and my mother made fig preserves and sealed the syrupy fruit in Mason jars with hot paraffin lids.

It is tempting to look back at this time and to remember only those images of ripeness and joy.

Many evenings my father was drinking whiskey. He never drank before he was bathed and clean at the end of a day's work—he smelled of Lifebuoy soap and Fitch's shampoo and Wildroot Cream Oil, and of course of the Four Roses bourbon, masculine and sweet as wooden barrels.

Sometimes my parents fought their strange fight. The day I am remembering was a Friday.

The three of us were in the kitchen. My mother said to my father, "I wish you wouldn't do that, Gilbert."

I was standing in front of the refrigerator with the door open, looking for nothing in particular.

My father was at the sink with the water running. He held a tall water glass beneath the spigot and allowed it to fill up, and then he poured the glass of water into the sink. He filled the glass again, and then poured it into the sink again. And as the water ran from the tap, he filled the glass and poured out its contents, over and over, glass after glass, maybe twenty times without speaking.

My mother could only say, "I wish you wouldn't do that, Gilbert," as she watched him, silent and withdrawn, filling and pouring, filling and pouring at the sink.

I closed the refrigerator door and watched my father pour out one final glass of water. Then he stopped. This was a thing he did every day, and it gave my mother distress. When he was finished, he did as always—he placed the glass on the sink and stood for a while longer and watched the water run from the pipe into the drain. Then slowly, deliberately, he turned the handle and shut off the flow.

That was the end of it. After the water-pouring episode, my father went to his room and closed the door and my mother went into her own room—she called it a guest bedroom, but it was her own, with her underwear in the drawers, her bobby pins on the dresser—and lay across her bed and cried.

I could hear her from the kitchen, and I could hear music from my father's phonograph, and I knew that he was drinking from a bottle hidden in his chest of drawers and that he would not come out until morning.

I wanted to comfort my mother, but there was nothing to say. I stood by the kitchen sink and looked at the glass my father had been filling and emptying, and I believed for the one millionth time that if I looked at it long enough, tried hard enough, I could understand what my parents' strange fighting meant.

Tonight I went to my father's room, a thing I ordinarily never did after they fought, or after he closed the door and started to drink in earnest.

I knocked at his door and waited. I knew he would not answer and he did not. I knocked again and said, "Daddy," and waited again.

I heard movement inside his room, his chair, I supposed—a green-painted metal lawn chair, which he used as an easy chair—scraping against the hardwood floor. The chair sat on a rounded frame, which allowed it to rock back and forth.

After a silence the door opened and I could tell that my father was already very drunk. He looked at me and finally moved aside to let me in. He sat in his strange lawn chair and his record kept playing softly on the phonograph, a slow ballad sung by Elvis. The whiskey bottle was not in sight.

He said, "What is it, Sugar?"

My father was not a tall man, no more than five feet six inches, and his childlike shoes, with crepe soles and shiny uppers, were covered with tiny speckles of paint. His feet did not reach the floor except as the chair rocked forward. He was wearing Big Smith khakis and an open-necked shirt, and I noticed that the face of his watch was flecked with paint.

I said, "I bought a shovel." I had not known I was going to say this.

My father let a few seconds pass and then he said, "Is that right."

I said, "I've got it in my room."

He said, "Do you want a peppermint puff?" My father reached across the top of the phonograph to a cellophane bag filled with peppermint candy and brought out a small handful and put one piece of candy into his mouth. I held out my hand and received a piece.

I said, "I haven't dug anything with it yet." I put the candy in my mouth, the peppermint puff, and it was light and airy as magic. It seemed almost to float instead of melt inside my mouth.

And then, as unexpectedly as I had announced the existence of the shovel, my father said, "The Delta is filled up with death."

Now that I look back on this moment I think that he meant nothing at all by this remark. Probably the mention of a shovel made him think of graves and that made him think of death, which was his favorite drunken subject anyway. Self-pity, self-dramatization—the boring death-haunted thoughts of an alcoholic, nothing more.

And yet at the time the words that he spoke seemed directly related to my accidental, unintentional mention of the shovel, the way advice is related to a problem that needs to be solved.

I said, "It is?"

He said, "Yep. To the brim."

The conversation was over. I stayed a little longer, but already my father was growing irritable and restless, and I knew he wished I would leave so that he could drink from the bottle in the chest of drawers.

The Delta was filled with death. The information came like a summons, a moral imperative to search.

And so that day, and for many days afterwards, I took the shovel outside and started to dig. In the front yard the shovel blade cut through the grass and scarred the lawn. I replaced the squares of sod before my mother could see the damage, but already I knew I was doing the right thing. Earthworms retreated to cooler, safer depths. Roly-polies curled up into little balls. The blade of the shovel shone at the edges, the dirt was fragrant and cool to my touch.

My first serious digging was a trench alongside the back of the chicken yard, near the fence. The earth there was loamy and soft and worm-rich and easy to dig. I threw spadefuls of loose dirt at the busy old hens and watched them scatter and puff out their feathers as large as beach balls.

What was I digging for? Indians had lived on this land, Chickasaws and Choctaws. Slaves had died here. There might be bones. A well-digger once dug up a Confederate mortar shell near the dog pen, and it was still on display in the Plantation Museum in Leflore. Sometimes a kid would find an arrowhead or spearpoint. My father was right—the remains of other civilizations did still occasionally poke through into our own.

So there was a sense in which I was only following my father's advice—I was digging for evidence of other worlds. And for a while the hard work of digging, and the work of hiding its consequences, were enough.

The trench by the fence was a mistake. A neighborhood dog crawled under and killed my father's blue Andalusian rooster, and I had to fill the trench and get the dog out before anyone could figure out that I was responsible. I threw the dead rooster into some tall weeds near the trailer where the midgets lived, and so my father thought it had flown the coop and been killed as a result of its own restlessness and vanity. So that was good.

I kept on digging. All the holes I dug were in some way unsatisfactory.

Beneath the walnut tree the earth was rock hard and root-congested and I was afraid of breaking the shovel handle.

The last of several holes I dug on the lake bank, which was softer ground, finally yielded a few bones, but they were in a plastic garbage bag and, though it took me a while, I finally understood that they were the skeleton of a big tomcat that belonged to a neighbor-woman, Mavis Mitchum. The cat had been hit by a car last winter.

Along the ditch at the back of the house I dug up a nest of ground-hornets and was stung seven times. I dug each day and found a good deal of unpleasantness but little death in the Delta.

I have to ask the question again: What was I digging for?—skeletons?—Indians? Not really, not at first, though I thought of those things in a general way. I think I was only playing, only digging for fun. I was a child, and I enjoyed child's play, as I had enjoyed the games behind my closet, in the crawl space.

And yet the more I dug—the greater number of holes I emptied and refilled, the more often I heard the shovel blade cut the soil and breathed the mold-and-mulch-rich fragrance of overturned earth and felt its heft in my hands, and watched the retreat of the earthworms and the vivid attack of the hornets and the other evidences of life beneath the surface of the earth—mole tunnels and rabbit holes—the more I feared and was driven to discover evidence of death.

And so by some process I became not the soldier or prisoner I had pretended to be in the crawl space, not a child with a game, but a person driven by some need born of my father's pain, my mother's despair.

My occupation became not only more necessary but more real, more dark in character. I was no longer pretending to be a soldier or prisoner, but now, without the protection of fantasy at all, I was a real-life grave digger, possessed and compulsive—and not merely a grave digger but a hopeful grave robber, a sad innocent little ghoul spading my way through the Delta looking for God knows what, some signal or symbol, I don't know, whatever a child in need and fear is capable of looking for after talking to his drunken father about a shovel.

I don't blame my father. What would be the point? There is a sense in which I blame the geography itself, though that, of course, is useless as well.

The more I dug in the Delta earth, the more it seemed to call me to dig, the more certain I became that it would finally yield up some evil treasure.

I turned over spadeful after spadeful. I dug all over our small property—backyard and front yard and chicken yard. I dug out by Roebuck Lake, and even in Mavis Mitchum's yard, the neighborwoman. Some of the holes were deep, some were long shallow trenches. I looked in each spadeful of earth for some sign—a toe, a tooth, some small thing, a knuckle. There was nothing.

I moved underneath the house—(Delta houses have no basements)—and here beneath the floorboards and water pipes, in the slick, sun-untouched hard-packed earth, my digging took new meaning. No longer frantic, no longer directionless, my entire body slowed down, the way a body is slowed down by age. I was a strong child—thin but sturdy—and I had the will to dig, the iron will of a child's burden of his parents' unhappiness. I would dig to China if necessary. I was digging a hole beneath my house, and I knew I would find whatever I had been looking for.

The underside of the house was a different world to me. Suddenly plumbing made sense—pipes going in and coming out. The light was filtered and cool. The dirt was slick and ungrassed for half a century. The outside world, glimpses of it, was allowed into my vision only through chinks in the brick foundation. Above me were the boards of the floor where my parents walked. Refuse had been thrown under here, a slick tire, a bald baby-doll, a wood case of Coke bottles. The house was an old structure, sixty or seventy years old, and other families had lived here before my own. Even in the refuse—the broken glass, a dog food can, two cane poles —there was a sense that lives had been lived here, that death had defeated them.

I kept on digging. I could not stand up to dig—the floor was directly above me—so I lay on my side. I stabbed the blade into the earth and, with the strength of my arms, lifted out the dirt. The work was slow and laborious. Spadeful after spadeful I dragged dirt out of the hole and piled it away from me in a mound.

Each day I was tired and filthy, the muscles of my arms were hot with strain. I worried that my mother would stop me from what I was doing.

She did not. She only knew that I was playing under the house. She warned me about broken bottles, she grouched at me about the dirt in my jeans. But our lives went on. I continued to dig.

There were happy days, with watermelon, and sad days of whiskey. The hole beneath the house grew deeper and wider, and the mound beside the hole grew taller. My father continued to pour glasses of water down the sink, my mother begged him not to. "I wish you wouldn't do that, Gilbert." I had a sense of doing something worthwhile, or at least necessary in the face of the many things I could not otherwise control.

I kept on, possessed I would say, and sometimes fear of what I was looking for would overtake me. I would sit beside the hole and cry—*weep* is a better word, since there was as much drama in this as there was sadness—and often I would wish that I had never heard of this hole, that I had never bought this shovel, that I had bought the wicked canteen instead.

I was afraid that whatever I found—joint, knuckle, or tooth—would be too personal to endure. Suddenly, or rather gradually, this became no abstraction I was searching for, not merely *death*. I believed now that whatever bone I found—and I had no doubt I would find something, however small—was not without a human history, that a single bone was a person, someone whose life was as filled with madness and loss as the lives of my father and mother.

I believed I could not endure knowing more about such sadness than I already suspected. My throat ached. I imagined that whatever relic I found would contain within it the power to reconstruct an entire self, a finger joint becoming a hand, the hand re-creating an arm, the arm a torso, with chest hair and a head and knees. Dry bones becoming meat and, immediately, the meat reclaiming the right and capacity to rot and fall away, the bones to be scattered and lost.

So I continued to dig underneath the house. I dug long past the time when I enjoyed it. It was a job to me, this digging, it was medicine necessary in some way to my continued life, neither joyful nor joyless, a thing to be done, a hole to be dug.

The underside of my house became as familiar to me as the crawl space behind my closet. I stopped digging sometimes and lay on my back beneath the house, beside the hole, which now was deep —two feet deep and two feet wide, and then wider and deeper. I dug down to three feet, and the hole was squared off, like the grave of a child. I kept on digging. I lay in exhaustion, down in the hole, and looked up at the floorboards of the house. I heard my mother's footsteps above me in the kitchen. I heard the boards make their small complaint. Water ran through the pipes around me—surging up through pipes into the house and into the sink, or going the other way, out of the house through the larger pipes, down into the earth and away.

I lay in the dirt and looked at the floorboards, as sweat drained out of me, my back and arms, and soaked down into the same earth. I imagined that my sweat flowed under the earth like a salty river, that it entered the water table and into a seepage of sand grains and clay and, from there, into Roebuck Lake, its dark still waters. Around me sunlight broke through the cracks in the foundation in points as brilliant as diamonds, and underneath my house was always twilight, never day and never dark.

One day in my digging—who can remember which day, a Thursday, a Saturday?—all the summer days were the same—my shovel struck something and my heart stopped, seemed to stop, tried to stop. I had found whatever I had been destined to find. Directed to find: by the man at the junk store, by the canteen, which had whispered *take the shovel not me,* by my father at the sink. My shovel struck something—hard, solid, long, like a sheet of heavy glass, a tabletop—and my heart, stopped dead by fear and awe, cried out for this to be some innocent thing, a pirate's chest, a sewer line.

I took only one look, and never looked again, and so what I tell you is only what I saw, not what I know to have been there. I was lying in the hole I had dug, this grave, its dark dirt walls on four sides of me. I was comfortable with my entrenching tool. I touched the earth again with the shovel, and again heard the noise of its blade against a sheet of heavy glass.

I thought, in that moment before I brushed away the dirt and took one brief look through a glass window into the past, or into my own troubled heart, whichever it really was, of a nursery rhyme my mother had said to me many times at night, beneath the fake stars.

It was the tale of a woman who goes to the fair and falls asleep beneath a tree and, while she sleeps, has the hem of her petticoat cut off and stolen by a thief. Without her petticoat she doesn't recognize herself when she wakes up, and she wonders who this strange woman with no petticoat can be. Even when she gets home and looks in the mirror, she is unfamiliar to herself. She says, "Dearie dearie me, is it really I?"

I could not believe that I was the person with this shovel, on this brink.

I brushed the dirt off the sheet of glass and allowed my eyes their one second of looking. Beneath the glass was a dead woman, beautiful, with auburn hair and fair skin. Her head was resting on a blanket of striped ticking.

One second, less than a second, and I never looked again. I averted my eyes and put down the shovel and crawled up out of the hole. Without looking down into the hole again, I filled the hole with the dirt I had taken out. I pushed it with my hands until it spilled over the sides of the grave and covered the shovel and whatever else was there or not there.

The dress she was wearing was red velvet, down to her ankles. Her shoes were tiny, with pointed toes. The slipper was leather and the boot was of some fabric, silk I thought. On one finger was a gold ring in the shape of a bent spoon.

It is impossible that I saw all this in one glance—her whole length, her tiny feet and fingers. It is impossible that I brushed away a bit of dirt and saw her entirely, her fingers, her hair, an exposed calf that showed the fabric of her boot.

And yet I know that I did see this, and that one second later I covered it up and did not look again.

I sat there in the dirt, beneath the floorboards of my parents' home, and I saw another thing, a gaggle of white geese being chased by a fox, but I knew even then that these were not real geese but only the erratic beating of my heart made visible. The woman in the glass coffin?—still I am not sure what was real and what my mind invented.

The sound of my parents' footsteps was above me, where I sat in the twilight of this cloistered world. In the dead woman's face I had seen my mother's beauty, the warm blood of her passion, as my father had once known her and had forgotten. I heard water running in the sink above me and imagined, whether it was true or not, that it was my father filling and emptying tumblers of water, and all around me I heard this poured-out water gurgling down through pipes, headed for sewers, the water table, the gills of gars in Roebuck Lake. Through the floorboards I could hear voices, the sound not the words, and I believed it was my mother's voice begging my father not to pour his life down this sad drain, glass after glass, day after day, until she too was empty of life and hope.

I kept sitting there, thinking of the dead woman, and I imagined her in a church pew with a songbook on her lap. I imagined her on a riverboat (if she was real she might have died a hundred years before and been buried here, pickled, perfectly preserved in alcohol or some other fluid, mightn't she?—could she not have died on one of the riverboats that once floated from the Yazoo into the Roebuck harbor?), on the deck of a boat and holding a yellow parasol. I imagined her in a green backyard, hanging out sheets on a line. I saw her eat cantaloupe and spit out the seeds, secret and pretty, into a bed of bright flowers. I saw her leading a horse by a blue bridle from an unpainted barn.

I named her pretty names. Kate and Molly and Celia, even Leda, and I called her none of these names for fear of changing something too fragile ever to be named, the same reason I did not look at her longer, for fear she could not exist in the strength of more than a second's looking. In my mind, as I named her, my father's name kept ringing, over and over, with a sound like wooden ducks in a carnival shooting gallery when they are knocked over, the ding and ding and ding, and the slap of their collapse.

I left the underside of the house and never went back.

I went inside and surprised my mother by bathing and washing my hair with Fitch's shampoo in the middle of the afternoon, and without being told. I put my dirty clothes into the washer and set the dial, and while the machine made them clean, I dressed in fresh blue jeans and a button-up shirt and dug the dirt out from under my fingernails and cleaned the mud off my shoes.

In my mind I gave the woman gifts. I gave her a candle stub. I gave her a box of wooden kitchen matches. I gave her a cake of Lifebuoy soap. I gave her a ceilingful of glow-in-the-dark planets. I gave her a bald baby-doll. I gave her a ripe fig, sweet as new wood, and a milkdrop from its stem. I gave her a peppermint puff. I gave her a bouquet of four roses. I gave her fat earthworms for her grave. I gave her a fish from Roebuck Lake, a vial of my sweat for it to swim in.

I combed my hair with Wildroot Cream Oil and ate an entire package of my father's peppermint candy and puked in the toilet.

My mother said, "Sugar, are you all right?"

I said, "You bet," and walked boldly into my father's room and stole two rubbers from a box of Trojans in the drawer of his bedside table, and as long as I had the drawer open, took out his pistol and spun the cylinder and aimed it at the green lawn rocker and cocked the hammer with my thumb and then eased it back down. I stole two bullets from a box of cartridges in the drawer.

Later I walked beside Roebuck Lake and threw away the rubbers and the bullets and hated my father and myself.

* * *

The summer was long and its days were all the same. The poison in the ditches was sweet, the mosquitoes were as loud as violins, as large as owls. The cotton fields smelled of defoliant, and the cotton stalks were skeletons in white dresses. As summer deepened, the rain stopped, and so the irrigation pumps ran night and day in the rice paddies. My father took my mother dancing at the American Legion hut, and I went with them and put a handful of nickles in the slot machine near the bar and won enough money to keep on playing for hours.

The black man behind the bar—his name was Al, and he drove an Oldsmobile—took me to the piano and showed me an eight-beat measure with his left hand and said it was the boogie-woogie beat and that if I listened right I could hear it behind every song ever written, every song that for a lifetime would ever make my toes feel like tap-tap-tapping.

That night it was true, and I still listen for it. I could hear it, this under-music, like a heartbeat, in the tunes my parents were dancing to. I could hear it in the irrigation pumps in the rice paddies. I could hear it in the voice of the preacher at the Baptist church, and in the voices of the pigeons in the church rafters. I heard it in the voice of a carny who barked at the freak show. I heard it in the stories my mother told me at night. I heard it in the tractors in the fields and in the remembered music of my shovel, my entrenching tool, its blade cutting into the earth, and in the swarm of hornets, and in the bray of mules, and in the silence of earthworms.

I watched my father and mother dance in the dim light of the dance floor, the only two dancers that night, and I fell in love with both of them, their despair and their fear and also their strange destructive love for each other and for some music I was growing old enough to hear, that I heard every day in the memory of the woman in her private grave. My father was Fred Astaire, he was so graceful, and my mother—though before this night I had seen her only as a creature in a frayed bathrobe standing in the unholy light of my father's drinking—she was an angel on the dance floor. The simple cotton dress that she wore was flowing silk—or was it red velvet?—and her sensible shoes were pointy-toed leather slippers with a silk boot. I understood why the two of them had been attracted to each other. I understood, seeing them, why they continued in their mutual misery. Who can say it was not true love, no matter how terrible?

In this dim barnlike room—the felt-covered poker tables, the dark bright wood of the dance floor, the upright piano, a lighted Miller sign turning slowly on the ceiling, a nickle slot by the bar —here I loved my parents and the Mississippi Delta, its poisoned air and rich fields, its sloughs and loblollies and coonhounds and soybeans. In everything, especially in the whisk-whisk-whisk of my parents' feet on the sawdusty dance floor, I heard the sound of the boogie-woogie beat, eight notes—five up the scale and three down—I heard it in the clash and clatter of the great machines in the compress, where loose cotton, light as air, was smashed into heavy bales and wrapped in burlap and tied with steel bands. I held onto my secret, the dead woman under our house, and wished that I could have known these things about my parents and our geography and its music without first having looked into the dead woman's face and held inside me her terrible secret.

My father and mother danced and danced, they twirled, their bodies swayed to the music, their eyes for each other were bright. My father sang to my mother an old tune, sentimental and frightening, crooning his strange love to her, *oh honeycomb won't you be my baby oh honeycomb be my own,* he sang, this small man enormous in his grace, *a hank of hair and a piece of bone my honeycomb.* My mother placed her head on his shoulder as they danced, and when she lifted her face he kissed her lips and they did not stop dancing.

There is one more thing to tell.

Late in the summer, deep in August, when the swamps were steam baths, and beavers as big as collies could be seen swimming in Roebuck Lake from a canebreak to a willow shade, I passed my tenth birthday.

I still had told no one about the corpse, if it was a corpse and not something equally terrifying, a vision or hallucination born of heartbreak and loss, beneath our house. The shovel was a forgotten toy.

My mother made me a birthday cake in the shape of a rabbit —she had a cake pan molded in that shape—and she decorated it with chocolate icing and stuck on carrot slices for the eyes. It was a difficult cake to make stand up straight, but with various props it would balance on its hind legs on the plate, so that when I came into the room it looked almost real standing there, its little front feet tucked up to its chest.

At the sight of the rabbit I started to cry. My mother was startled by my tears. She had been standing in the doorway between the kitchen and the dining room. The table was set with a white table-cloth and linen napkins, three settings for my birthday dinner.

I could not stop crying, looking at that rabbit cake. I knew that my mother loved me, I knew something of her grief—something in the desperate innocence of the rabbit, its little yellow carrot eyes. I thought of the hopelessness of all love, and that is why I was crying I think.

My mother came to me and held me to her and I felt her warmth and smelled her woman-smell. I wanted to dance with her at the Legion Hut. I wanted to give her a gift of earthworms.

I kept crying.

My mother said, "Oh, Sugar-man . . ."

I kept on crying, sobbing, trying to talk between the sobs. I said, "There's a woman under the house."

She said, "I know, Sugar-man, I know, hush now . . ."

I said, "I don't want to listen to the boogie-woogie beat."

She said, "I know, darling, I know . . ."

She kept on holding me, rocking me where we stood.

I said, "It's a dead woman. Under our house."

She said, "I know, Sugar-man, I know . . ."

I said, "In a grave."

She said, "I know, darling, you hush now . . ."

I said, "I don't want my toes to go tap-tap-tapping."

Annette Sanford

SIX WHITE HORSES

(from *The Ohio Review*)

In the summer of 1947, Lila Bickell took an interest in a salesman named Terrence V. Dennis.

Her brother Hector said, "*Terrence,* for God's sake!"

Hector was thirty-eight, a teller at the Farmers Union Bank and nice enough looking except for a certain hardness of heart that showed up as a scowl on his nice looking face.

"If I were named Hector," Lila said, "I wouldn't throw stones."

Lila, at forty, was pretty in a careless sort of way that kept people from noticing how small and fine-boned she was, and how generally appealing. She wore any old thing and when she got up in the morning, if her hair misbehaved, she pulled a tam over it and went off to her job at The Quality Shoe Mart, about as content as she would have been otherwise.

Lila and Hector shared a home, a yellow stone cottage that had belonged to their parents until their parents died. Hector grew vegetables in the rambling old garden, and Lila raised flowers she put around in the dark rooms to lighten the furniture.

They each had their chores. Lila cooked and shopped, and Hector did the laundry and cleaned the house. At night they read in two chairs by the fireplace.

They might have gone on that way for a long time except for Terrence, who came one day and knocked on the door when Lila was at home nursing a summer cold.

She thought at first she might ignore the knock. "If I were at work," she told herself, "whoever is there would give up and go away." Then she got out of bed and put on a dilapidated bathrobe and went to see who it was.

Terrence V. Dennis was an honorably discharged veteran selling reconditioned vacuum cleaners. He wasn't as tall as Lila would have liked, and he had a mole on his chin that she intended to suggest he have burned off as soon as they were married.

"Married!" Hector said. "You aren't thinking of that, are you?"

Lila replied, "If Terrence proposes, I'll accept."

That was later, of course, after she found out more about him and kissed him in the grape arbor a number of times.

"A great many men my age have died, Hector." In the war, she meant, but she steered clear of the war because of Hector's embarrassment at not having gone due to a punctured eardrum.

"I think Terrence and I can be happy," she went on. "And that's all anyone wants, isn't it? Just to be happy?"

"I thought we were."

"How can we be, Hector? We aren't fulfilled."

Through the rest of June, Terrence showed up once a week at least to take Lila to the movies. On the Fourth of July he asked her to marry him and after that he came regularly to dinner on Saturday night.

On these occasions he wore a nice jacket of houndstooth tweed and slicked back his hair with some kind of tonic that smelled like chrysanthemums. Hector inhibited him, sitting like a bulldog at the end of the table, but after dessert he usually said something memorable.

One evening he said, "Four out of five women open their doors wearing pink kimonos."

Lila said in surprise, "Mine is tan."

"Four out of five," Terrence reminded.

After he was gone Hector said, "Have you thought about eating with him day after day?"

"He'll be easy to cook for," Lila said. "He eats whatever I put on the table." She was doing what she always did, which was to hum something catchy while she put away the leftovers.

"Does he read at all?"

"Of course he reads."

"I'd like to know what."

"Then ask him, why don't you?"

By then, Hector had let up a little about the vacuum cleaner Lila had bought without consulting him.

The first afternoon he took on terribly. "*I* clean the house. Why should you choose the vacuum?"

"As a little surprise." Lila brought him his gardening boots. "Do you know who you remind me of? Silas Marner, when he smashed his water pot."

"Why didn't you call me? You knew where I was."

"He was about to break down," Lila continued, "and then he found Eppie under the furze bush."

"Under what kind of bush have you hidden my Hoover?"

"This is a good machine, Hector, with quality parts. Terrence sprinkled wet sand on the carpet and it sucked up the whole mess with only one passover."

Lila went on humming and storing what was left from the Saturday night dinner. Hector swept around the table, particularly around Terrence's chair where crumbs of biscuits were strewn like dandruff.

He called out to the kitchen. "Terrence V. Dennis thinks all he has to do to support a wife is knock on doors."

"Well," Lila called back, "that's how he found one."

She hung up her apron and went upstairs to look over the trousseau she was assembling in their parents' bedroom.

The trousseau consisted so far of one white nightgown with flowing peignoir, two peach-colored slips, shoes both black and brown, a serviceable coat that wouldn't show spots and a print blouse with roses on it.

While she was trying the blouse on, Hector appeared with a new pronouncement. "You'll be at The Quality Shoe Mart for the rest of your life."

"I might have been anyway," Lila said. "But if that's the way it works out, I won't mind too much. We aren't planning on babies."

"Babies!" said Hector. "You're too old for that."

"Oh, do you think so?" She slipped on the coat. "Well, anyway I don't want any. I wouldn't make a good parent, and neither would Terrence."

"I can't think of anything Terrence would be good at."

"You aren't fair, Hector. You're rude to him, in fact."

"He asks for rude treatment. He's oily, Lila."

"Oily? What does that mean?"

"Slick," Hector said. "He can't be trusted."

"How do you know?"

"It sticks out all over him."

Lila folded the nightgown and the peignoir and laid them again with the peach-colored slips in a drawer smelling of lavender leaves she had picked from the garden. "You'd better get used to him. We may live nearby." She hung up the coat. "We could live here if you like."

"Here!" said Hector.

"There's plenty of room. He could help with the vegetables."

Lila went off to take her bath. When she came out after a while wearing her worn-out robe, Hector was downstairs reading in their father's chair.

Lila hunted up the book she was halfway through and sat down across from him in their mother's chair.

"I think you hold it against Terrence that he grew up in a carnival."

Hector breathed through pinched nostrils. One of their rules was that neither of them talked while the other was reading. "I thought it was a circus."

"Oh, maybe it was." Lila leaned forward to do a little house-keeping on one of the ferns banking the fireplace.

"No," she reconsidered. "I think it was a carnival. I remember being surprised that a carnival had a band."

"What does a band have to do with it?"

"Terrence's father directed it."

"Terrence's father sold tickets. You told me that yourself."

Lila explained patiently. "He sold tickets first, while the crowd was coming in. Then he put on his uniform and directed the band." Lila moved around in the chair until her spare frame fit it. "It was interesting really. They played from a collapsible platform set up in the midway to keep things lively. When a crowd feels lively, they spend more money."

Hector said sullenly, "What did Terrence do while the band was playing?"

Lila shrugged. "Lessons, I guess. What other children do." She nibbled her lip. "His mother was the circus seamstress."

"Which was it, for God's sake? A circus or a carnival?"

"There's not much difference, is there? Except for the animals. And the trapeze artists. Terrence sang now and then. Have I told you that?"

"No," Hector said, as if more on the subject was too much to bear.

"One of his songs we used to sing ourselves. You remember it, don't you? It went like this." Lila looked toward the rug where Terrence had thrown out the wet sand. " 'She'll be coming a-round the moun-tain when she comes—' " She labored with the melody like a train having trouble going up and down hills. " 'She'll be dri-ving six white hor-ses when she comes—' "

She went through all the verses, the one about killing the red rooster and all the rest, and then she was quiet.

Hector revived slowly. "Terrence sang that? To a crowd who paid money to get on a Ferris wheel?"

Lila shifted her glance to Niagara Falls, confined in a brown frame since 1920. "He did very well, I think, standing up singing in front of people who were eating and talking and not paying attention."

She looked again at Hector. "What do you think about when you hear those words?"

"I don't think of anything. They bore me senseless."

"I think of us when we were children. We never had celebrations."

"We were too poor for celebrations," Hector replied. "The whole world was poor."

"The woman in the song wasn't. Or if she was, it didn't matter." Lila's gaze glazed over with dreamy absorption. "She was just jouncing along in that empty wagon, rushing into town, rushing toward excitement."

Hector scowled. "What empty wagon?"

"The one the horses are pulling. Can't you hear it rattling?" She looked brightly at Hector slumped in his chair. "Everything to fill it is waiting ahead. Like in marriage," she said.

He burst out suddenly, "I hate this damned business with Terrence V. Dennis!"

"Yes. Why is that?" She peered at him closely. "Is it because I'm your sister and you feel you ought to protect me? Or because when I'm married you'll be discommoded?"

She blew out her breath in a despairing little puff. "It's both, I suspect—though I've never been sure just how much you care for me."

"What does that mean?" Hector asked tensely.

"Oh, it's not your fault. No one in this house was ever demonstrative."

She flung out something else as carelessly as a dropped handkerchief. "Our parents never kissed. Have you thought about that?"

Hector got to his feet. "I'm going to bed."

"Oh, do sit down. You ought not to run off when we're finally getting to something."

"Getting to what?"

"To sex," Lila said. "That's why I'm marrying, you know. To experience sex." She watched him sink down again. "Well, haven't *you* ever wanted to?"

"This is not a topic I care to discuss."

Lila said peevishly, "You didn't shy away from it when you showed me those horses—the ones across the creek that we watched through the fence."

"That was thirty years ago!" Hector said in astonishment.

"I know when it was. I remember everything about it—and it's not a happy prospect, realizing I could go to the grave knowing only about horses."

Hector closed his eyes. "Do I owe all this to a summer cold?"

"Terrence would have come along anyway," Lila said. "He was just slow turning up because of the war." She saw Hector flinch and went on more strongly. "That's something else, Hector. We've tiptoed too long around the war."

"For pity's sake, Lila!"

"You were classified 4-F for a legitimate reason. You aren't a coward who has to slink around ashamed for the rest of your life."

"This is worse than the Johnstown flood!"

"You're making it worse," Lila told him crossly. "But why not, I suppose. Look how we've lived—like two dill pickles shut up in a jar."

Lila brooded with her chin in her hand. "If it hadn't been for

Terrence prying the lid off, we might have had a blow-up instead of this civilized conversation."

"Our *life* is civilized because we don't have conversations."

"We're opening locked closets, Hector." Lila gazed dispiritedly at the pale line of his lips. "The trouble is, most of them are empty."

"You can't possibly judge the extent of my experience!"

"When would you have managed any?" Lila asked. "In all your life you've spent three nights away from this house. Two for your tonsils and that one other time when you camped on the river and the bears chased you home."

"It was coyotes, dammit!" Hector leaped from his chair. "You think you know so much. You don't even know that a man and a woman don't necessarily require darkness."

Lila sighed. "If you know it, I know it. We've read the same books."

The following Saturday while Lila was stuffing cabbage for Terrence's dinner, Hector went out in the back garden and ripped up a pear tree. He left a hole the size of an icebox where the roots had been, and green, ruined fruit all over the lawn.

"Our tree!" cried Lila when she stepped out at five to pick mint for the tea. "What's the matter with you, Hector? Are you having a breakdown?"

Hector lay on his back, panting like a lizard. "Can't a man hate pears?"

"You never hated them before. What about in pear marmalade?"

He said from the grass, "The worst thing in the world is pear marmalade."

The week after that, he took to wearing red socks and calling up girls.

On Saturday evening he sailed through the kitchen at five minutes to five. "Tell Terrence I'm bowling," he said to Lila.

"I will," said Lila, watching him go. "If he happens to ask, that's just what I'll say."

Hector continued his Saturday night absences. Summer wore down and fall came on before he perceived that the situation with Terrence had altered somehow.

The first thing he noticed was Lila going to work in her serviceable coat. Next he was dripped on by a peach-colored slip drying in the bathroom. Then he spotted the print blouse with the roses on it laid out for pressing.

He said to Lila, "What's happened to Terrence?"

"Nothing that I know of." Lila hummed. She was putting away meat loaf and *au gratin* potatoes with nice little beans out of Hector's garden.

"You're wearing your trousseau."

"Yes," she said. She didn't explain. She went off upstairs and ran enough water to drown a crocodile. When she came down again, she had on her lace nightgown and matching peignoir.

She smiled at Hector, owlish by the fire, and then at the pear logs, smoking and popping. "Have you seen my book?"

"Your book!" said Hector. "I want to hear about Terrence."

"Oh," said Lila. She took her time sitting down in her mother's chair. "He's off in Oklahoma selling Watkins vanilla."

"Since when?" Hector asked.

"Since the last week in August."

"Well, you might have mentioned it!" Hector recalled wrenchingly the Saturday nights wasted eating restaurant stew and hanging around pool halls until the coast was clear. "Is he gone for good?"

"Yes," said Lila.

He could scarcely believe it. Terrence was gone! In deference to Lila in her celebration raiment with nothing to celebrate, he summoned his scowl. "It's too bad," he said. "The dolt threw you over. But of course he would, anybody fool enough to wear tweed in the summer."

Lila cleared her throat lightly. "He didn't read either—only the funnies."

Hector observed her. She was lovely in white—like a slice of angel food cake—and not at all dampened by her sad experience.

"What was the *V* for?" he brought out of nowhere.

"Victor," said Lila. She consulted the ceiling. "Or perhaps it was Vincent. Or Vernon or Virgil."

Hector stared at her, pop-eyed. "You never asked?"

"I intended to once. But he wasn't around."

"Well," said Hector. "It was plain from the start he had nothing to offer."

"Plain to you maybe. You have a man's eye for things." A piece of bright hair tumbled over her shoulder. "To me he seemed interesting. He grew up in a circus."

"In a carnival, Lila."

"Whatever it was, he had a very good childhood. He was out in the world, having adventures."

"Now he's selling vanilla. In Oklahoma."

The hall floor creaked. Geese gabbled in the sky.

"I should tell you, Hector." Lila looked toward Niagara in its tame brown frame. "Terrence is gone because I asked him to go."

"You ran him off, Lila?" Hector's neck bowed forward. "When you were so bent on marrying him?"

"I was bent on fulfillment."

"It's the same thing, isn't it?"

"It's not the same thing at all."

Hector sat still. Once in a fall on the stairs he was knocked unconscious. The way he felt now, he was just coming to.

"Lila," he said after a suitable pause. "If you've sent Terrence off, you realize, don't you, that you'll have to forget—whatever you hoped for."

"Maybe," said Lila. She twiddled with her hair. "Or maybe I'll find it somewhere else."

The room heaved gently, like the sealed-down crust of a steam-filled pie. "Where?" he asked.

"Wherever it is."

She rearranged her white skirts, revealing to Hector's numbed gaze a number of pink toes and pink painted toenails.

"Terrence," he said. "Terrence upset things."

"He did," said Lila as softly and smoothly as if she were slipping on slippers at The Quality Shoe Mart. "But he cleared the air too. We can be grateful for that."

Hector shuddered. "Grateful to Terrence." He had breathed ether once. It was nothing to this.

Finally he said, "It's too late, I suppose, to back up and start over."

Lila smiled on him kindly. "It was too late for that when you hacked down the pear tree."

Larry Brown

SAMARITANS

(from *St. Andrews Review*)

I was smoking my last cigarette in a bar one day, around the middle of the afternoon. I was drinking heavy, too, for several reasons. It was hot and bright outside, and cool and dark inside the bar, so that's one reason I was in there. But the main reason I was in there was because my wife had left me to go live with somebody else.

A kid came in there unexpectedly, a young, young kid. And of course that's not allowed. You can't have kids coming in bars. People won't put up with that. I was just on the verge of going out to my truck for another pack of smokes when he walked in. I don't remember who all was in there. Some old guys, I guess, and probably, some drunks. I know there was one old man, a golfer, who came in there every afternoon with shaky hands, drank exactly three draft beers, and told these crummy dirty jokes that would make you just close your eyes and shake your head without smiling if you weren't in a real good mood. And back then, I was never in much of a good mood. I knew they'd tell that kid to leave.

But I don't think anybody much wanted to. The kid didn't look good. I thought there was something wrong the minute he stepped in. He had these panicky eyes.

The bartender, Harry, was a big muscled-up guy with a beard. He was washing beer glasses at the time, and he looked up and saw him standing there. The only thing the kid had on was a pair of green gym shorts that were way too big for him. He looked like maybe he'd been walking down the side of a road for a long time, or something similar to that.

Harry, he raised up a little and said, "What you want, kid?" I could see that the kid had some change in his hand. He was standing on the rail and he had his elbows hooked over the bar to hold himself up.

I'm not trying to make this sound any worse than it was, but to me the kid just looked like maybe he hadn't always had enough to eat. He was two or three months overdue for a haircut, too.

"I need a pack of cigrets," he said. I looked at Harry to see what he'd say. He was already shaking his head.

"Can't sell em to you, son," he said. "Minor."

I thought the kid might give Harry some lip. He didn't. He said, "Oh," but he stayed where he was. He looked at me. I knew then that something was going on. But I tried not to think about it. I had troubles enough of my own.

Harry went back to washing his dishes, and I took another drink of my beer. I was trying to cut down, but it was so damn hot outside, and I had a bunch of self-pity loading up on me at that time. The way I had it figured, if I could just stay where I was until the sun went down, and then make my way home without getting thrown in jail, I'd be okay. I had some catfish I was going to thaw out later.

Nobody paid any attention to the kid after that. He wasn't making any noise, wasn't doing anything to cause people to look at him. He turned loose of the bar and stepped down off the rail, and I saw his head going along the far end toward the door.

But then he stuck his face back around the corner, and motioned me toward him with his finger. I didn't say a word, I just looked at him. I couldn't see anything but his eyes sticking up, and that one finger, crooked at me, moving.

I could have looked down at my beer and waited until he went away. I could have turned my back. I knew he couldn't stay in there with us. He wasn't old enough. You don't have to get yourself involved in things like that. But I had to go out for my cigarettes, eventually. Right past him.

I got up and went around there. He'd backed up into the dark part of the lounge.

"Mister," he said. "Will you loan me a dollar?"

He already had money for cigarettes. I knew somebody outside had sent him inside.

I said, "What do you need a dollar for?"

He kind of looked around and fidgeted his feet in the shadows while he thought of what he was going to say.

"I just need it," he said. "I need to git me somethin."

He looked pretty bad. I pulled out a dollar and gave it to him. He didn't say thanks or anything. He just turned and pushed open the door and went outside. I started not to follow him just then. But after a minute I did.

The way the bar's made, there's a little enclosed porch you come into before you get into the lounge. There's a glass door where you can stand inside and look outside. God, it was hot out there. There wasn't even a dog walking around. The sun was burning down on the parking lot, and the car the kid was crawling into was about what I'd expected. A junky-assed old Rambler, wrecked on the right front end, with the paint almost faded off, and slick tires, and a rag hanging out of the grill. It was parked beside my truck and it was full of people. It looked like about four kids in the backseat. The woman who was driving put her arm over the seat, said something to the kid, and then reached out and whacked the hell out of him.

I started to go back inside so I wouldn't risk getting involved. But Harry didn't have my brand and there was a pack on the dash. I could see them from where I was, sitting there in the sun, almost close enough for the woman to reach out and touch.

I'd run over a dog with my truck that morning and I wasn't feeling real good about it. The dog had actually been sleeping in the road. I thought he was already dead and was just going to straddle him until I got almost on top of him, when he raised up suddenly and saw me, and tried to run. Of course I didn't have time to stop by then. If he'd just stayed down, he'd have been all right. The muffler wouldn't have even hit him. It was just a small dog. But, boy, I heard it when it hit the bottom of my truck. It went *WHOP!* and the dog—it was a white dog—came rolling out from under my back bumper with all four legs stiff, yelping. White hair was flying everywhere. The air was full of it. I could see it in my rearview mirror. And I don't know why I was thinking about that dog I'd killed while I was watching those people, but I was. It didn't make me feel any better.

They were having some kind of terrible argument out there in that suffocating hot car. There were quilts and pillows piled up in there, like they'd been camping out. There was an old woman on the front seat with the woman driving, the one who'd whacked hell out of her kid for coming back empty-handed.

I thought maybe they'd leave if I waited for a while. I thought maybe they'd try to get their cigarettes somewhere else. And then I thought maybe their car wouldn't crank. Maybe, I thought, they're waiting for somebody to come along with some jumper cables and jump them off. But I didn't have any jumper cables. I pushed open the door and went down the steps.

There was about three feet of space between my truck and their car. They were all watching me. I went up to the window of my truck and got my cigarettes off the dash. The woman driving turned all the way around in the seat. You couldn't tell how old she was. She was one of those women that you can't tell about. But probably somewhere between thirty and fifty. She didn't have liver spots. I noticed that.

I couldn't see all of the old woman from where I was standing. I could just see her old wrinkled knees, and this dirty slip she had sticking out from under the edge of her housecoat. And her daughter—I knew that was who she was—didn't look much better. She had a couple of long black hairs growing out of this mole on her chin that was the size of a butter bean. Her hair kind of looked like a mophead after you've used it for a long time. One of the kids didn't even have any pants on.

She said, "Have they got some cold beer in yonder?" She shaded her eyes with one hand while she looked up at me.

I said, "Well, yeah. They do. But they won't sell cigarettes to a kid that little."

"It just depends on where they know ye or not," she said. "If they don't know ye then most times they won't sell em to you. Is that not right?" I knew I was already into something. You can get into something like that before you know it. In a minute.

"I guess so," I said.

"Have you got—why you got some, ain't you? Can I git one of

them off you?" She was pointing to the cigarettes in my hand. I opened the pack and gave her one. The kid leaned out and wanted to know if he could have one, too.

"Do you let him smoke?"

"Why, he just does like he wants to," she said. "Have you not got a light?"

The kid was looking at me. I had one of those Bics, a red one, and when I held it out to her smoke, she touched my hand for a second and held it steady with hers. She looked up at me and tried to smile. I knew I needed to get back inside right away, before it got any worse. I turned to go and what she came out with stopped me dead in my tracks.

"You wouldn't buy a lady a nice cold beer, would you?" she said. I turned around. There was this sudden silence, and I knew that everybody in the car was straining to hear what I would say. It was serious. Hot, too. I'd already had about five and I was feeling them a little in the heat. I took a step back without meaning to and she opened her door.

"I'll be back in a little bit, Mama," she said.

I looked at those kids. Their hair was ratty and their legs were skinny. It was so damn hot you couldn't stand to stay out in it. I said, "You gonna leave these kids out here in the sun?"

"Aw, they'll be all right," she said. But she looked around kind of uncertainly. I was watching those kids. They were as quiet as dead people.

I didn't want to buy her a beer. But I didn't want to make a big deal out of it, either. I didn't want to keep looking at those kids. I just wanted to be done with it.

"Lady," I said. "I'll buy you a beer. But those kids are burning up in that car. Why don't you move it around there in the shade?"

"Well." She hesitated. "I reckon I could," she said. She got back in and it cranked right up. The fan belt was squealing, and some smoke farted out from the back end. But she limped it around to the side and left it under a tree. Then we went inside together.

The first Bud she got didn't last two minutes. She sucked the can dry. She had on some kind of military pants and a man's long-sleeved work shirt, and house shoes. Blue ones, with a little fuzzy white ball on each. She had the longest toes I'd ever seen.

Finally I asked her if she wanted another beer. I knew she did.

"Lord yes. And I need some cigrets too if you don't care. Marlboro Lights. Not the menthol. Just reglar lights."

I didn't know what to say to her. I thought about telling her I was going to the bathroom, and then slipping out the door. But I really wasn't ready to leave just yet. I bought her another beer and got her some cigarettes.

"I'm plumb give out," she said. "Been drivin all day."

I didn't say anything. I didn't want anybody to think I was going with her.

"We tryin to git to Morgan City, Loozeanner. M'husband's sposed to've got a job down there and we's agoin to him. But I don't know," she said. "That old car's about had it."

I looked around in the bar and looked at my face in the mirror behind the rows of bottles. The balls were clicking softly on the pool tables.

"We left from Tuscalooser, Alabama," she said. "But them younguns has been yellin and fightin till they've give me a sick headache. It shore is nice to set down fer a minute. Ain't it good and cool in here?"

I watched her for a moment. She had her legs crossed on the bar stool and about two inches of ash hanging off her cigarette. I got up and went out the door, back to the little enclosed porch. By looking sideways I could see the Rambler parked under the shade. One of the kids was squatted down behind it, using the bathroom. I thought about things for a while and then went back in and sat down beside her.

"Ain't many men'll hep out a woman in trouble," she said. "Specially when she's got a buncha kids."

I ordered myself another beer. The old one was hot. I set it up on the bar and she said, "You not goin to drank that?"

"It's hot," I said.

"I'll drank it," she said, and she pulled it over next to her. I didn't want to look at her anymore. But she had her eyes locked on me and she wouldn't take them off. She put her hand on my wrist. Her fingers were cold.

"It's some people in this world has got thangs and some that ain't," she said. "My deddy used to have money. Owned three service stations and a sale barn. Had four people drove trucks fer him. But you can lose it easy as you git it. You ought to see him now. We cain't even afford to put him in a rest home."

I got up and went over to the jukebox and put two quarters in. I played some John Anderson and some Lynn Anderson and then I punched Narvel Felts. I didn't want to have to listen to what she had to say.

She was lighting a cigarette off the butt of another one when I sat down beside her again. She grabbed my hand as soon as it touched the bar.

"Listen," she said. "That's my mama out yonder in that car. She's seventy-eight year old and she ain't never knowed nothin but hard work. She ain't got a penny in this world. What good's it done her to work all her life?"

"Well," I said, "she's got some grandchildren. She's got them."

"Huh! I got a girl eighteen, was never in a bit a trouble her whole life. Just up and run off last year with a goddamn sand nigger. Now what about that?"

"I don't know," I said.

"I need another beer!" she said, and she popped her can down on the bar pretty hard. Everybody turned and looked at us. I nodded to Harry and he brought a cold one over. But he looked a little pissed.

"Let me tell you somethin," she said. "People don't give a shit if you ain't got a place to sleep ner nothin to eat. They don't care. That son of a bitch," she said. "He won't be there when we git there. If we ever git there." And she slammed her face down on the bar, and started crying, loud, holding onto both beers.

Everybody stopped what they were doing. The people shooting pool stopped. The guys on the shuffleboard machine just stopped and turned around.

"Get her out of here," Harry said. "Frank, you brought her in here, you get her out."

I got down off my stool and went around to the other side of her, and I took her arm.

"Come on," I said. "Let's go back outside."

I tugged on her arm. She raised her head and looked straight at Harry.

"*Fuck* you," she said. "You don't know nothin about me. You ain't fit to judge."

"Out," he said, and he pointed toward the door. "Frank," he said.

"Come on," I told her. "Let's go."

It hadn't cooled off any, but the sun was a little lower in the sky. Three of the kids were asleep in the backseat, their hair plastered to their heads with sweat. The old woman was sitting in the car with her feet in the parking lot, spitting brown juice out the open door. She didn't even turn her head when we walked back to the car. The woman had the rest of the beer in one hand, the pack of Marlboro Lights in the other. She leaned against the fender when we stopped.

"You think your car will make it?" I said. I was looking at the tires and thinking of the miles they had to go. She shook her head slowly and stared at me.

"I done changed my mind," she said. "I'm gonna stay here with you. I love you."

Her eyes were all teary and bitter, drunk-looking already, and I knew that she had been stomped on all her life, and had probably been forced to do no telling what. And I just shook my head.

"You can't do that," I said.

She looked at the motel across the street.

"Let's go over there and git us a room," she said. "I want to."

The kid who had come into the bar walked up out of the hot weeds and stood there looking at us for a minute. Then he got in the car. His grandmother had to pull up the front seat to let him in. She turned around and shut the door.

"I may just go to Texas," the woman said. "I got a sister lives out there. I may just drop these kids off with her for a while and go on out to California. To Los Vegas."

I started to tell her that Las Vegas was not in California, but it didn't matter. She turned the beer up and took a long drink of it, and I could see the muscles and cords in her throat pumping and working. She killed it. She dropped the can at her feet, and it hit with a tiny tinny sound and rolled under the car. She wiped her mouth with the back of her hand, tugging hard at her lips, and then she wiped her eyes.

"Don't nobody know what I been through," she said. She was looking at the ground. "Havin to live on food stamps and feed four younguns." She shook her head. "You cain't do it," she said. "You cain't hardly blame nobody for wantin to run off from it. If they was any way I could run off myself I would."

"That's bad," I said.

"That's terrible," I said.

She looked up and her eyes were hot.

"What do you care? All you goin to do is go right back in there and git drunk. You just like everybody else. You ain't never had to go in a grocery store and buy stuff with food stamps and have everbody look at you. You ain't never had to go hungry. Have you?"

I didn't answer.

"Have you?"

"No."

"All right, then," she said. She jerked her head toward the building. "Go on back in there and drank ye goddamn beer. We made it this far without you."

She turned her face to one side. I reached back for my wallet because I couldn't think of anything else to do. I couldn't stand to look at them anymore.

I pulled out thirty dollars and gave it to her. I knew that their troubles were more than she'd outlined, that they had awful things wrong with their lives that thirty dollars would never cure. But I don't know. You know how I felt? I felt like I feel when I see those commercials on TV, of all those people, women and kids, starving to death in Ethiopia and places, and I don't send money. I know that Jesus wants you to help feed the poor.

She looked at what was in her hand, and counted it, jerking the bills from one hand to the other, two tens and two fives. She folded it up and put it in her pocket, and leaned down and spoke to the old woman.

"Come on, Mama," she said. The old woman got out of the car in her housecoat and I saw then that they were both wearing exactly the same kind of house shoes. She shuffled around to the front of the car, and her daughter took her arm.

They went slowly across the parking lot, the old woman limping a little in the heat, and I watched them until they went up the steps that led to the lounge and disappeared inside. The kid leaned out the window and shook his head sadly. I pulled out a cigarette and he looked up at me.

"Boy you a dumb sumbitch," he said.

And in a way I had to agree with him.

Bobbie Ann Mason

WISH

(from *The New Yorker*)

Sam tried to hold his eyes open. The preacher, a fat-faced boy with a college degree, had a curious way of pronouncing his "r"s. The sermon was about pollution of the soul and started with a news item about an oil spill. Sam drifted into a dream about a flock of chickens scratching up a bed of petunias. His sister Damson, beside him, knifed him in the ribs with her bony elbow. Snoring, she said with her eyes.

Every Sunday after church, Sam and Damson visited their other sister, Hortense, and her husband, Cecil. Ordinarily, Sam drove his own car, but today Damson gave him a ride because his car was low on gas. Damson lived in town, but Hort and Cecil lived out in the country, not far from the old homeplace, which had been sold twenty years before, when Pap died. As they drove past the old place now, Sam saw Damson shudder. She had stopped saying "Trash" under her breath when they passed by and saw the junk cars that had accumulated around the old house. The yard was bare dirt now, and the large elm in front had split. Many times Sam and his sisters had wished the new interstate had gone through the homeplace instead. Sam knew he should have bought out his sisters and kept it.

"How are you, Sam?" Hort asked when he and Damson arrived. Damson's husband, Porter, had stayed home today with a bad back.

"About dead." Sam grinned and knuckled his chest, pretending heart trouble and exaggerating the arthritis in his hands.

"Not again!" Hort said, teasing him. "You just like to growl, Sam. You've been that way all your life."

"You ain't even knowed me that long! Why, I remember the night you was born. You come in mad at the world, with your stinger out, and you've been like that ever since."

Hort patted his arm. "Your barn door's open, Sam," she said as they went into the living room.

He zipped up his fly unself-consciously. At his age, he didn't care.

Hort steered Damson off into the kitchen, murmuring something about a blue dish, and Sam sat down with Cecil to discuss crops and the weather. It was their habit to review the week's weather, then their health, then local news—in that order. Cecil was a small, amiable man who didn't like to argue.

A little later, at the dinner table, Cecil jokingly asked Sam, "Are you sending any money to Jimmy Swaggart?"

"Hell, no! I ain't sending a penny to that bastard."

"Sam never gave them preachers nothing," Hort said defensively as she sent a bowl of potatoes au gratin Sam's way. "That was Nova."

Nova, Sam's wife, had been dead eight and a half years. Nova was always buying chances on Heaven, Sam thought. There was something squirrelly in her, like the habit she had of saving out extra seed from the garden or putting up more preserves than they could use.

Hort said, "I still think Nova wanted to build on that ground she heired so she could have a house in her own name."

Damson nodded vigorously. "She didn't want you to have your name on the new house, Sam. She wanted it in her name."

"Didn't make no sense, did it?" Sam said, reflecting a moment on Nova. He could see her plainly, holding up a piece of fried chicken like a signal for attention. The impression was so vivid he almost asked her to pass the peas.

Hort said, "You already had a nice house with shade trees and a tobacco patch, and it was close to your kinfolks, but she just *had* to move toward town."

"She told me if she had to get to the hospital the ambulance would get there quicker," said Damson, taking a second biscuit. "Hort, these biscuits ain't as good as you usually make."

"I didn't use self-rising," said Hort.

"It wouldn't make much difference, with that new highway," said Cecil, speaking of the ambulance.

On the day they moved to the new house, Sam stayed in bed with the covers pulled up around him and refused to budge. He was still there at four o'clock in the evening, after his cousins had moved out all the furniture. Nova ignored him until they came for the bed. She laid his clothes on the bed and rattled the car keys in his face. She had never learned to drive. That was nearly fifteen years ago. Only a few years after that, Nova died and left him in that brick box she called a dream home. There wasn't a tree in the yard when they built the house. Now there were two flowering crab apples and a flimsy little oak.

After dinner, Hort and Cecil brought out new pictures of their great-grandchildren. The children had changed, and Sam couldn't keep straight which ones belonged to Linda and which ones belonged to Donald. He felt full. He made himself comfortable among the crocheted pillows on Hort's high-backed couch. For ten minutes, Hort talked on the telephone to Linda, in Louisiana, and when she hung up she reported that Linda had a new job at a finance company. Drowsily, Sam listened to the voices rise and fall. Their language was so familiar; his kinfolks never told stories or reminisced when they sat around on a Sunday. Instead, they discussed character. "He's the stingiest man alive." "She was nice to talk to on the street but *H* to work with." "He never would listen when you tried to tell him anything." "She'd do anything for you."

Now, as Sam stared at a picture of a child with a Depression-style bowl haircut, Damson was saying, "Old Will Stone always referred to himself as me. '*Me* did this. *Me* wants that.'"

Hort said, "The Stones were always trying to get you to do something for them. Get around one of them and they'd think of something they wanted you to do." The Stones were their mother's people.

"I never would let 'em tell me what to do," Damson said with a laugh. "I'd say, 'I can't! I've got the nervous trembles.'"

Damson was little then, and her Aunt Rue always complained

of nervous trembles. Once, Damson had tried to get out of picking English peas by claiming she had nervous trembles, too. Sam remembered that. He laughed—a hoot so sudden they thought he hadn't been listening and was laughing about something private.

Hort fixed a plate of fried chicken, potatoes, field peas, and stewed apples for Sam to take home. He set it on the back seat of Damson's car, along with fourteen eggs and a sack of biscuits. Damson spurted out of the driveway backwards, scaring the hound dog back to his hole under a lilac bush.

"Hort and Cecil's having a time keeping up this place," Sam said, noticing the weed-clogged pen where they used to keep hogs.

Damson said, "Hort's house always smelled so good, but today it smelled bad. It smelled like fried fish."

"I never noticed it," said Sam, yawning.

"Ain't you sleeping good, Sam?"

"Yeah, but when my stomach sours I get to yawning."

"You ain't getting old on us, are you?"

"No, I ain't old. Old is in your head."

Damson invited herself into Sam's house, saying she wanted to help him put the food away. His sisters wouldn't leave him alone. They checked on his housekeeping, searched for ruined food, made sure his commode was flushed. They had fits when he took in a stray dog one day, and they would have taken her to the pound if she hadn't got hit on the road first.

Damson stored the food in the kitchen and snooped in his refrigerator. Sam was itching to get into his blue jeans and watch something on Ted Turner's channel that he had meant to watch. He couldn't remember now what it was, but he knew it came on at four o'clock. Damson came into the living room and began to peer at all his pictures, exclaiming over each great-grandchild. All Sam's kids and grandkids were scattered around. His son worked in the tire industry in Akron, Ohio, and his oldest granddaughter operated a frozen-yogurt store in Florida. He didn't know why anybody would eat yogurt in any form. His grandson Bobby had arrived from Arizona last year with an Italian woman who spoke in a sharp accent. Sam had to hold himself stiff to keep from laughing. He wouldn't let her see him laugh, but her accent tickled him. Now Bobby had written that she'd gone back to Italy.

Damson paused over an old family portrait—Pap and Mammy and all six children, along with Uncle Clay and Uncle Thomas and their wives, Rosie and Zootie, and Aunt Rue. Sam's three brothers were dead now. Damson, a young girl in the picture, wore a lace collar, and Hort was in blond curls and a pinafore. Pap sat in the center on a chair with his legs set far apart, as if to anchor himself to hold the burden of this wild family. He looked mean and willful, as though he were about to whip somebody.

Suddenly Damson blurted out, "Pap ruined my life."

Sam was surprised. Damson hadn't said exactly that before, but he knew what she was talking about. There had always been a sadness about her, as though she had had the hope knocked out of her years ago.

She said, "He ruined my life—keeping me away from Lyle."

"That was near sixty years ago, Damson. That don't still bother you now, does it?"

She held the picture close to her breast and said, "You know how you hear on the television nowadays about little children getting beat up or treated nasty and it makes such a mark on them? Nowadays they know about that, but they didn't back then. They never knowed how something when you're young can hurt you so long."

"None of that happened to you."

"Not that, but it was just as bad."

"Lyle wouldn't have been good to you," said Sam.

"But I loved him, and Pap wouldn't let me see him."

"Lyle was a drunk and Pap didn't trust him no further than he could throw him."

"And then I married Porter, for pure spite," she went on. "You know good and well I never cared a thing about him."

"How come you've stayed married to him all these years then? Why don't you do like the kids do nowadays—like Bobby out in Arizona? Him and that Italian. They've done quit!"

"But she's a foreigner. I ain't surprised," said Damson, blowing her nose with a handkerchief from her pocketbook. She sat down on Sam's divan. He had towels spread on the upholstery to protect it, a habit of Nova's he couldn't get rid of. That woman was so practical she had even orchestrated her deathbed. She had picked out her burial clothes, arranged for his breakfast. He remembered holding up hangers of dresses from her closet for her to choose from.

"Damson," he said. "If you could do it over, you'd do it different, but it might not be no better. You're making Lyle out to be more than he would have been."

"He wouldn't have shot hisself," she said calmly.

"It was an accident."

She shook her head. "No, I think different."

Damson had always claimed he killed himself over her. That night, Lyle had come over to the homeplace near dark. Sam and his brothers had helped Pap put in a long day suckering tobacco. Sam was already courting Nova, and Damson was just out of high school. The neighborhood boys came over on Sundays after church like a pack of dogs after a bitch. Damson had an eye for Lyle because he was so daresome, more reckless than the rest. That Saturday night when Lyle came by for her, he had been into some moonshine, and he was frisky, like a young bull. Pap wouldn't let her go with him. Sam heard Damson in the attic, crying, and Lyle was outside, singing at the top of his lungs, calling her. "Damson! My fruit pie!" Pap stepped out onto the porch then, and Lyle slipped off into the darkness.

Damson set the family picture back on the shelf and said, "He was different from all the other boys. He knew a lot, and he'd been to Texas once with his daddy—for his daddy's asthma. He had a way about him."

"I remember when Lyle come back late that night," Sam said. "I heard him on the porch. I knowed it must be him. He was loud and acted like he was going to bust in the house after you."

"I heard him," she said. "From my pallet up there at the top. It was so hot I had a bucket of water and a washrag and I'd wet my face and stand in that little window and reach for a breeze. I heard him come, and I heard him thrashing around down there on the porch. There was a loose board you always had to watch out for."

"I remember that!" Sam said. He hadn't thought of that warped plank in years.

"He fell over it," Damson said. "But then he got up and backed down the steps. I could hear him out in the yard. Then—" She clasped her arms around herself and bowed her head. "Then he yelled out, 'Damson!' I can still hear that."

A while later, they had heard the gunshot. Sam always remembered hearing a hollow thump and a sudden sound like cussing, then the explosion. He and his brother Bob rushed out in the dark, and then Pap brought a coal-oil lantern. They found Lyle sprawled behind the barn, with the shotgun kicked several feet away. There was a milk can turned over, and they figured that Lyle had stumbled over it when he went behind the barn. Sam had never forgotten Damson on the living-room floor, bawling. She lay there all the next day, screaming and beating her heavy work shoes against the floor, and people had to step around her. The women fussed over her, but none of the men could say anything.

Sam wanted to say something now. He glared at that big family in the picture. The day the photographer came, Sam's mother made everyone dress up, and they had to stand there as still as stumps for about an hour in that August heat. He remembered the kink in Damson's hair, the way she had fixed it so pretty for Lyle. A blurred chicken was cutting across the corner of the picture, and an old bird dog named Obadiah was stretched out in front, holding a pose better than the fidgety people. In the front row, next to her mother, Damson's bright, upturned face sparkled with a smile. Everyone had admired the way she could hold a smile for the camera.

Pointing to her face in the picture, he said, "Here you are, Damson—a young girl in love."

Frowning, she said, "I just wish life had been different."

He grabbed Damson's shoulders and stared into her eyes. To this day, she didn't even wear glasses and was still pretty, still herself in there, in that puffed-out old face. He said, "You wish! Well, wish in one hand and shit in the other one and see which one fills up the quickest!"

He got her. She laughed so hard she had to catch her tears with her handkerchief. "Sam, you old hound. Saying such as that—and on a Sunday."

She rose to go. He thought he'd said the right thing, because she seemed lighter on her feet now. "You've got enough eggs and bacon to last you all week," she said. "And I'm going to bring you some of that popcorn cake my neighbor makes. You'd never guess it had popcorn in it."

She had her keys in her hand, her pocketbook on her arm. She was wearing a pretty color of pink, the shade of baby pigs. She said, "I know why you've lived so long, Sam. You just see what you want to see. You're like Pap, just as hard and plain."

"That ain't the whole truth," he said, feeling a mist of tears come.

That night he couldn't get to sleep. He went to bed at eight-thirty, after a nature special on the television—grizzly bears. He lay in bed and replayed his life with Nova. The times he wanted to leave home. The time he went to a lawyer to inquire about a divorce. (It turned out to cost too much, and anyway he knew his folks would never forgive him.) The time she hauled him out of bed for the move to this house. He had loved their old place, a wood-frame house with a porch and a swing, looking out over tobacco fields and a strip of woods. He always had a dog then, a special dog, sitting on the porch with him. Here he had no porch, just some concrete steps, where he would sit sometimes and watch the traffic. At night, drunk drivers zoomed along, occasionally plowing into somebody's mailbox.

She had died at three-thirty in the morning, and toward the end she didn't want anything—no food, no talk, no news, nothing soft. No kittens to hold, no memories. He stayed up with her in case she needed him, but she went without needing him at all. And now he didn't need her. In the dim light of the street lamp, he surveyed the small room where he had chosen to sleep—the single bed, the bare walls, his jeans hanging up on a nail, his shoes on a shelf, the old washstand that had belonged to his grandmother, the little rag rug beside the bed. He was happy. His birthday was two months from today. He would be eighty-four. He thought of that bird dog, Obadiah, who had been with him on his way through the woods the night he set out to meet someone—the night he first made love to a girl. Her name was Nettie, and at first she had been reluctant to lie down with him, but he had brought a quilt, and he spread it out in the open pasture. The hay had been cut that week, and the grass was damp and sweet-smelling. He could still feel the clean, soft, cool cotton of that quilt, the stubble poking through and the patterns of the quilting pressing into his back. Nettie lay there beside him, her breath blowing on his shoulder as they studied the stars far above the field—little pinpoint holes punched through the night sky like the needle holes around the tiny stitches in the quilting. Nettie. Nettie Slade. Her dress had self-covered buttons, hard like seed corn.

Madison Smartt Bell

CUSTOMS OF THE COUNTRY

(from *Harper's Magazine*)

I don't remember much about that place anymore. It was nothing but somewhere I came to put in some pretty bad time, though that was not what I had planned on when I went there. I had it in mind to improve things, but I don't think you could fairly claim that's what I did. So that's one reason I might just as soon forget about it. And I didn't stay there all that long, not more than about nine months or so, about the same time, come to think, that the child I was there to try to get back had lived inside my body.

It was a cluster-housing thing a little ways north out of town from Roanoke, on a two-lane road that crossed the railroad cut and went about a mile further up through the woods. The buildings looked something like a motel, a little raw still, though they weren't new. My apartment was no more than a place that would barely look all right and yet cost me little enough so I had something left over to give the lawyer. There was fresh paint on the walls and the trim in the kitchen and bathroom was in fair shape. And it was real quiet mostly, except that the man next door used to beat up his wife a couple of times a week. The place was soundproof enough I couldn't usually hear talk but I could hear yelling plain as day and when he got going good he would slam her bang into our common wall. If she hit in just the right spot it would send my pots and pans flying off the pegboard where I'd hung them above the stove.

Not that it mattered to me that the pots fell down, except for the noise and the time it took to pick them up again. Living alone like I was, I didn't have the heart to do much cooking and if I did fix myself something I mostly used an old iron skillet that hung there on the same wall. All the others I only had out for show. The whole apartment was done about the same way, made into something I kept spotless and didn't much care to use. I wore my hands out scrubbing everything clean and then saw to it that it stayed that way. I sewed slipcovers for that threadbare batch of Goodwill furniture I'd put in the place, and I hung curtains and found some sunshiny posters to tack on the walls, and I never cared a damn about any of it. It was an act, and I wasn't putting it on for me or for Davey, but for all the other people I expected to come to see it and judge it. And however good I could get it looking, it never felt quite right.

I felt even less at home there than I did at my job, which was waitressing three snake-bends of the counter at the Truckstops of America out at the I-81 interchange. The supervisor was a man named Tim that used to know my husband Patrick from before we had the trouble. He was nice about letting me take my phone calls there and giving me time off to see the lawyer, and in most other ways he was a decent man to work for, except that now and then he would have a tantrum over something or other and try to scream the walls down. Still, it never went beyond yelling, and he always acted sorry once he got through. The other waitress on my shift was an older lady named Prissy, and I liked her all right in spite of the name.

We were both on a swing shift that rolled over every ten days, which was the main thing I didn't like about that job. The six-to-two I hated the worst because it would have me getting back to my apartment building around three in the morning, not the time it looked its best. It was the kind of place where at that time of night I could expect to find the deputies out there looking for somebody, or else some other kind of trouble. I never got to know the neighbors any too well, but a lot of them were pretty sorry—small-time criminals, dope-dealers and thieves, none of them much good at whatever it was they did. There was one check forger that I knew of, and a man who would break into the other apartments looking for whiskey. One thing and another, along that line.

The man next door, the one that beat up his wife, didn't do

crimes or work either that I ever heard. He just seemed to lay around the place, maybe drawing some kind of welfare. There wasn't a whole lot of him, he was just a stringy little man, hair and mustache a dishwater brown, cheap green tattoos running up his arms. Maybe he was stronger than he looked, but I did wonder how come his wife would take it from him, since she was about a head taller and must have outweighed him an easy ten pounds. I might have thought she was whipping on him—stranger things have been known to go on—but she was the one that seemed like she might break out crying if you looked at her crooked. She was a big fine-looking girl with a lovely shape, and long brown hair real smooth and straight and shiny. I guess she was too hammered down most of the time to pay much attention to how she dressed, but still she had pretty brown eyes, big and long-lashed and soft sort of like a cow's eyes, except I never saw a cow that looked that miserable.

At first I thought maybe I might make a friend of her, she was about the only one around there I felt like I might want to. Our paths crossed pretty frequent, either around the apartment building or in the Kwik Sack back toward town, where I'd find her running the register some days. But she was shy of me, shy of anybody, I suppose. She would flinch if you did so much as say hello. So after a while I quit trying. She'd get hers about twice a week, maybe other times I wasn't around to hear it happen. It's a wonder all the things you can learn to ignore, and after a month or so I was that accustomed I barely noticed when they would start in. I would just wait till I thought they were good and through, and then get up and hang those pans back on the wall where they were supposed to go. And all the while I would just be thinking about some other thing, like what might be going on with my Davey.

The place where he had been fostered out was not all that far away, just about ten or twelve miles up the road, out there in the farm country. The people were named Baker. I never got to first names with them, just called them Mr. and Mrs. They were older than me, both just into their forties, and they didn't have any children of their own. The place was only a small farm but Mr. Baker grew tobacco on the most of it and I'm told he made it a paying thing. Mrs. Baker kept a milk cow or two and she grew a garden and canned in the old-time way. Thrifty people. They were real sweet to Davey and he seemed to like being with them pretty well. He had been staying there almost the whole two years, which was lucky too, since most children usually got moved around a whole lot more than that.

And that was the trouble, like the lawyer explained to me, it was just too good. Davey was doing too well out there. He'd made out better in the first grade than anybody would have thought. So nobody really felt like he needed to be moved. The worst of it was the Bakers had got to like him well enough they were saying they wanted to adopt him if they could. Well, it would have been hard enough for me without that coming into it.

Even though he was so close, I didn't go out to see Davey near as much as I would have liked to. The lawyer kept telling me it wasn't a good idea to look like I was pressing too hard. Better take it easy till all the evaluations came in and we had our court date and all. Still, I would call and go on out there maybe a little more than once a month, most usually on the weekends, since that seemed to suit the Bakers better. They never acted like it was any trouble, and they were always pleasant to me, or polite might be a better word yet. The way it sometimes seemed they didn't trust me did bother me a little. I would have liked to take him out to the movies a time or two, but I could see plain enough the Bakers wouldn't have been easy about me having him off their place.

But I can't remember us having a bad time, any of those times I went. He was always happy to see me, though he'd be quiet when we were in the house, with Mrs. Baker hovering. So I would get us outside quick as ever I could and, once we were out, we would just play like both of us were children. There was an open pasture, a creek with a patch of woods, a hay barn where we would play hide-and-go-seek. I don't know what all else we did, silly things mostly. That was how I could get near him the easiest, he didn't get a whole lot of playing in, way out there. The Bakers weren't what you would call playful and there weren't any other children living near. So that was the thing I could give him that was all mine to give. When the weather was good we would stay outside together most all the day and he would just wear me out. But over the winter those visits seemed to get shorter and shorter, like the days.

Davey called me Momma still, but I suppose he had come to

think your mother was something more like a big sister or just some kind of a friend. Mrs. Baker was the one doing for him all the time. I don't know just what he remembered from before, or if he remembered any of the bad part. He would always mind me but he never acted scared around me, and if anybody says he did they lie. But I never really did get to know what he had going on in the back of his mind about the past. At first I worried the Bakers might have been talking against me, but after I had seen a little more of them I knew they wouldn't have done anything like that, wouldn't have thought it right. So I expect whatever Davey knew about that other time he remembered on his own. He never mentioned Patrick hardly and I think he really had forgotten about him. Thinking back I guess he never saw that much of Patrick even when we were all living together. But Davey had Patrick's mark all over him, the same eyes and the same red hair.

Patrick had thick wavy hair the shade of an Irish setter's, and a big rolling mustache the same color. Maybe that was his best feature, but he was a good-looking man altogether, still is I suppose, though the prison haircut don't suit him. If he ever had much of a thought in his head I suspect he had knocked it clean out with dope, yet he was always fun to be around. I wasn't but seventeen when I married him and I didn't have any better sense myself. Right to the end I never thought anything much was the matter, all his vices looked so small to me. He was good-tempered almost all the time, and good with Davey when he did notice him. Never once did he raise his hand to either one of us. In little ways he was unreliable, late, not showing up at all, gone out of the house for days sometimes. Hindsight shows me he ran with other women, but I managed not to know anything about that at the time. He had not quite finished high school and the best job he could hold was being an orderly down at the hospital, but he made a good deal of extra money stealing pills out of there and selling them on the street.

That was something else I didn't allow myself to think on much back then. Patrick never told me a lot about it anyhow, always acted real mysterious about whatever he was up to in that line. He would disappear on one of his trips and come back with a whole mess of money, and I would spend up my share and be glad I had it too. I never thought much about where it was coming from, the money or the pills either one. He used to keep all manner of pills around the house, Valium and ludes and a lot of different kinds of speed, and we both took what we felt like whenever we felt in the mood. But what Patrick made the most on was Dilaudid. I used to take it without ever knowing what it really was, but once everything fell in on us I found out it was a bad thing, bad as heroin they said, and not much different, and it was what they gave Patrick most of his time for.

I truly was surprised to find out that it was the strongest dope we had, because I never really even felt like it made you all that high. You would just take one and kick back on a long slow stroke and whatever trouble you might have, it would not be able to find you. It came on like nothing but it was the hardest habit to lose, and I was a long time shaking it. I might be thinking about it yet if I would let myself, and there were times, all through the winter I spent in that apartment, I'd catch myself remembering the feeling.

You couldn't call it a real bad winter, there wasn't much snow or anything, but I was cold just about all the time, except when I was at work. All I had in the apartment was some electric baseboard heaters, and they cost too much for me to leave them running very long at a stretch. I'd keep it just warm enough so I couldn't see my breath, and spend my time in a hot bathtub or under a big pile of blankets on the bed. Or else I would just be cold.

There was some kind of strange quietness about that place all during the cold weather. If the phone rang it would make me jump. Didn't seem like there was any TV or radio ever playing next door. The only sound coming out of there was Susan getting beat up once in a while. That was her name, a sweet name, I think. I found it out from hearing him say it, which he used to do almost every time before he started on her. "*Susan*," he'd call out, loud enough I could hear him through the wall. He'd do it a time or two, he might have been calling her to him, and I suppose she went. After that would come a bad silence that reminded you of a snake being somewhere around. Then a few minutes' worth of hitting sounds and then the big slam as she hit the wall, and the clatter of my pots falling on the floor. He'd throw her at the wall maybe once or twice, usually when he was about to get through. By the time the pots had quit spinning on the floor it would be real quiet over there again, and the next time I saw Susan she'd be walking in that ginger way people have when they're hiding a hurt, and if I said hello to her she'd give a little jump and look away.

After a while I quit paying it much mind, it didn't feel any different to me than hearing the news on the radio. All their carrying on was not any more to me than a bump in the rut I had worked myself into, going back and forth from the job, cleaning that apartment till it hurt, calling up the lawyer about once a week to find out what was happening, which never was much. He was forever trying to get our case before some particular doctor or social worker or judge who'd be more apt to help us than another, so he said. I would call him up from the TOA, all eager to hear what news he had and every time it was another delay. In the beginning I used to talk it all over with Tim or Prissy after I hung up, but after a while I got out of the mood to discuss it. I kept ahead making those calls but every one of them just wore out my hope a little more, like a drip of water wearing down a stone. And little by little I got in the habit of thinking that nothing really was going to change.

Somehow or other that winter passed by, with me going from one phone call to the next, going out to wait on that TOA counter, coming home to shiver and hold hands with myself and lie awake all through the night, or the day, depending what shift I was on. It was springtime, well into warm weather, before anything really happened at all. That was when the lawyer called *me*, for a change, and told me he had some people lined up to see me at last.

Well, I was all ready for them to come visit, come see how I'd fixed up my house and all the rest of my business to get set for having Davey back with me again. But as it turned out, nobody seemed to feel like they were called on to make that trip. "I don't think that will be necessary" was what one of them said, I don't recall which. They both talked about the same, in voices that sounded like filling out forms.

So all I had to do was drive downtown a couple of times and see them in their offices. That child psychologist was the first and I doubt he kept me more than half an hour. I couldn't tell the point of most of the questions he asked. My second trip I saw the social worker, who turned out to be a black lady once I got down there, though I never could have told it over the phone. Her voice sounded like it was coming out of the TV. She looked me in the eye while she was asking her questions, but I couldn't tell a thing about what she thought. It wasn't till I was back in the apartment that I understood she must have already had her mind made up.

That came to me in a sort of a flash, while I was standing in the kitchen washing out a cup. Soon as I walked back in the door I saw my coffee mug left over from breakfast, and I kicked myself for letting it sit out. I was giving it a hard scrub with a scouring pad when I realized it didn't matter anymore. I might just as well have dropped it on the floor and got what kick I could out of watching it smash, because it wasn't going to make any difference to anybody now. But all the same I rinsed it and set it in the drainer, careful as if it was an eggshell. Then I stepped backward out of the kitchen and took a long look around that cold shabby place and thought it might be for the best that nobody was coming. How could I have expected it to fool anybody else when it wasn't even good enough to fool me? A lonesomeness came over me, I felt like I was floating all alone in the middle of cold air, and then I began to remember some things I would just as soon have not.

No, I never did like to think about this part, but I have had to think about it time and again, with never a break for a long, long time, because I needed to get to understand it at least well enough to believe it never would ever happen anymore. And I had come to believe that, in the end. If I hadn't, I never would have come back at all. I had found a way to trust myself again, though it took me a full two years to do it, and though of course it still didn't mean that anybody else would trust me.

What had happened was that Patrick went off on one of his mystery trips and stayed gone a deal longer than usual. Two nights away, I was used to that, but on the third I did start to wonder. He normally would have called at least, if he was going to be gone that long of a stretch. But I didn't hear a peep until about halfway through the fourth day. And it wasn't Patrick himself that called, but one of those public-assistance lawyers from downtown.

Seemed like the night before Patrick had got himself stopped on the interstate loop down there. The troopers said he was driving like a blind man, and he was so messed up on whiskey and ludes I suppose he must have been pretty near blind at that. Well, maybe he would have just lost his license or something like that, only that the backseat of the car was loaded up with all he had lately stole out of the hospital.

So it was bad. It was so bad my mind just could not contain it, and every hour it seemed to be getting worse. I spent the next couple of days running back and forth between the jail and that lawyer, and I had to haul Davey along with me wherever I went. He was too little for school and I couldn't find anybody to take him right then, though all that running around made him awful cranky. Patrick was just grim, he would barely speak. He already knew pretty well for sure that he'd be going to prison. The lawyer had told him there wasn't no use in getting a bondsman, he might just as well stay on in there and start pulling his time. I don't know how much he really saved himself that way, though, since what they ended up giving him was twenty-five years.

That was when all my troubles found me, quick. Two days after Patrick got arrested, I came down real sick with something. I thought at first it was a bad cold or the flu. My nose kept running and I felt so wore out I couldn't hardly get up off the bed and yet at the same time I felt real restless, like all my nerves had been scraped bare. Well, I didn't really connect it up to the fact that I'd popped the last pill in the house a couple of days before. What was really the matter was me coming off that Dilaudid, but I didn't have any notion of that at the time.

I was laying there in bed not able to get up and about ready to jump right out of my skin at the same time when Davey got the drawer underneath the stove open. Of course he was getting restless himself with all that had been going on, and me not able to pay him much mind. All our pots and pans were down in that drawer then, and he began to take them out one at a time and throw them on the floor. It made a hell of a racket, and the shape I was in, I felt like he must be doing it on purpose to devil me. I called out to him and asked him to quit. Nice at first: "You stop that, now, Davey, Momma don't feel good." But he kept right ahead. All he wanted was to have my attention, I know, but my mind wasn't working right just then. I knew I should get up and just go lead him away from there, but I couldn't seem to get myself to move. I had a picture of myself doing the right thing, but I just wasn't doing it. I was still lying there calling to him to quit and he was still banging those pots around and before long I was screaming at him outright, and starting to cry at the same time. But he never stopped a minute. I guess I had scared him some already and he was just locked into doing it, or maybe he wanted to drown me out. Every time he flung a pot it felt like I was getting shot at. And the next thing I knew I got myself in the kitchen someway and I was snatching him up off the floor.

To this day I don't remember doing it, though I have tried and tried. I thought if I could call it back then maybe I could root it out of myself and be shed of it for good and all. But all I ever knew was one minute I was grabbing a hold of him and the next he was laying on the far side of the room with his right leg folded up funny where it was broke, not even crying, just looking surprised. And I knew that it had to be me that threw him over there because as sure as hell is real there was nobody else around that could have done it.

I drove him to the hospital myself. I laid him straight on the front seat beside me and drove with one hand all the way so I could hold on to him with the other. He was real quiet and real brave the whole time, never cried the least bit, just kept a tight hold on my hand with his. Well, after a while, we got there and they ran him off somewhere to get his leg set and pretty soon the doctor came back out and asked me how it had happened.

It was the same hospital where Patrick had worked and I even knew that doctor a little bit. Not that being connected to Patrick would have done me a whole lot of good around there at that time. Still, I have often thought since then that things might have come out better for me and Davey both if I just could have lied to that man, but I was not up to telling a lie that anybody would be apt to believe. All I could do was start to scream and jabber like a crazy person, and it ended up I stayed in that hospital quite a few days myself. They took me for a junkie and I guess I really was one too, though I hadn't known it till that very day. And I never saw Davey again for a whole two years, not till the first time they let me go out to the Bakers'.

Sometimes you don't get but one mistake, if the one you pick is bad enough. Do as much as step in the road one time without looking, and your life could be over with then and there. But during those two years I taught myself to believe that this mistake of mine could be wiped out, that if I struggled hard enough with myself and the world I could make it like it never had been.

Three weeks went by after I went to see that social worker, and I didn't have any idea what was happening, or if anything was. Didn't call anybody, I expect I was afraid to. Then one day the phone rang for me out there at the TOA. It was the lawyer and I could tell right off from the sound of his voice I wasn't going to care for his news. Well, he told me all the evaluations had come in now, sure enough, and they weren't running in our favor. They weren't against *me*, he made sure to say that, it was more like they were *for* the Bakers. And his judgment was it wouldn't pay me anything if we went on to court. It looked like the Bakers would get Davey for good anyhow, and they were likely to be easier about visitation if there wasn't any big tussle. But if I drug them into court, then we would have to start going back over that whole case history—

That was the word he used, *case history,* and it was around about there that I hung up. I went walking stiff-legged back across to the counter and just let myself sort of drop on a stool. Prissy had been covering my station while I was on the phone and she came right over to me then.

"What is it?" she said. I guess she could tell it was something by the look on my face.

"I lost him," I said.

"Oh, hon', you know I'm so sorry," she said. She reached out for my hand but I snatched it back. I know she meant it well but I just was not in the mood to be touched.

"There's no forgiveness," I said. I felt bitter about it. It had been a hard road for me to come as near forgiving myself as I ever could. And Davey forgave me, I really knew that, I could tell it in the way he acted when we were together. And if us two could do it, I didn't feel like it ought to be anybody else's business but ours. Tim walked up then and Prissy whispered something to him, and then he took a step nearer to me.

"I'm sorry," he told me.

"Not like I am," I said. "You don't know the meaning of the word."

"Go ahead and take off the rest of your shift if you feel like it," he said. "I'll wait on these tables myself, need be."

"I don't know it would make any difference," I said.

"Better take it easy on yourself," he said. "No use in taking it so hard. You're just going to have to get used to it."

"Is that a fact?" I said. And I lit myself a cigarette and turned my face away. We had been pretty busy, it was lunchtime, and the people were getting restless seeing all of us standing around there not doing a whole lot about bringing them their food. Somebody called out something to Tim, I didn't hear just what it was, but it set off one of his temper fits.

"Go on and get out of here if that's how you feel," he said. He was getting red in the face and waving his arms around to include everybody there in what he was saying. "Go on and clear out of here, every last one of you, and we don't care if you never come back. There's not one of you couldn't stand to miss a meal anyhow. Take a look at yourselves, you're all fat as hogs. . . ."

It seemed like he might be going to keep it up a good while, and he had already said I could leave, so I hung up my apron and got my purse and I left. It was the first time he ever blew up at the customers that way, it had always been me or Prissy or one of the cooks. I never did find out what came of it all because I never went back to that place again.

I drove home in such a poison mood I barely knew I was driving a car or that there were any others on the road. I was ripe to get killed or kill somebody, and I wouldn't have cared much either way. I kept thinking about what Tim had said about having to get used to it. It came to me that I was used to it already, I really hadn't been all that surprised. That's what I'd been doing all those months, just gradually getting used to losing my child forever.

When I got back to the apartment I just fell in a chair and sat there staring across at the kitchen wall. It was in my mind to pack my traps and leave that place, but I hadn't yet figured out where I could go. I sat there a good while, I guess. The door was ajar from me not paying attention, but it wasn't cold enough out to make any difference. If I turned my head that way I could see a slice of the parking lot. I saw Susan drive up and park and come limping toward the building with an armload of groceries. Because of the angle I couldn't see her go into their apartment but I heard the door open and shut and after that it was quiet as a tomb. I kept on sitting there thinking about how used to everything I had got. There must have been generous numbers of other people too, I thought, who had got themselves accustomed to all kinds of things. Some were used to taking the pain and the rest were used to serving it up. About half of the world was screaming in misery, and it wasn't anything but a habit.

When I started to hear the hitting sounds come toward me through the wall, a smile came on my face like it was cut there with a knife. I'd been expecting it, you see, and the mood I was in I felt satisfied to see what I had expected was going to happen. So I listened a little more carefully than I'd been inclined to do before. It was *hit hit hit* going along together with a groan and a hiss of the wind being knocked out of her. I had to strain pretty hard to hear that breathing part, and I could hear him grunt too, when he got in a good one. There was about three minutes of that with some little breaks, and then a longer pause. When she hit the wall it was the hardest she had yet, I think. It brought down every last one of my pots at one time, including that big iron skillet that was the only one I ever used.

It was the first time they'd managed to knock that skillet down, and I was so impressed that I went over and stood looking down at it like I needed to make sure it was a real thing. I stared at the skillet so long it went out of focus and started looking more like a big black hole in the floor. That's when it dawned on me that this was one thing I didn't really have to keep on being used to.

It took three or four knocks before he came to the door, but that didn't worry me at all. I had faith, I knew he was going to come. I meant to stay right there till he did. When he came, he opened the door wide and stood there with his arms folded and his face all stiff with his secrets. It was fairly dark behind him, they had all the curtains drawn. I had that skillet held out in front of me in both my hands, like maybe I had come over to borrow a little hot grease or something. It was so heavy it kept wanting to dip down toward the floor like a water witch's rod. When I saw he wasn't expecting anything, I twisted the skillet back over my shoulder like baseball players do their bats, and I hit him bang across the face as hard as

I knew how. He went down and out at the same time and fetched up on his back clear in the middle of the room.

Then I went in after him, with the skillet cocked and ready in case he made to get up. But he didn't look like there was a whole lot of fight left in him right then. He was awake, at least partly awake, but his nose was just spouting blood and it seemed like I'd knocked out a few of his teeth. I wish I could tell you I was sorry or glad, but I didn't feel much of anything really, just that high lonesome whistle in the blood I used to get when I took all that Dilaudid. Susan was sitting on the floor against the wall, leaning down on her knees and sniveling. Her eyes were red but she didn't have any bruises where they showed. He never did hit her on the face, that was the kind he was. There was a big crack coming down the wall behind her and I remember thinking it probably wouldn't be too much longer before it worked through to my side.

"I'm going to pack and drive over to Norfolk," I told her. I hadn't thought of it before but once it came out my mouth I knew it was what I would do. "You can ride along with me if you want to. With your looks you could make enough money serving drinks to the sailors to buy that Kwik Sack and blow it up."

She didn't say anything, just raised her head up and stared at me kind of bug-eyed. And after a minute I turned around and went out. It didn't take me any time at all to get ready. All I had was a suitcase and a couple of boxes of other stuff. The sheets and blankets I just pulled off the bed and stuffed in the trunk all in one big wad. I didn't care a damn about that furniture, I would have lit it on fire on a dare.

When I was done I stuck my head back into the other apartment. The door was still open like I had left it. What was she doing but kneeling down over that son of a bitch and trying to clean off his face with a washrag. I noticed he was making a funny sound when he breathed, and his nose was still bleeding pretty quick, so I thought maybe I had broke it. Well, I can't say that worried me much.

"Come on now if you're coming, girl," I said. She looked up at me, not telling me one word, just giving me a stare out of those big cow eyes of hers like I was the one had been beating on her that whole winter through. And I saw then that they were both of them stuck in their groove and that she would not be the one to step out of it. So I pulled back out of the doorway and went on down the steps to my car.

I was speeding on the road to Norfolk, doing seventy, seventy-five. I'd have liked to gone faster if the car had been up to it. I can't say I felt sorry for busting that guy, though I didn't enjoy the thought of it either. I just didn't know what difference it had made, and chances were it had made none at all. Kind of a funny thing, when you thought about it that way. It was the second time in my life I'd hurt somebody bad, and the other time I hadn't meant to do it at all. This time I'd known what I was doing for sure, but I still didn't know what I'd done.

David Huddle

PLAYING

(from *Quarterly West*)

Billy Hyatt is a prodigy of the alto saxophone. The summer between eighth grade in Rosemary and ninth grade in Madison, Billy's mother drives him to Madison High School so that he can practice with the band. Before practice and after practice and during practice if it's possible Billy talks to girls, plays games with girls, chases girls across the fields of mown grass that surround the brick school building. One day just after the morning marching session, Billy finds himself shoved up against the rough wall outside the band-room door, Bob Kerns holding him there with one hand against Billy's chest and the other hand held back like he means to make a fist and maybe decorate the bricks with Billy's brains.

"Frieda Goforth is my girl," Bob Kerns instructs him. "You need to know that."

Billy nods. It wouldn't be something he'd argue even if Bob Kerns didn't seem ready to snuff out the bright flame of his candle. But he understands Bob Kerns's reasons. Billy, after all, has noted the billowing curls of Frieda's reddish brown hair and her skin, which is the color of a just-peeled apple. Billy has had the nerve, once when he peeped down the collar of her blouse, to imagine the whole shape of one of Frieda's breasts, though in this moment of confronting Bob Kerns and Bob's anger, he reminds himself that he did not imagine them both, only the one most apparent to him in the instant of her bending over to pick up a dropped piece of sheet music.

Bob drops both his held-back hand and the one pushing Billy's chest. Billy guesses he looked so afraid that Bob is ashamed of himself. He should be. Bob Kerns is a junior, a big boy who plays a sousaphone. He hasn't so much as spoken to Billy before this, and now with deep contempt he's saying, "You really like the girls, don't you, Hyatt?" Bob shakes his head and walks away before Billy has a chance to answer him.

But he wouldn't have answered anyway. What Bob Kerns says to him falls on him like prophecy. In the core of his fourteen-year-old brain he knows it's true, he's a fool for girls. This is the moment he realizes that it's O.K. to like them but not as much as he does.

God knows why any girls are interested in gangly, pimply-faced Billy anyway, though they are. Every day at these band practices they call out his name when his mother lets him out of the car. When the whole band loads up on buses and goes to band camp for ten days, Bob Kerns's sad mockery still rings in Billy's ears every time he catches himself trying to look up the skirt of one of the flute players or that sleepy-eyed eighth-grade girl in the clarinet section.

"The saxophone is the sexiest instrument," Valerie Williams tells him one day during a break, squinting her eyes against the sun to be able to look up at him, a light sweat broken out across her freckly forehead.

If somebody like Valerie Williams says something like that it must be true. She's thirteen, the new majorette. She's short, with curly blond hair, and a shape like those cartoon girls he studies in his grandfather's *Esquire* magazines. She's Larry O'Dell's girlfriend, but she's been recently discussed intently by every boy Billy knows—by now he's fifteen and already the first-chair tenor saxophone—with the consensus opinion being that Valerie Williams is something else.

Something else, something else, his mind chants for him all the rest of that afternoon. It's August. They're practicing their marching routines in a dry, stubbled field. Out in front of the band the majorettes prance, twirl their batons, pitch them up at the cloudless sky, fail to catch them, grimace and say shit not quite loud enough to have Mr. Banks yell at them. They get tired. Only Valerie Williams lifts her knees almost to her chin every time they go through the show. By four-thirty the others are walking through it, Valerie is still lifting those knees, and Billy, back in the fourth rank, is still listening to his old brain chant for him, something else, something else.

Nighttime at band camp is hot, and the air smells like the sassafras leaves are cooking in the dark. "What do you think?" Valerie whispers to Billy. He's got a hand up underneath her blouse, her breast in its bra-cup in his palm. Billy's in a state. If he speaks or moves, he's going to shoot off a load in his pants. They're sitting out on the steps at the back of the main building, where they can hear the music from the scratchy forty-fives somebody's playing so that kids can dance in the little social area around front. "One early morning . . . ha-ooo . . . I met a woman . . . ha-ooo . . . we started talking. . . ."

"Cigarette?" Billy asks Valerie. He calmly removes his hand from her blouse at the same time he discharges enough sperm into his jockey shorts to impregnate every mildly fertile female within a radius of thirty miles. He lets his face show nothing, but wonders if she'll be able to smell it. Leaning forward, unintentionally over his crotch, she's tucking her blouse back in her shorts. "Yeah, sure," she says.

He drops several smokes, shaking them up then out of the pack, but it's dark, and probably she can't see anyway, and so he lets them lie there. Hospitably he extends the pack toward her, and she takes one. He has a lighter. His hand shakes. She coughs. He cautions her against inhaling if she hasn't done it much before.

VALERIE WILLIAMS! WILLIAM HYATT! Like a figure from the Old Testament Mr. Banks bursts upon them. He confiscates Billy's pack of Chesterfields. He extracts a vow from Valerie that she will never, ever smoke again. He dispatches them around the building into the lighted area where Billy can't stay because he has to go change his pants.

But they are impelled toward each other. When the band comes back to town, school starts, and Billy starts riding the bus twenty miles there and twenty miles back every day. Most of the hours of the day he's got a hard-on and Valerie floating through his frontal lobe.

Valerie lives in Madison. Her mother won't let her wear shorts downtown. After school Billy finds excuses to stay in town so that he can walk home with her, drink milk and eat cookies with her in the kitchen, then go downstairs with her to play Whistle-Stop in the basement. That girl can't whistle worth a damn. Billy's fingers make it all the way up under the hem of her shorts before she so much as raises one faint note. Billy's hand goes behind her back untucking her blouse, and she gets a pensive look on her face like she's thinking about something else.

Valerie's little sisters sneak around and spy on them through the windows. Valerie plays Peggy Sue on the record player again and again, Billy trying to sing along, never getting it right. In shorts Valerie walks him downtown where he catches his ride home with Walter Sawyers, whom he must pay a quarter each trip. Billy rides with his books in his lap, figuring out how to explain to his parents why he stayed in town this afternoon. Valerie's mom raises a holy ruckus when she hears Valerie was downtown in her shorts again. Valerie's dad, the manager of Piggly-Wiggly, gives Billy that look every time he sees him; they both know what the look means, but they make their manners just the same.

Billy gets into a dance band. These guys his brother knows at the radio station need a sax man. Billy can play a couple of jazzy tunes, but he hasn't tried it much. They say they'll teach him. They buy him sheet music they can't read but he can. What they can do is fake it behind him. They practice and work up a program, make a date to put it on the air on Saturday at four o'clock.

Billy tries to tell Valerie who they are. Al Kravic, the news man, claims he's learning how to play this expensive set of drums he bought in Abingdon. Johnny Wilson, the station engineer, plays steel guitar, leans heavily toward hillbilly stuff and those Hawaiian numbers that make Billy want to puke every time he hears them, but Johnny's a virtuoso of his own kind, even Billy can discern that. And Birdy Z. Pendergast, the station's morning man: Billy can't make him clear to Valerie at all, a little rat-faced man you just know was a sissy all the time he was growing up, moody, fastidious, mildly effeminate, high-pocketed, pot-bellied genius of the cheap piano not tuned for years.

"I'm serious," Billy tells her, liking the way she's laughing at him, "if it was a new Steinway somebody had just tuned, Birdy Z.

would sound like the clunker he really is." It's Saturday afternoon and they're buying popcorn and Pepsis to take into the two o'clock movie at the Millwald Theatre. It's September but hot as July. Valerie talked her mother into letting her wear Bermuda shorts to the movie. Billy'd rather she wore a skirt, he keeps his druthers to himself.

"Birdie Z., Birdie Z.," she says and laughs loud enough to make people turn around and look at her. Valerie wants the rest of his popcorn. She's got an appetite. When the movie starts—it's a western—they slump down in their seats and hold hands and lightly rub the goosey insides of their arms together.

It's five minutes until four when they walk into the radio station together, rubbing sweaty palm to sweaty palm, Billy's ears ringing and Valerie's face crimson. Up in the studio Al Kravic and Johnny Wilson take one look at the kids and commence grinning at each other, but Birdy Z. is in a fury. When they go on the air (Birdy Z. telling the audience out there, "Ladies and gentlemen, a new musical organization in the area . . ."), Billy's sticking the neck into his sax and going to have to try to get it tuned while they're playing the first number.

When they switch off the studio mike to run a couple of commercials, Birdy Z. bursts out, "God almighty, that sounded like a piece of warmed over rat shit!" He's looking straight at Billy. Billy knows Valerie is watching them all through the studio window. He blows a cute little riff she can't hear, looks up at the acoustic tiles of the ceiling, tries to act like nothing's wrong. "Don't know as I would dignify it to that extent," murmurs Johnny, giving Billy a wink and echoing Billy's riff on the steel guitar, using it as a segue into one of his Hawaiian numbers. "Come on, Bird," Kravic cautions. Red light over the door goes on, and Birdy tries to smooth it all out with his lilting tenor voice, "Just getting warmed up here, folks, let me introduce you to the members of . . ."

Billy notices the faces of his old mom and dad bob up beside Valerie's in the studio window. Thank God, they'll introduce themselves. Billy's relieved he doesn't have to perform his manners for his mother. The old man will ground him for the week if he hears Billy was late for the job. Billy wails out two choruses of O When the Saints, Johnny takes his two, making it sound like something you ought to strum along to with a ukulele, Birdy harangues the studio with about thirty-thousand piano notes, and they yield to Kravic's pitiful version of a drum solo. When the program's over, Billy hauls his sax case out into the waiting room and finds Valerie and his mom, their legs crossed and leaning forward toward each other, sitting on vinyl seats by a plastic fern in the corner.

Birdy Z. comes out, all sociable and Mr. Public Personality, and makes a joke out of it, but he damn sure lets Billy's old man know Billy was late getting there for the program. Taller than Birdy by an inch or two, Billy hates him standing here in his rat-man glasses.

Billy's old man doesn't say anything to him when they're giving Valerie a ride home, country folk in town, driving slow as farmers in a field, Billy leaning forward in the back seat doing all he can to give the car forward momentum, Valerie and his mom carrying on their chatting like a little song they both make up as they go along. It's all deeply, deeply embarrassing. Billy walks her to the door but they don't touch so much as an arm hair when they say goodbye with his parents watching them from the car.

Coda for the day is the lecture Billy's old man has for him on the slow, slow drive back out into the country to their house: Billy's heritage of six known generations of responsible and decent men on both sides of his family is what he'd better be carrying on his shoulders for the foreseeable and so on. Billy bites the inside of his jaw to keep himself from offering any smart mouth. What he does not wish to be denied is going home with Valerie after school, the milk, the cookies, the basement, the spying little sisters, his fingers walking high up Valerie's downy thigh.

"So he told, did he?" she says. "The damned old queer." Valerie says she never cared for Birdy Z., even when all she knew about him was his voice on her mom's radio in the kitchen. "You can just hear it in somebody's voice, somebody like that. A thirty-five-year-old tattletale. What're you doing, Billy? Listen, let's turn him on now and spit on the radio," she says, but it's not Birdy on the air, it's Kravic stumbling through the news like it was written in a foreign language. And what Billy's doing is backing Valerie up against her mom's refrigerator. They don't know what it is about that refrigerator, but they like it against her butt bracing them pelvis to pelvis. "Let's go downstairs," Billy whispers. "What do you guess is down there?" she asks him and pulls his mouth toward hers again so that he can't answer.

Her little sisters' names are Connie and Florence, Coco and Flossie. Eight and ten. Geniuses of hiding places with an angle of vision on Billy and Valerie. They could be down there doing their homework all afternoon and never hear a peep from the siblings, but let Billy get a hand up under Valerie's sweater or let them lie down on the sofa and from somewhere there'll come a twitter. Or else one bright little girl's blue eye looking straight down on them when Billy chances a glance toward the door or the window. "What would we do without them?" Billy says, standing up, trying to re-arrange his pants to get some comfort.

Valerie opines she has to go outside and practice her baton routine anyway. Goes up to her room, puts on shorts and a spiffy little white T-shirt. From the porch Billy watches, torn between admiration for her physical skill and resentment of the energy Valerie devotes to keeping that two-foot rubber-tipped aluminum rod spiking through the air.

"I gotta go," he says, finally. She's out of breath anyway, talks him into staying and having some lemonade with her on the porch. She's worked up a light sweat. He marvels at the fragrance of her. They talk about how much they hate the Z. "Let's go turn him on," she says, and they go into the kitchen and snap the switch on. He isn't. "Shit," Valerie says, lacking authority in her swearing, because she's just turned fourteen. Billy likes it anyway, gets a thrill from her trash mouth. "What're you doing, Billy?" she asks, but he knows she knows what he's doing. Behind her, the refrigerator makes its barely discernible humming. "Mom's gonna come in here any minute," she whispers. "That's cool," he says.

Billy turns sixteen and gets his drivers' license the very next day. The band gets a job playing for the Moose in Hillsville. "God, I didn't even know they had the Moose in Hillsville," says Birdy Z., chortling, "but the man calls me up and offers us a hundred and fifty dollars. He heard us on the air."

"I'm surprised he didn't send us a bill for a hundred and fifty dollars, if he heard us on the air Saturday," Johnny says, diddling that little chrome bar up and down the strings.

"We're getting better all the time," pipes up Kravic, but he's not.

The man has reached a permanent plateau at the zero-beginner's level.

Birdy Z. and the D-Jays is the name Birdy gives them. Kravic can't argue because he has no status, Johnny doesn't argue because he doesn't give a fat rat's ass, and Billy makes a face at the name because secretly he wanted it to be Billy Hyatt and the High Notes.

Besides, Birdy is the one doing the driving. "Can you believe a Studebaker?" Billy asks Valerie. She says she wouldn't have believed anything else. It's October. She has on a sky-blue sweater that spot-welds her torso into the base of Billy's brain. Mythic, downright mythic: if he could have her both naked and in that sky-blue sweater at the same time, that's what he'd choose for his deathbed vision, for the last image his eyeballs would ever shoot to his brain.

In the Studebaker, the four D-Jays drive to Hillsville, Galax, Max Meadows, Rural Retreat, all around the county. They get a reputation, not for being good, but for being cheap and for taking short breaks. All these dances are the same: boozy old guys and dames with bottles in brown bags they set on the floor under the tables, stepping through dances that went out before Billy was born. "Trying to drink themselves back to your age," Birdy Z. tells Billy. Nowadays Billy doesn't hold back his smart mouth. "How do you know, Bird? You don't drink."

"Reason I don't is that I do," Birdy Z. tells him. "Or I did." Then he tells Billy all about it.

Through a snowstorm, Birdy Z. crawled from the street, where somebody had dumped him on the sidewalk, around back of his house, and up onto the porch where he slept, got frostbite, almost lost a couple of fingers. He takes a hand off the steering wheel now and wiggles its fingers for Billy. Lost a job somewhere, got a job somewhere else, showed up drunk, lost that one, too, and no money to get home with. His wife wouldn't let him back in the house when he did get there.

It's a long drive through those mountains from Galax to Madison. Johnny and Kravic sleep in the back with Kravic's tom-tom on the seat between them. Birdy Z. tells Billy places in the house a drunk will hide his bottles. Highway's empty; nobody's out that time of night. Talk in the front seat of a car takes on intimacy. How can you hate a man who explicates for you the three dozen ways he has been humiliated?

But Billy can't explain it to Valerie. Something about the man she can't stand, takes him as her personal enemy. Another night he's meeting her late, after the D-Jays get back to Madison and let him out at the bus station where he's parked his dad's car. Instead of heading straight home—it's after two now—he drives up near her house, douses the lights, parks, sneaks into her back yard, taps on her window. Her face appears, her lips move, she's gone again. In three minutes she's slipping out the screen door of the back porch. He can't hold enough of her to keep her warm. She's in shorty pajamas, not even slippers on her feet. Can't stay, can't stay, crazy whispering out by the swing-set in the back yard.

He's never encountered her without her bra on, now he doesn't want to stop touching her breasts under the thin material of that pajama top (they're free, he says, they're so free!), but if he lets her go to do that she gets cold immediately, the pale, almost full moon over them both the ice and fire of the moment. He holds her, wraps the sides of his dumb band jacket around her, tells her about Birdy Z. crawling through the snowstorm to his back porch, but Valerie's feet and legs are so cold she's about to cry. The story and how cold she is, how mean it is that she has to go in, make her hate Birdie Z. even more.

Monday morning, standing by her locker at school, Billy tells her, "Valerie, he doesn't care what we do," but she's sure he does, sure he's the one who called and told her mom she was with him downtown in her shorts that day. "He's a queer, Billy, don't you know that?" she tells him, and Billy says no, he's not, suspects immediately that maybe Birdy is, but then a queer is somebody despicable, and now that Billy carries with him these stories Birdy has told him, he holds responsibility for the man, feels he must defend him, says again no, he's not. When Valerie tells him everybody in town has known that about Birdy Z. for years, it's only because Billy's from Rosemary that he doesn't know that, Billy argues that maybe Birdy used to be queer when he was a drunk but he isn't now, he's certain of it. He isn't at all.

Birdy Z. and the D-Jays need somebody else, another horn player or something. Elliott Pugh, this big-lipped kid in Billy's classes at school, is a clarinet player the band director is trying to switch to alto sax. Birdy Z. knows the kid, lives near him, asks Billy about him. Billy says the kid knows no music but classical, which he knows is an exaggeration, but he doesn't care. He reminds Bird that Elliott has taken piano lessons since he was old enough to sit up by himself. "Beethoven is the kid's personal hero, if you can feature it," Billy says. Birdy shrugs, says all they need is somebody who can play the harmony part, a second sax. "Might be just the man for us," Bird says, "talk to him, see what he says, see what you think." Billy's the one who makes the contact. Billy's the one who actually hires Elliott Pugh to play sax and clarinet with them.

Valerie can't believe it. "Elliott Pugh?" she says. She took ballroom dancing with Elliott from old Mrs. Tyson when she was eight and he was ten. "No one I ever met had less rhythm," she tells Billy, tossing the baton twenty yards straight over her head and catching it already spinning in her hands. Billy lugs her books, the price he pays for the milk and cookies he's got coming to him. The baton twiddles in the air around Valerie, going hand to hand to hand, cutting swathes of air around her, buzz-saw, propeller, finger-bruiser if you so much as reach to touch her. Valerie doesn't like Birdy Z. Billy doesn't like the baton. Elliott Pugh they figure doesn't matter to anybody.

Elliott himself couldn't be happier. He's humbled by the invitation and gives Billy more big-lipped grins than Billy has seen on his face in a year's worth of knowing the kid.

"Why'd they get me to hire him?" Billy asks Valerie. She doesn't have the slightest. "Can't be because of your looks," she tells him, running a finger down his cheekbone. "You gotta start shaving closer, you know that?" she says.

Billy's had a hell of a time getting his pants pegged exactly right. Whenever he stands up, he has to shake his pants down. But Elliott Pugh is the only kid in the whole school who wears un-pegged —pleated, for God's sakes!—pants, beltbuckle riding about navel high.

"They're both high-pockets," Valerie tells him. "Probably queering each other every chance they get." She and Billy are riding the second of two band buses back from the Martinsville football game. Good bus to ride, Susan Sweeney and Annabell Sparks up front picking out the songs and getting them going, telling who to sing what part: Blue Moon, Tell Me Why, Down By the Riverside, Try to Remember. Sweet voices come out of even the toughest kids, Maynard Johnson and Delano Phillipi doing the doom-da-da-dooms of Blue Moon pretty as can be. Best bus to ride, no doubt about it. The couples kiss for long miles of highway, boys in the darkest seats getting as much bare titty as the girls will allow. Billy doesn't want to talk about Elliott Pugh and Birdy Z. Pendergast, wants instead to be carrying out an inventory of the goosebumps on the inside of Valerie's thigh.

"What do queers do, Billy?" Valerie seems struck suddenly by the intellectual aspect of the whole thing. Billy's got vague ideas, but he guesses he doesn't know. "Play Whistle-Stop?" he suggests, puts a hand on her knee. She whistles three notes, loud and clear. "I mean really," she says.

"They're not queers," Billy whispers into the curly hairs around her ear. "They're just . . ." But he doesn't know what they are.

Elliott and Bird do have this understanding. Rarely do they have to talk. But two more disparate musicians couldn't exist. Elliott so stiff, precise, not an ounce of fudge, fake, or syncopate in his bones, and Birdy Z., who never in his life read a note or hit the right note on the right beat but on pure intuition could fake a Mahler symphony. Rehearsing Woodchopper's Ball, Billy witnesses at one and the same time Elliott tapping a big foot like a metronome, Birdy Z. diddling both heels and slapping randomly at the pedals with his toes.

Stars Fell On Alabama, Blue Hawaii, Little Brown Jug, Rock Around the Clock, Your Cheating Heart, Night and Day, Cherry Pink and Apple Blossom White, Stardust, Laura, Blue Monday—Birdy Z. and the D-Jays have no shame about what they'll play. No matter what the tune, there's one of them in the band who can sabotage it, Johnny being the great spoiler of musical integrity, but Billy beginning to understand and imitate the wit of Johnny's ever so slight alterations. If you don't like the tune, trash it, is the unspoken motto Billy shares with Johnny Wilson—except they end up trashing each other's tunes most of the time. At the kind of dances they play, nobody cares; you could take a dishpan and a hammer in those places and somebody'd pay you to knock one against the other so they could get out there and step around the floor with their arms around somebody.

They fire Kravic and get Cecil Taylor, a kid who looks like he was put together with drinking straws, to become the rhythm section. Kravic holds no grudges, sells his drums cheap to Cecil, and Cecil turns out to have an instinct for the cymbal, the snare, and the tom-tom. A certain ruthlessness sets in as a result of how they improve themselves. Billy and Elliott, tenor and alto, loose and stiff, reckless and cautious, not such a bad pair on two or three numbers, but Elliott can't ad-lib, no matter what they tell him to try to help, just can't do it, would rather sit, red-faced, with the sax in his lap and study his charts than to stand up and try to make up some ditty as it goes along. Something about that failure pisses Billy off way down deep. He commences a sabotage on Elliott, making him look bad, making him sound bad, mocking him, overtly condescending to him. "Stand up and blow that thing, sucker!" he'll shout when he knows Elliott's going to sit there, big-lipped, hair combed like an old-timey photograph, eyes cast down like a shy girl's.

"Don't pick on him," Birdy Z. tells him.

"You're the one they made hire him, why don't you fire him?" Valerie asks him at lunchtime, out in Billy's dad's car, the two of them out there fooling around, sneaking cigarettes. Would be a hell of a thing, damn right it would be, Billy allows, chortling to himself, slumped down in the driver's seat. "You're fired, Elliott Pugh, your ass is gone!"

"You're fired, Elliott Pugh, your ass is gone!" Billy says Wednesday afternoon in the studio where they're rehearsing. Elliott's just said he's not going to play harmony or anything else on Burn That Candle, he's sorry. To air the words, Billy has said he's fired. Elliott blinks at him. Nobody else says a word. Johnny slides the chrome on his strings, evokes the swaying hips of Hawaiian girls in grass skirts, pays no attention to anybody. Cecil's new, keeps his mouth shut, looks into the other studio where the evening man is holding forth at the board. Birdy watches, watches, a look on his face like he's ready to start slavering at the mouth and taking bites out of somebody's arm or leg. Elliott looks around at them. Nobody's got anything to say. "Haul your ass on home, Elliott," Billy tells him and knows now he's got the power to do it, knows he is in fact doing it and getting by with it.

Elliott starts blubbering while he packs up the alto. If Billy had a gun he doesn't know whether he'd aim it at Elliott or himself, but he wishes he had the choice.

Small-town dances are on Billy's mind. How the women put their arms up around a man's neck and let their breasts lift up against his chest is the gesture Billy begins to dream about, again and again, fat women, thin women, all of them reaching upward in that heartbreaking willingness to give themselves over to some man and politely dance with him.

Teenage master of sneaking-around foreplay, Billy's destiny is blue-balls, sperm-spotted underwear, stained crotches of his khaki pants, wet dreams, the rightful heritage of any high school boy. He's sixteen, Valerie's fourteen, they're so clearly too young for it that even they, had they been asked to speak responsibly, would have said of course they shouldn't do it!

They do it. On a rainy night in the spring in the front seat of Billy's dad's Dodge, they park out behind the Madison Country Club, so close to the clubhouse door that from its window the light from the Coke machine shines on them. It's after a concert for which Valerie has ushered. She has on crinolines, stockings, a garter belt. Billy has on a suit that six months ago fit him pretty well. They stretch across that seat, managing legs and clothes and body parts as best they can, and somehow manage a penetration. To neither one of them does it feel even as good as a dry-lipped kiss on the cheek. They talk a little and lie sweetly to each other and disguise their disappointment. The rubber he probably didn't even need Billy throws out the window for the club pro to find in the morning when he opens the shop.

Nothing changes. Billy drives home and next morning wakes up with a hard-on and smelling lilacs from the front yard. At school, standing at her locker, talking with Annie B. Loomis, Valerie gives him a grin that tightens the muscles in Billy's thighs. He has English first period and tries to change his seat so he won't have to sit beside Elliott Pugh. It's been three days since Billy fired him, but Elliott's face, like some weepy girl's, still looks tear-stained, bruised. Miss Lancaster won't let him change. Elliott hands him an envelope with Billy's name typed on the front. He doesn't open it until lunchtime, in the car by himself now, Valerie not able to sneak past Mr. Banks, who from the band-room doorway keeps an eye on the parking lot. Dragging hard on his Marlboro—Billy's brand now—he makes himself read a sentence or two—*want to know what right you have . . . think you are such a . . . let me tell you what a real musician would . . . will never know*—of Elliott's typed letter to him, but he can't go on with it or he'll be crying out there himself. He'll go in and find Elliott before Algebra and apologize and hire him back—if they gave him the power to hire and fire Elliott, then he knows he has the power to re-hire him—but when he sees the goddamned high-pocketed, big-lipped queerball standing and scowling just outside the door to Miss Damron's room, just waiting for Billy to say one word to him, why then Billy stares him down, walks right past him without speaking, and takes his seat.

Billy's cool, he's got his collar turned up, his tightest pegged pants on and slung low down on his hips, he smells like cigarette butts and he's got money in his pockets from last week's gig, money coming to him this Friday and Saturday night from gigs in Abingdon and Fries. But what cool he's got he needs—and maybe a little more besides—when he has to face Birdy at rehearsal that night. The man has a way of beaming his eyeballs through those thick-lensed glasses of his like he means to blow-torch straight through Billy's zit-pocked forehead. "I thought Elliott might come tonight," he finally says quietly.

"You want him to come," Billy says, putting a cigarette in the corner of his mouth and pretending he's got on sunglasses, "call him up."

The Bird says nothing, nor does he move toward the door to go call Elliott. Mechanically they work through the rehearsal, hardly a sociable word among the four of them. Once running through Till There Was You, Billy hears Elliott's harmony and for a moment thinks he's hallucinating it until he sees Johnny is playing it exactly with Elliott's play-it-by-the-numbers phrasing, grinning as he runs the chrome bar over the strings. It's tasteless of Johnny to make a joke like that, Billy feels, but he says nothing when at the end of the thing, Johnny winks at him. "Billy, you want to stay a minute?" Bird asks him when they're packing up, and Billy dreads it.

In the studio alone with Birdy now, Billy is aware of how the place cuts off every sound from outside, and he's jumpy, trying to face down the Bird, who's just looking at him in that pursemouthed way. "I think we need somebody else, Billy," Birdy finally says. "The sound's too thin. Don't you think so?"

In about three seconds flat, Billy has to reevaluate everything he thinks about Birdy and himself and his place in the band and the world. That Birdy would consult him, would actually talk with him as if his, Billy's, opinion were the one that determined how things would go is simply outside the territory of Billy's imaginings. He's thought they were letting him hire and fire Elliott as a joke, because he's the kid of the group and because they didn't want to take responsibility for dealing with another kid besides himself.

"What do you think of Jack Lamereaux?" Birdy asks him.

Billy hasn't heard him play, but he's heard Mr. Banks talking about him, and so Billy has some opinions about Jack Lamereaux, the new band director at Rural Retreat High School, the main one being that Jack won't want to join up because he's a college-trained trumpet-man who probably wouldn't want the D-Jays even to play for his old cat. But he doesn't release that particular opinion to the Bird. Instead he allows that what he's heard is that Jack Lamereaux's real talents and inclinations are toward concert trumpet-playing, or at the very least big band stuff. He says he'd be surprised if Jack would be interested in becoming a D-Jay. Birdy nods slowly, holds onto his rat-man philosopher face, and assures Billy that Jack would like the chance to play with them.

Before Billy makes it out the studio door, Birdy turns half around on the piano bench, with his right hand plinks out a tacky little riff, sighs, and says he wishes he was a drinking man again, he's got a hankering for a cold one. Billy wants to get out of there and so doesn't even pause. "Yeah, well, good night, Bird," he says, already clearing his mind for the project of meeting Valerie at the Shaefers' apartment where she's baby-sitting.

"These guys think I'm better than I am," is how he explains it to Valerie. Still it doesn't add up for him. "It's true, I read music, and they can't. And it's true I'm the coolest one ever to grace the corridors of that sorry radio station," he tells her, walking toward her in mock pursuit while she backs away in mock retreat all around the kitchen.

"Oh yeah?" She parks herself against the Shaefers' refrigerator, lifting her eyebrows and giving him to understand she's waiting for him there, but when he lunges toward her, quick as a single-wing tailback she's gone. Billy acts like all he meant to do was take a peek inside the fridge. He pulls out a can of Miller High Life, closes the door, rummages in a couple of drawers until he finds an opener; though he's never done it before, he punches holes in the thing, turns it up and takes a big swig.

"See?" he says, but then the foam backs up in his throat.

"Yeah, I see." Valerie points a finger at him. "The coolest one ever to grace the corridors of Anna Shaefer's kitchen can't handle a little sip of beer. Give me that," she tells him. When he hands it over, she takes two reasonable sips. "That's how you do it, young fella." She sets the can on the counter in front of him. "Want me to get you a bowl of Cheerios?" she asks. When he comes toward her again, she's out the door and down the corridor, telling him no, leave her alone, she didn't mean it. Then they're rassling around on the Shaefers' big bed, trying to stifle their giggles so as not to awaken and traumatize the sweet-dreaming little infant in the next room. With Valerie flat on the bed, Billy half on the floor and half on top of her with his head pillowed on her beskirted, beslipped, and bepantied pubic bone, he says, "Hey, Val, you think this is what queers do to each other?" He kisses her skirt right there and feels her relax, her whole body go loose.

"Don't do that," softly, dreamily, she tells the ceiling above her. "Don't you even think about doing that."

So he doesn't.

Jack Lamereaux knows a lot of good jokes to tell in the car on the way home from dance jobs. The one of Jack's that Billy likes best is about the tall, dark stranger; it takes miles and miles of highway to tell it, and the punchline is "You better cut that shit out." Johnny Wilson knows a lot of jokes, too, and with his intellect aroused by the jokes Jack tells, Johnny takes to matching Jack joke for joke. He makes it even tougher on himself by sticking only to farmer's-daughter jokes. Billy's never heard men do this before, but he recognizes that he is being included in some significant way. Birdy's jokes, mostly puns, seem to him insipid, but he snickers politely along with the others.

So Billy tells the one joke he knows himself, about this retarded guy trying to seduce this extremely seducible girl, the punchline being the retarded guy's repeating after the girl, "lower, lower," in a bass voice. If Billy begins telling his joke in the spirit of manly fellowship, as he tells it, he feels himself drifting out into intense isolation and ends it feeling deeply humiliated. He tells the joke badly, his voice won't go down to anything approaching a bass register, and he's a sixteen-year-old boy performing for grown men. They don't laugh, not even politely. Billy has the middle seat in the back, between Jack Lamereaux and Cecil Taylor. His neck and ears burn. He'd like to die. Short of that, he'd like to machine gun Birdy Z. and the other three D-Jays. They ride for a long time without saying anything. Then Jack Lamereaux tells a joke about queers, lisping and making an effeminate gesture with his hand. Billy makes a point of not laughing at that one, not saying a word to any of them all the rest of the way back to Madison.

Parked with her down by Brice Memorial Middle School, he explains to Valerie his relief at having the decision-making responsibility pass on to Jack Lamereaux. Jack really does know the music, really does know what kinds of arrangements they can play, how to set up the numbers in a set, even how to use Johnny's steel guitar to the band's advantage. Billy is happy to be just one among them again, but he wonders about it a lot. "It was like for a little while I was the boss of these grown men. I didn't want to be, and they didn't want me to be, but it just came about. I don't know why."

"You're the coolest one," Valerie tells him, with an edge to her voice that Billy knows is not generous. She is smoking a Marlboro now, one of her own, and they're working on a six-pack of Schlitz that earlier tonight Birdy bought for Billy at Billy's request. Valerie and Billy have had sex again a couple of times. Tonight they could have it if they wanted to, and they're choosing not to, because it's like an appliance they've bought that just doesn't work. Instead of screwing, they've taken to sitting in the car and talking, smoking cigarettes and drinking beer if Billy has been able to get it.

He knows something that he's not supposed to know officially, though they both know that he knows: Valerie has been out several times with Pete Ratcliffe. It stands to reason because lots of times when there are parties and dances at their school, Billy is out with Birdy Z. and the D-Jays in some godawful Odd Fellows Hall playing from nine until one and even later if the old dames and geezers can come up with the cash to keep the D-Jays going. Pete's a nice enough guy, and Billy figures Valerie's entitled to a decent time. He has no doubt that Valerie only likes Pete while she loves him.

Later, he explains all this about Valerie to Birdy Z. while the two of them sit in Billy's dad's car after a Friday night dance job. Birdy has surprised him by joining him for a beer before Billy drives home. Billy was just joking when he invited the Bird, and he thought the Bird's saying all right, he would do that, was also just playing around. But now Billy works the church key on the little can of Country Club and hands it over. Birdy holds it, grins at it, shakes his head, and then turns the can up for a hell of a big swig. He belches, and tells Billy he ought not to be sure of anything with any woman, he's here to tell him that. Billy watches Birdy grin at the beer can again and wonders if now that he's drinking with him Birdy Z. is getting ready to propose queering him. On the contrary, Birdy tells Billy he's going to have to come home with him some night soon and meet his wife. If he's going to be having a beer every now and then with Billy, he's going to have to tell his old lady; it'll be easier if Billy is there with him.

So after the gig on Saturday night they go up to Birdy's house and Billy meets Lannie. She's a big, loose-jointed woman, taller than the Bird by a good three or four inches, with blond hair going dark at the roots, buck teeth, and blue plastic-rimmed glasses. Billy likes her a lot in her faded blue pajamas and maroon bathrobe. Lannie looked really worried when the Bird brought in this bottle and set it on the counter and asked her if she'd like to join him and Billy in a little nightcap. But then she sighed and said, "Oh God, Birdy, if you just knew how tired I was getting of drinking that Sanka with you at this time of night anyway. I guess I'll have one with you." So now they're standing in her kitchen at two-thirty of a Sunday morning, the three of them finishing off a fifth of Smirnoff's vodka, mixing it with the breakfast juice from the refrigerator.

The house is a mess, as far as Billy can tell, at least the downstairs is, evidence of kids messing into everything, scattering toys everywhere, even into real stuff like the Pendergasts' magazines, the jars under the kitchen counter, the books, and ashtrays. Billy wonders why Lannie didn't clean some of the mess up while she was waiting to have Sanka with Birdy Z. She fires a lot of questions at him, about where they play and how the people act and dance. While he's telling her, she gets this dreamy look on her face and sighs and says she wishes she could get out and go to these things with Birdy Z. Before they had kids, she used to go with him and have a great time. She gives Billy this big horsey grin and winks at him. He can just imagine Lannie out there on the floor, dancing to a fast one, letting it all out, flinging those long arms and legs of hers every which way.

"I guess that's the last of this," Birdy says, pulling the bottle down from his mouth. Billy watches Lannie's face change when she sees what the Bird has done. It does occur to him that the bottle was at least half full when they brought it in, and he and Lannie have had just one drink apiece.

"How do you feel, Bird?" Billy asks him, swirling what's left of his ice in the Bugs Bunny glass Lannie gave him.

Birdy Z. grins at them both. "I feel fine, kids, I feel goddamn terrific."

Over the next several months Billy sees a good deal of Birdy and Lannie. It's a little deal they've struck, Billy wanting to be careful not to let his parents find out he's drinking, Birdy and Lannie not wanting anybody to know they've gone back to drinking, and so they drink with each other after rehearsals, after gigs, once or twice just when Billy comes up and has supper with them and the kids. They're full of good cheer, as if they've come into money or found a secret pleasure. One night Billy takes Valerie over there, but she doesn't have a good time and doesn't change her mind about the Bird one bit. "So what if he's got kids and that goony-goony wife? So what if he's nice to you? I don't have to like him, do I?"

Well, she doesn't. And the truth is, Billy has begun to wonder if she even likes him. Nowadays, without milk and cookies, they go straight down to her basement. When he untucks a blouse and reaches a hand back there to unhook her bra, she sighs, sits up straight, and says, "Here, let me do that, for goodness sakes." Then she sits back, looks at the ceiling while Billy puts his hands on her. Billy still likes her breasts, but he can feel little messages being passed from every cell of her skin to the palms of his hands: "Get away from me, get away."

"Val, have I done something to you to make you mad?" He backs his hands to his own self.

"No, but I'll tell you what." She starts crying like she just realized she was in pain.

He's ready for her to tell him something he won't like, such as she's sick and tired of him and she's decided to accept Pete Ratcliffe's invitation to go steady. What in fact she does tell him is that she's pregnant. He feels like she's taken a sledgehammer to his forehead.

"And I'll tell you what else," she says, too, from this posture she has taken of leaning forward with her face in her hands. Billy can't imagine what else there could be after what she's just said.

"It could be your baby or Pete's, I don't know which." Until this moment, Billy has never imagined sex between Valerie and Pete; now the image of them doing it in a car seat stuns him into a long silence during which he merely gapes at Valerie. She won't look back at him.

Billy goes through the motions of asking her questions—yes, she's seen a doctor; yes, her mother knows; no, her father doesn't know yet; no, she hasn't told Pete yet, but she's going to tonight —but all his mind will do for him is chant *you're not even seventeen yet, she won't be fifteen until March, you're not even* . . .

Billy slides through a couple days like a brain-damaged kid. In the hallways at school, his pals are constantly putting their hands on him and pushing him this way, directing him that way. His teachers are bemused. "Go sit down back there, Billy," Mrs. Lancaster, his English teacher tells him, and he does. But the next thing he knows is he's in Pete Ratcliffe's dad's car with Pete driving and Valerie sitting between them, and they're heading out to the Pendleton stone quarry after school to figure out what's to be done, all three of them smoking Valerie's cigarettes and shaking so bad it doesn't even occur to them to get nasty with each other.

Billy hears himself yelping, "A goddamn coin-flip? I cannot goddamn believe this!"

He could write the script for Valerie—cry at length while sitting between the two boys—and for Pete, too—"If you know a better way to . . ."

He and Pete get out of the car. It's a Ford, a new one, pretty, with the sun glazing its waxed hood, shining on the chrome bumper up there where he and Pete stand to do the flip. It's Pete's quarter. They agree that Pete gets to flip it, Billy gets to call it while it's in the air, they'll let it fall in the grass beside the road. One throw will decide the whole thing. One throw, one toss, what the hell, Billy feels like he's about to float out into space. Just before Pete flips that thing up in the air, he looks Billy in the eye and asks, "Did you use rubbers?"

Billy nods, then asks, "Did you?"

"Damn straight I did!" Pete spits to the side. They shake their heads at each other and press their lips together hard. Pete tosses the quarter, Billy calls tails just before it hits, then they're both leaning down to look at it, little metal disk in the scrubby grass. It's tails. When they get back in the car Pete is the one who has to tell Valerie that he is the one.

On the way back into town not one of the three of them has a word to say. Billy has scooted over as close to the door as he can, and Valerie has scooted over beside Pete as far as she can. Billy asks Pete to take him to Birdy Z.'s place. When he steps out and says, "See ya," it's as if he's a hitchhiker they're just dropping off.

Inside the Pendergasts' house, Lannie sits him down at the kitchen table and tells him she should have known it, she's a fool, she's got to get Bird on the wagon again or he's going to lose his job at the station. They smelled it on him the other morning, and they warned him. The Bird is out for a walk, mulling it over. Billy and Lannie sit there and smoke. Billy wants to tell her what he's just gone through but knows better than to put that on her shoulders. He knows she wouldn't like what he really feels about the whole thing, as if he's been accused of some crime but found innocent in court. And while he sits there with her, he knows Lannie knows the Bird would have never started drinking again if Billy hadn't gotten him going. He tries to think back over the night when he joked and asked the Bird to have a beer with him and the Bird joked and said, well all right.

When Birdy Z. comes in from his walk, he's chewing gum and smells like Juicy Fruit. Billy and Lannie know he's loaded. While he goes to wash up, sitting there at the table like parents of a wayward kid, Billy and Lannie give each other a long look. "Stashed a bottle in the garage, I expect," Lannie murmurs.

"Do you want me to go look?" Billy offers.

Lannie tells him he won't know where to look, and Billy tells her a long time ago Birdy told him all about stashing bottles. She tells him to go find it then and pour it out and come on back in for supper. Out there, behind a can of charcoal lighter fluid, Billy finds a half-full pint of Old Mr. Boston gin. He takes a big slug of the stuff, grimaces, decides what the hell, he wasn't hungry anyway. He finishes it in three more swigs, and starts walking out to the edge of town where he can hitchhike home.

The next day Pete and Valerie are absent from school, and the day after that it's all over school about them running off to Sparta, North Carolina, to get married. Kids look at Billy funny in the hallway. He feels resentful and smug at the same time. Next week they're back. Billy and Pete manage to nod grimly at each other when their paths cross, but he goes out of his way not to see Valerie, and he expects she's doing her best, too, to keep from seeing him.

Billy feels like he's chasing his life. Jack Lamereaux raises the fee the D-Jays charge for playing a dance, and they get more jobs. He raises it again, and they get still more jobs, at higher-class places. "We are goddamn much in demand," Birdy Z. says in the car on the night of the day he has received final notice from the radio station. "I can make a living on my music."

"You can't do any such goddamn thing," Johnny Wilson leans forward from the back seat to tell him. They are headed to the Hotel Roanoke where they will make a hundred dollars apiece for their night's work, a little dance for the Southwest Virginia Hollins Alumnae. Jack Lamereaux is the one who drives them to the jobs now, though because they all still defer to him, the Bird always rides shotgun.

The Bird turns up his bottle for a quick swig and chortles and says, "Johnny, you old fart, you just lack the guts to set yourself free."

Johnny sits back. He's not saying anything, but he's grinning at Billy and Cecil Taylor on either side of him.

By eleven-thirty, Birdy Z. can't sit up straight at the piano bench. They have been hired to play until one. Two numbers too soon Jack declares the band to be on a break and helps Billy escort the Bird outside where they walk him around in the parking lot. "Can't fire me, you fuckers," Birdy tells them, giggling, his arms pulling heavily on their shoulders. "Band's named after me."

"Yeah, Bird, yeah," Jack Lamereaux tells him. Jack's pretty disgusted. "Can you handle him, Billy?" Jack needs to go back in and stall for time before they start the next set. Billy keeps walking the Bird up and down the aisles of cars under the streetlights that make everything look bluish-grey, especially the skin of Birdy's face and hands.

"Billy?" the Bird says, hauling his arm away from across Billy's shoulder.

Billy's happy to see him getting hold of himself this much. "Yeah, Bird?"

"You love me, Billy?" Bird stops suddenly and stands there in the parking lot with his eyes locked on Billy. His shirt's untucked; his tie's loose and skewed around under his collar.

"Let's keep walking, Bird." Billy reaches for him to turn him back in the right direction.

Birdy brushes his hand away. "I asked you a question, Billy." He's even put a little parental authority into his voice, so that Billy has to shake himself to get a hold of exactly what the situation is.

Billy studies the Bird and knows he's not going to get off easy here. Now is the time that Birdy Z. is going to try to queer him. He isn't afraid of it anymore. He sighs and says, "You're my pal, Bird."

"Goddamn it, Billy."

"Lannie loves you, Bird."

"You like Lannie, Billy?" Birdy's voice takes on a smooth, interested quality that sends shivers up Billy's back.

"Hey, Bird," Billy tells him, no-nonsense now. "Time to go back in and play the last set, man."

The Bird stands there and stares at him. Finally he does say, "You're not my pal, Billy. I don't want anything to do with you. I don't want to see you around my house anymore. You understand?"

Billy's relieved. He figures it's just drunken palaver, just what came into the Bird's brain at the moment. And if it isn't that, then what the hell, he can do without the whole mess of Birdy Z. and his drinking. "You ready to go back in and play the last set, Bird?" Billy asks him.

"You're goddamn right I am," Bird says and takes a step. Billy reaches toward him to steady him. "Keep your goddamn hands off me, O.K.?" Birdy says and walks into the back of an Oldsmobile, falls forward onto its trunk, then slides backward onto the asphalt. Billy can't get him up and so trots back into the hotel to get help.

All the D-Jays come out and have a look at Birdy Z. laid out like a dead man in the parking lot.

"You free now, Bird?" Johnny murmurs while they are lifting him into Jack's car, but of course the Bird can't respond.

They try playing out the job without a piano player, but nobody argues with Johnny Wilson when he starts packing up and says that even by his standards they sound embarrassing. Politely angry, in their pretty dresses, the officers of the Southwest Virginia Hollins Alums pay them half the fee they agreed to originally, and the D-Jays head home early. By the time they pull up in front of his house, Bird has awakened and sobered somewhat, but he has nothing to say until he's out and standing on the sidewalk, glaring down at the car full of them. "You fuckers are fired!" he shouts at them. "Lousy goddamn musicians anyway!" Jack pulls away, but they can hear the Bird shouting after them, "And I don't want you using my name anymore! You understand that?"

"Set us free, too," Johnny Wilson murmurs, looking back at him, as they all are, even Jack Lamereaux, using the rearview mirror. Billy is the only one of them who giggles, but he thinks it may be because he feels almost crazy. Jack will drop him off at his father's car, and he'll drive the twenty miles to Rosemary because it is no longer possible for him to drive up to Valerie's house and knock on her window, and he can't go into Birdy's kitchen to have a nightcap with him and Lannie.

Jack stops beside Billy's dad's car, parked in front of the bus terminal. The four of them sit there talking for a little while, finally agreeing that it's not worth it to try to keep the D-Jays going with Birdy Z. but that Jack will look into the matter of finding another piano man and starting over again under another name. "We're disbanded, man," Johnny says, laughing. Jack says, "Yeah, man, that's exactly what we are, disbanded as hell."

Before he gets on the road, Billy walks into the bus terminal to take a leak. While he's in the men's room facing the urinal, he hears a stall door slowly creak open behind him. He turns to see a man's face slowly extend toward him from one of the stalls. It is an unremarkable male face, not one Billy has ever seen before, but the sight of it scares Billy. He hears himself saying in a voice he hardly knows to be his own, "You son of a bitch, you fuck around with me, I'll fucking kill you!" The face recedes into the stall, the stall door creaks closed, Billy rushes his urination and leaves without washing his hands.

Driving home at three in the morning, he's wide awake now, shivering and wondering about the voice that came out of his own chest and throat in the bus terminal. When he said what he said, he knows he felt a power in his arms, hands, and fingers; whether or not he actually had it in him to kill the man who peered at him, he knows he spoke out of animal certainty that he could do it. Would do it, he whispers to the green light of the dashboard, would do it. He wonders what Birdy Z. would have done if Billy had spoken to him that way. Then he feels a gush of affection for the Bird, imagines himself back in the parking lot, admitting to the Bird that he did indeed love him, walking toward him and embracing him. It wouldn't have had to be queer, he thinks. He entertains the idea that if he had done that, they could have gone back in and finished the gig and ridden home telling each other jokes.

At school Valerie is absent for an entire week. Pete is out of school, too, one day, back another, then absent another. Billy's friends and acquaintances talk about Valerie and Pete so much that the hallways ring with their names, every laugh sounding to Billy as if it must be on Pete and Valerie's account. But he himself is not included in their conversations, hears no information, asks no one about them. He's almost seventeen. His days now seem full of the grim injustice of his having been cut off from everyone.

On the day she comes back to school, before homeroom, Valerie walks straight up to Billy at his locker and hands him a note that instructs him to meet her outside the band room at lunchtime. She's so quick and definite about it that what she's done goes almost unremarked by anybody but Billy himself. She's pale and puffy-faced, doing what she can to smile and speak to kids who come up and ask her how she's doing. She looks back over her shoulder at him when he's had a chance to read the note. He nods at her.

He knows the place she means, out by a side door where people rarely pass by, even at lunchtime. She's waiting for him when he walks back there, but she's got no smile for him, not even a hello. It's late April, a damp day. Underneath her band jacket she's got on a new white sweater he likes, but the way she's standing there she looks like a tough girl. She drags hard on her cigarette, then starts speaking to him in what he figures is a speech she's worked on for a while. "The doctor was wrong," she says. "That bastard. Sunday afternoon I started hemorrhaging. What I have—what I had!—was a cyst! Can you believe that?"

Her eyes drill Billy as if she's holding him responsible for what's happened to her, but he knows it's just because she's willing herself not to cry. Or maybe she does think it's his fault. Maybe it is. He can't say anything, and so he reaches toward her to pat her shoulder or something, but she backs away from him and keeps looking at him. He can't say anything for more than a minute; then he gets some words up out of his throat: "Are you and Pete going to stay . . . ?"

"Yeah, we are," she says vehemently. "My parents don't want me to, but Pete thinks we've made fools enough of ourselves now, and he doesn't want a divorce. What he thinks is what I go by since he was the one who was man enough to—"

"Valerie, it was a coin flip!"

"Yeah, tell me about it," she says and keeps her eyes on him, waiting. Billy feels the weight of enormous injustice coming down on him, but he knows better than to complain about it to her. He tries to hold her eyes, looks away, tries again.

"I just wanted you to know," she says finally.

"Yeah," Billy says.

"Can you keep it to yourself?" she asks him, and he nods. She reaches toward him—for a second he thinks she means to punch him in the ribs—clasps his hand and squeezes it. "Take care," she says, then walks away from him fast, stretching her navy-blue skirt with every stride.

Just before marching-band practice that afternoon, Elliott Pugh, like a soldier reporting for duty, walks over and stands in front of Billy. "I'm playing with Mr. Pendergast now," he says.

Billy drags on his cigarette and looks at Elliott but doesn't make an effort to meet his eyes. In the last couple of days he's had about all the hostile eye contact he can stand. Still, he can't help witnessing Elliott's presence here in front of him. Billy would still like to take back his betrayal of Elliott those months ago. He figures he has some options: one, he can warn Elliott of Birdy's drinking and tarnish the prize Elliott thinks he's won, or two, he can politely wish Elliott luck. He chooses number three and tells Elliott to go fuck himself. When he sees Elliott grin maliciously at him, he knows that number three was the best for both of them.

Billy puts his cigarette in the corner of his mouth and keeps standing off more or less by himself, comfortable with the horn at his waist hooked to his neck strap like a little attached shelf for him to rest his arms on. Elliott's down at the other end of the ranks with the clarinet section, all of them toodling like free-lance musical idiots. If for no other reason than that the big queer is a clarinet player, Billy knows he was right in what he told Elliott. He snorts to himself, drops his cigarette and stomps it. Up front chatting with the other majorettes, Valerie has changed into shorts but she's still got on her band jacket, and Billy imagines she's feeling the wind on her legs. "Val, Val," Billy hums to himself and shakes his head and smiles.

More than a hundred kids are in this marching band with Billy. He is one among them. He thinks of Birdy, home at this moment, probably sleeping off one binge, getting ready for another one, and Lannie, probably sitting at her kitchen table, smoking a cigarette and trying to figure out what she's going to do about the Bird and the kids and her life—their lives. That's the thought that comes to him just about the time Mr. Banks hollers at them that break is over, put out the cigarettes, dress right dress! Billy takes his place in ranks, still thinking about how Lannie really does have to look after her kids, how she probably figures she has to do what she can for the Bird. Elliott has just hitched himself to the Bird's fate for at least a little while. Valerie is up there in front, a married woman, but bouncing her baton on her toe now like a kid.

Mr. Banks pokes the whistle into his mouth, lifts his arms and gives them a shrill blast. Billy puts his teeth to the mouthpiece of the saxophone, ready to play. He's in the center of a rank, kids in front of him, behind him, and to either side of him. Mr. Banks blasts the whistle again, plunging his arms downward, and in unison with them all Billy steps forward, releasing a huge exhalation into the horn. The sound that comes forth is an enormous, rich billowing of vibration that swells up out of the moving formation of more than a hundred musicians. He keeps perfectly square in his rank and in his file. Stepping out crisply to John Philip Sousa's King Cotton, Billy's exhilarated. He feels so free he can hardly stand it.

Sandy Huss

COUPON FOR BLOOD

(from *TriQuarterly*)

For a brain, Phin had to cope with hard-baked clay. This he owed to his maker, who—though he had blown Phin up tight as a rubber raft, inspiring every chamber of his body with pure and lucid air—hadn't thought to give Phin much of anything else. In the beginning, moist and infused with oxygen, the lush gritty clay of his cerebrum had been good enough to eat, rich in salubrious minerals—food, indeed, for thought. But from the time Phin turned thirteen he had tried to jazz it up, had bled out the air, had baked and fired, with the result that now his head rattled with potsherds and jagged bits of roofing tile. Occasionally his inner eye, working like the mirrors of a kaleidoscope, trained itself upon this chaos, reflecting some seeming order out of this substance for thinking that could no longer support a thought. But the mirrors too had been damaged over the years, their silver scratched and charred, so that the images they presented were crazed and dim, and what passed in this brain for memories, information, or ideas were often chimerical—and sometimes alien even to Phin, who had given them birth.

But he had no doubts about what he saw just then. Even from the box canyon of the bus's back seats, Phin could tell that a coupon for blood waited to board. While the driver (out on the street, babysitting her children over the phone) held the payphone's metal cord to her heart, the coupon for blood kept its tail to the wind. While the passengers already aboard the idling bus clucked to each other about company time, the coupon for blood stamped its feet and pressed its great hooked fingers to its lips. Phin, temporarily out of the late November cold and agog that a coupon for blood was headed his way, hugged himself and clapped the soles of his sneakered feet.

Everyone waited while the driver changed a diaper over the phone. She wiped her fingers over and over through the hair at her temple, explaining to her daughter how to charge the safety pin with static, so that the pin—filmed with deposits of urea or not—would glide. Phin didn't mind the delay: as long as a nine-year-old struggled to pierce layered folds of diaper without stabbing her infant sister, as long as she fumbled against the tension of the gaping pin, Phin could picture himself stretched out on a narrow table, tethered only by dreams of what his pint of blood (worth two bucks more than usual, once he got his hands on the coupon) would buy.

Next to lying on the table itself, nothing made Phin more light-hearted than imagining himself there, his blood draining through a rubber tube that lay in a loop across his forearm like an out-of-body vein, the loop counter-balancing the drag of gravity that sucked his red and white cells into a little plastic pouch. At the same time that the loop's weight kept the end of the hollow needle buried in his skin, its precise curve prevented the tube from kinking and impeding the flow. Every technician at every blood bank made the same loop, as regular as a coil in a handwriting exercise, as practiced and legible (even to Phin for whom sentences had become a chore) as an *l* or an *e,* rising and backtracking across his forearm, one after another, for as many months and years as his marrow could crank the hemoglobin out. Phin reveled in the regeneration of his blood. It was a wonderful world, he thought, that would give him money for something he couldn't hold in his hand.

When Phin slapped his feet together, Deedee, catty-corner across the aisle, had been startled and relieved. Until then she had read in his face prostitution and unrelenting pain. Phin was ravishingly poor: his skin, the color of a tarnished penny, clung to his cheekbones, and his sparse curly lashes tossed diaphanous veils before his eyes. His cheap tight pants bound his thighs and genitals, and his skimpy T-shirt, its pieces stamped out haphazardly along the bias by machine, hung in a skewed line that barely covered him. He was nineteen, Deedee's age, and his remaining beauty had the fragility of a pear ripe too long by a day, a pear whose skin is still thin and promising, still so primed to yield that the gentlest thumb-smear can skim it away, but whose flesh beneath is pocked with rotting translucence so that it no longer tempts the tongue, so that its only use is as a matrix for seed. Sitting modestly upright, his tapered fingers caging his knees, Phin had seemed to Deedee to be awaiting absolution, to be dogged by regret for having loosed all evil upon the world. Deedee (white, enrolled in one of the better state universities, and hungry for her lunch) had been glum, having recently been taught how she caused Phin's poverty, how it profited her. She took heart at his little leap.

She was so relieved that she unzipped the knapsack propped between her feet and felt through it until something crackled in her hand. With both hands buried in the knapsack she forced apart stubborn cellophane welds. Casually she lifted a barbecued chip to her lips. Even as she broke its back with her teeth she knew she was rude, but now that Phin wasn't starving there was only one other person near enough for Deedee to offend—a woman of fifty, straight across the aisle—who probably already thought of Deedee as a slob: the older woman was magnificent. Black as basalt with a cast of blue, her skin seemed to have just lately cooled, and the light in her eyes suggested that she yet smoldered within. Katy (for that was her name) had anchored herself in her seat with her severe Etta Jenicks, with her own sense of worth.

Even when a bus is idling, its backmost passengers brace themselves. In the bench seats above the wheels, they, like Deedee and Katy, like Deedee and Phin, face each other—usually there are mothers with strings of children (and strollers that won't collapse), indigents and evangelists, high-school kids with graffitied notebooks, sometimes a bold unattended child—and they brace themselves against their own sidelong hurtling, unrestrained by each other's arms (even if arms were offered, there'd be too much open space in which to fall). They brace themselves against their roll to the front like so many thudding cabbages, where they would lie in a heap beneath a box of shifting coins.

This bus made its last stop within two blocks of the Greyhound station, and Katy—like Deedee—was headed there: beneath her seat a gray cardboard suitcase lay, ancient and ungainly, like something beached and stoically smothering beneath its own weight. Deedee, untucked and overslept, her student pallor unvaried by any blush of health, her own luggage a collection of knapsacks and canvas bags splotched with coffee and ballpoint ink—felt she must seem a flibbertigibbet in Katy's eyes. The woman was a monolith. How had she made that of herself? Deedee wanted her approval, but saw no chance of it, so pulled the little cellophane bag out into the open and munched away. The chips were stale, but Deedee accepted their staleness as a punishment: they were half gone by the time the driver and the coupon for blood climbed aboard.

Deedee, not in the market herself, naturally didn't realize that a coupon for blood was about to enter her life. She saw only middle-aged Harper in his green all-weather coat, clamping the *Post-Dispatch* under his arm. He must habitually have carried a paper there: a smeary stain had swallowed his armpit and spread halfway down his side. Deedee had the meanness of spirit to be ashamed of him, being guilty of such carelessness herself: she often left a thumbprint of chocolate or cheese dust on a library page. She sometimes felt that at any moment she too could become a walking stain.

For the length of the aisle Harper ducked his head, one hand lifting his green plaid hat by the crown—in obeisance to the ladies, it seemed. Yet he swaggered at the same time, trilled unselfconsciously, and flapped his hand in the pocket of his coat so violently that the hem knocked away Deedee's little cellophane bag. She said, "Hey!"—but as she spoke, Harper heedlessly punted the chips all the way to the back of the bus, and as Deedee said, "Hey!" again, Harper stepped on the bag, pivoting as he sat down on the bench that faced the front. Barbecued crumbs spilled from the bag's mouth beneath his shoe.

Deedee rolled her eyes and gave out an exaggerated sigh. She saw Katy turn her face toward the back of the driver's head. At least they were finally on their way.

Harper dropped his paper next to himself on the seat within reach of Phin, who—oblivious to Deedee's little disaster—bent toward the newsprint dotingly. He'd been prepared to change his seat if necessary, but the coupon had come straight to him.

"So sorry." Harper lifted his hat to Deedee, higher than before, revealing an oily baldness marked by parallel tracks of surgical scar. They ran from his eyebrows across his crown toward his nape as if he were a waxwork whose pate had served as a toy truck's proving ground. His hat back on, he bent over and with fastidious fingers swept the broken chips, a cigarette filter and a scrap of religious tract into the bag. Meanwhile, Phin's hand hovered above the neglected paper, but he did not touch.

Harper held the little bag out to Deedee, who took it, though she pinched it by a corner, dangling it away from herself like someone else's trash. She looked over at Katy. Katy looked down.

"Shit." Deedee glowered at the floor.

Harper raised a disciplinary finger in the air. "No smoking, food or drink," he said, ticking his finger toward the posted rule. Ignoring the covetous Phin, Harper selected a section of his paper and snapped it open with a sharp crack, sealing himself away behind it as if the bus were his own living room. Poor Phin, the drudge wife, inclined toward the newsprint, his eyes bashful and full of need, one hand with its long fingers just barely raised.

Behind that paper Harper's flesh was pulpy, his skin squamous, and his chemical sweat might have come straight from the embalmer's gun, but he thought of himself as oozing vitality. Living either on the street or in the bin, he rarely saw himself in anything besides window glass or bumper chrome, but even if Harper's world had been filled with highly polished mirrors, his clamminess would have registered with himself as a glow. Harper had been repeatedly doctored: he almost always felt good.

Now that he had taught that girl a lesson he felt wonderful, and his face flushed with righteous blood—some of which (as you might expect) had once streamed (though with different perceptions) through poor Phin's arteries and veins. Last summer Harper had lectured a less docile mark than Deedee: a hospital attendant bearing Harper's dinner on a tray. The young man had taken offense at the word *jigaboo,* and couldn't be persuaded to approve it even after Harper explained that he had been set down on the planet expressly to assign the lower animals their names. The attendant likewise could not credit *shine, smoke, junglebunny* or *coon,* and didn't give a rat's ass what Harper had been taught in Sunday school. By the time the other workers separated the attendant from his heavy tray, Harper had lain in a coma and a slick of gore.

Harper remembered none of this, had even momentarily forgotten his mission to name (which he usually forgot when he took his Mellaril instead of trading it for sex or food), but that was how it had come to be that Harper had been transfused, that it was in part Phin's blood that Harper's heart now pumped, first to his lungs, then to his spackled brain, giving him a magnanimous idea.

"Here's the sports page, buddy," he said to Phin. "You can keep it, I'll just throw it away." He went back behind the business section, which he pretended to read.

Phin held the paper up in front of himself at arm's length as if it were sheet music and he would momentarily begin to sing. But he spoke, instead, in a voice that was soft and musical. "Does this here have a coupon for blood?"

Harper feigned absorption in the world of commerce for a moment, but then folded down the paper. "Well, I don't know . . . a coupon for blood?"

"Yeah. For two dollars."

"What do you want to buy blood for?"

Katy and Deedee looked for a heartless instant at each other, then away.

"Not buy. Sell."

"With a coupon they give you two dollars?"

"They give you eight dollars, but with a coupon they give you two more."

"Ten dollars?"

Phin poked around in his broken brain, looking first at eight dollars, then at two. He couldn't bring them together in any way, but he didn't want to disagree. He smiled slowly, keeping his lids down for a moment, then raising them languidly. Phin had sold sex as well as plasma, and could say yes wordlessly.

Harper didn't smile in return. "Well, you can look." He withdrew behind his paper and sat very still.

Phin peeled open his allotted section, still holding it at arm's length, still sitting expectantly straight. As he paged through, the bell rang, and an old woman in the middle of the bus who had been facing the front stood up, walked toward the back, and waited in the stairwell near the back door. She held a sack of groceries against her hip, and took a long look at the two raised walls of newsprint that were Harper and Phin. "Huh," she said, and got off.

Just as she closed the door behind the woman, the driver perceived a presence in her womb. From the time she'd been an adolescent she had set her inner ear to listen for change, so that even sleeping her body had always known when to wake itself with the news that she was about to bleed. And now she heard a familiar burgeoning, the forbidding sound of the division that is multiplication, and she knew what she had known for several days. For a long while this sound would only get louder, its frequency higher, until the train of transformations that would bring her new baby to her had passed. For a moment she allowed tears to gather, but by the time she had pulled back out into traffic and begun to inventory the cupboards at home (planning what her eldest could fix for lunch), her eyes were dry.

Phin had some ideas about the coupon: a shape, some dotted lines, its location on the page. Someone, he was sure, had recently shown him one. There would be a cross in each corner of a rectangle, he thought. Crosses hung before his mind's eye as if he had just sped past a family plot on the open road, could still see tracers of gold and blue.

He studied every page. The fine print of the box scores snaked before his bloodshot eyes. He squinted for some time at a photograph wherein a man holding a soccer ball seemed to be sitting on another man's head, a flagpole growing out of his own. Phin forgot for a horrible moment what he was looking for, but then he remembered, and felt a glow of good fortune returning to surround him like a divine cloud that would protect him and show him the way. A clip-and-save box in the classifieds gave his heart a little thrill, but there were no crosses, and the bold WORD PROCESSING meant, Phin was positive, that the coupon had nothing to do with him. There were pages of cars for sale, and Phin's eyes sucked the names of some of them into his crumbling brain: Phoenix, Aries, Delta 88. Electra . . . Electra . . . Phin had ridden once in a midnight-blue Electra—or had he just leaned on it in a blue and midnight street?

The coupon wasn't here. Phin took his bearings by looking

through a film of pomade on the window: they hadn't yet reached the numbered streets. He had seen Harper somewhere before, he was sure, maybe on this very bus. He bet that Harper would ride with him to the end of the line. There was plenty of paper still to check, and he had five—maybe six—more miles. Phin trued up the corners of the sports section, folded it precisely, and balanced it on his knees, waiting for Harper to notice him.

And Harper lowered his paper as if he had not been reading at all.

With Harper's eye on him, Phin spoke again, a music box in Harper's hands. This was as clear to Harper as it was to Deedee and Katy, more clear perhaps, because polluted by chemicals he was free to see the delicate porcelain ballerina twirling in Phin's throat. It gave him great pleasure to arouse such attentiveness and modesty in Phin, as if he were, by tiny increments, leading him from barbarism to light. Phin sounded more and more angelic to Harper's ear: "Would you mind if I just checked those?"

Phin pointed to the stack of paper on the seat, but Harper knew better than to relinquish anything. "I'll see if it's in here," he said, and flipped through the business section so fast that the back of the bus filled with the flapping of gigantic wings. "There's no coupon for blood in here, buddy. There's nothing in here but the Dow Jones." Harper shrugged his shoulders with a crackling of paper and withdrew again.

Phin brought the pads of his fingers together in imitation of the Praying Hands. Very slowly he turned his head away from Harper to look outside. Twenty-first street. When he checked back, Harper was watching him. "What about those?"

Harper, affected by Phin's pretty smile—a smile that Harper would like to keep on Phin's face if he could—graciously picked through the paper at his side and handed one more section over. "I guess you can have this, buddy. I'll just throw this away."

Deedee opened her mouth with a click of her tongue and a quick intake of breath, but closed it again and turned red.

Katy covertly kept an eye on her. Deedee had a pointed chin and two dark moles—one above each corner of her mouth—that gave her face a catlike triangularity. Her slit-eyed twitching heightened the effect. She seemed as tortured as a house cat spying on a pair of warring toms from the wrong side of a screen: The stink of hot fur, the sight of backs bristling and humped cause her heart to pound, oxygen to crowd her cells, and blood to stream, messianic, through her veins. But she sits, contained, on a windowsill, slapping at it with her tail, raising nothing but backlit, floating motes. Once the fight moves down the block she'll throw herself down from the window and charge—dishing throw rugs one after another out of her way—as far in one direction as the walls of her house will permit, then wheel and take another tack, crash behind the couch and end tables, bruise herself against the furniture.

Deedee for now was still at the window, and the poor stymied thing kept sneaking looks at Katy, wanting Katy to nanny her, wanting Katy to nanny the whole bus. But Katy intended to let those nasty boys run *each other* ragged—she had problems of her own.

Phin began to page through a thick sheaf of department-store ads as daintily as he had waded through the sports, and Deedee's heart went out to him. Someone who could read ought to step in. Phin, scrawny as he was, probably shouldn't be peddling drop one, but Deedee wanted him to do—to have—whatever he desired, for reasons even she was suspicious of: his blackness, his wasted beauty, that bastard Harper's lunacy. Deedee still clutched her trashed bag of chips out of a horror of littering. Yes, she wanted that smug son-of-a-bitch—crazy or not—to do the generous thing. She imagined herself commandeering the paper, finding —or not finding, definitively—the damn coupon. But every reaction she anticipated from Harper was withering. She couldn't bear to give him an opening.

If Deedee's mother had still been alive, Deedee would have had more to offer than the heroics of a busybody. If Deedee's mother had still been alive, Deedee wouldn't have been headed back to school the day after Thanksgiving with nothing in her luggage but half a round-trip bus ticket and a desiccated, bloodless meal: she had rice cakes and peanut butter left, stuff suited to the fitful stomach of chemotherapy. (The barbecued chips, Deedee figured, must have been a whim, mentioned by her mother wistfully, fetched by husband or son in a hell-bent car, then rejected from a pit of nausea.)

If Deedee's mother had still been alive, Deedee would have had a couple pounds of turkey in tow, half an apple cake and a fistful of cold hard cash—the price of her bus ticket and then some. But though Deedee had cooked the holiday meal, she had left it all behind, sure that control over the family larder didn't transfer to the temporary help. Taking the leavings of her mother's restricted diet couldn't possibly offend—no one still living in her father's house considered it food.

If Deedee had asked her father for groceries, for cash, he doubtless would have given her enough to tide her over until her check for work-study came in Monday's mail. But unless she asked, her father seemed to assume that she could chow down on the intellectual breeze. Her mother had been dead now for months, it was not as if her father were still hazy with grief. Deedee was simply out of sight—even when *in* sight—out of mind. She felt too insubstantial to ask for a loan. Deedee had expected to miss her mother when she died, but she hadn't expected that her mother's death would give birth to her own poverty.

Musing in this vein, Deedee hid from herself the fact that she had what Phin was looking for: in the shape of a two-dollar bill, a bill so new and crisp it could have held knife pleats. She kept it folded within a concealed compartment in her wallet, safe from even her own emergency. As far as Deedee was concerned it was a relic that wouldn't spend.

By the time her mother died, the sick woman's purse had long been out of her control, her cash spent on grieving people's groceries, her lists of things to do ticked off by grieving people's hands. Deedee had often carried the purse itself from house to hospital to market; her brothers had taken out their mother's wallet and crammed it into their jacket pockets; everyone in the family had had occasion to dig through the linen and leather bag, tallying check stubs, tracking down rolls of film and dry-cleaning or reading off strings of numbers from insurance cards. Her mother's purse had been an open book. So when Deedee, boxing things for the Goodwill, had discovered a stash of two-dollar bills wedged in the wallet's plastic album between a list of clinic phone numbers and an organ donor card, she had been annoyed with herself that she hadn't noticed it before. The little lump of cash wasn't so little that it shouldn't have been obvious all along.

With the lump unfolded and four two-dollar bills laid out on the floor, Deedee had felt contempt for her mother as she had suddenly felt contempt for all people who refuse to honor a certain kind of currency—then end up holding it all. People with caches of fifty-cent pieces and Susan B. Anthony coins, people whose imagination limited money to denominations for which there were slots in cash registers and vending machines. But at the same time she had felt a loopy joy that her mother had left this weird legacy. Like the marvelous irrelevancy of the donor card, the money seemed a symbol to Deedee that her mother had intended to save her own life—but Deedee blushed at the thought of saying as much to her father or to his sons. So she kept a single bill for herself and stuffed the rest inside the stand for her mother's best wig, which she hid in an attic trunk.

Everyone on that bus but Phin had at least two dollars, but everyone's money was already spent. The driver's roll of quarters was destined for pay-phones, and the woman wearing a sweatsuit would need the four ones in her pocket for a box of tampons—soon. The woman with blue hair, who had just gotten on, and who was painstakingly threading her gauzy headscarf through the top buttonhole of her coat, had only her weekly allowance from her sister for Bingo cards. The guy carrying a new fire extinguisher was saving to straighten his kid's teeth, and the couple reading the Bible together wanted someday to have furniture in their living room. Even Harper's three dollars from selling his Elavil (which was supposed to counteract his Mellaril) had been budgeted for lunch at Burger King. Phin may have had no cash, but then he had only a few needs that he could remember, and he took solace in what Deedee found appalling: he was a walking factory of sex and blood. He was always on line. And he knew he would get the coupon, it was meant to be.

Katy had more money on her than the rest of the riders combined—and it never occurred to her to share it with Phin. She needed it to put up her daughter's bail. Their phone conversation had been unsatisfactory because they'd been whispering on both ends of the line—her daughter to thwart her guard, Katy to let her husband sleep—but Katy knew for sure that her daughter had been picked up driving a stolen car, a car she had thought belonged to her new boyfriend. Her daughter had known he was AWOL—had even, she admitted, mostly approved—but she had never once doubted that the car was his. That much she had promised Katy, in an insistent whisper Katy had to believe.

Even from two states away, her daughter could fill Katy with disappointment and self-reproach, from two states away she could make Katy's wallet gurgle like an open drain. In the past year Katy had bought eyeglasses when her daughter's prescription changed, neutered her adopted cats, kept up the insurance on her car. Now this.

Her daughter seemed to have been spun out of her, but never to have detached from her, seemed in fact to contain *her* now, like a cocoon. As her daughter grew older, it was Katy who changed, who was forced to embrace her daughter's chaos if she were to embrace her daughter at all. Katy supposed it was inevitable that her daughter would lead a fitful and struggling life, having spent her childhood in Katy's steady shade. For her daughter Katy could leave her husband this once. He would survive: he loved the pork-chop sandwiches they made at the neighborhood bar.

Phin's progress through the paper went more and more slowly; he had to look repeatedly over his shoulder out the window—they were nearing the end of the line. The more the fragments of crockery in Phin's head tried to piece together a vessel that could contain Harper, the more Phin remembered Harper saying he loved him, saying that Phin was a beautiful bitch. Phin remembered Harper's pulse quickening, Harper's fingers at Phin's nape kneading Phin's hair. Harper had never *had* such raunchy sex before, he had said, that had been the *most lewd* experience of his entire life, Phin was a Grade A, floor-licking, cock-sucking whore.

Even if Harper hadn't tipped Phin while he still knelt at Harper's feet (without Phin having to dogtrot after him, flirting and begging just a bit), Phin would have remembered Harper fondly, would have preened himself over being called Grade A. It was what he had always thought about himself, when he could still think—that he was choice.

And here again was that smitten man.

That it might have been someone other than Harper who had been so good to him, Phin had no reason to believe. It seemed likely enough, as likely as the coupon itself, as likely as its ultimate transfer to his own hands. Phin had the optimism of bad memory. He shifted his seat next to Harper and looked up into his face. Harper had loved him once, he was sure. "Look," Phin said, thumping a health-club ad, "it looks something like this here."

Harper let the business section crumple in his lap as if his weary arms couldn't support it anymore. "Buddy," he said, "it ain't in here, I looked."

Harper felt the high drama of his beleaguerment, of his duty to be magnanimous and kind. He looked around for an audience. The girl and the nigger woman both looked at their hands, but the bus driver had an eyebrow cocked at him in the rearview mirror. Harper panicked: they were at the end of the line. Harper hated to give the driver a reason to cast her evil eye his way. "Sorry, buddy," he said, and scooped together his paper, including the sections he'd given to Phin. He lurched out the back door, holding onto his hat as he stepped into the wind. He heard Phin's footsteps behind him, rubber soles as hard as old erasers clunking on the stairs, but Harper didn't look back.

With the men's departure, Deedee roused herself, folded her chip bag over and over at one end, and stuffed it into the pocket of her parka where it slowly opened, making tiny rustles and pops as she gathered her book bags. With the men's departure, she had a little trouble believing what she'd just heard and seen. If she'd only done something, she'd know how it all turned out. When she got to the stairwell, she saw that in her bending and leaning she'd been hogging the aisle, making Katy wait to draw her suitcase from beneath her seat. Deedee might not be able to help anyone, but at least she shouldn't be getting in their way. She sighed and shrugged piteously, but refused to let herself wait for any look of tolerance—let alone forgiveness—in Katy's eyes.

She started down the stairs, and there was Phin in the street, bouncing up and down, a parade-struck child, one moment craning his head to watch Harper zigzag down the street like a pigeon, the next moment eyeing the door of the bus. He was waiting, it turned out, for her.

He looked up at her and showed his teeth, but his eyes were flat and expressionless, their color that of raw liver, of clotted menstrual blood. "Help me, baby," he said.

Deedee couldn't understand what Phin wanted from her. It was too late, she had nothing, she was no match for Harper after all.

But as she stood in the stairwell struggling with an answer for him, she became transfixed by the sudden knowledge of the two-dollar bill in her wallet, by the sound of her mother's hands folding it, by the image of the full white moons rising on the horizons of her mother's fingernails. Deedee felt that she could never step off the bus into the stream of trouble that was Phin: he was a sluice of one-way valves. She would pool forever in the loggy legs of the universe if she gave him anything.

But how could she refuse? Phin waited with the confidence of someone people loved.

All Deedee's life she would remain uncertain whether it was Katy's hand or the curved edge of Katy's suitcase in the small of Deedee's back that pushed Deedee from the bus and kept on pushing until she was well past Phin. She felt she deserved only the suitcase, the suitcase accidentally, at that, but she hoped for Katy's hand. When the pushing stopped, Deedee looked lovingly at the side of Katy's face, but the older woman surged by, her eyes on the sign that read BUS, one shoulder dipped to balance the suitcase in the opposite hand.

The bus's door closed, and in the driver's womb a blastula of cells implanted itself. The driver could give it only divided attention, being—always—otherwise occupied. She closed her doors, checked her mirrors, and began her shuttle back to the other end of the line.

Deedee, her lumpy luggage banging around her knees, followed a respectful distance behind Katy, and slipped forever through the dross of Phin's brain. He fixed his eyes on something at the end of a long city block: that hat and that dirty coat, that pale bald neck would be easy to track. Phin ambled along in his sneakers, waiting for Harper to throw the coupon away.

Paula Sharp

HOT SPRINGS

(from *Threepenny Review*)

Mrs. Hope Doherty sat in the front seat, tugging at the front of her dress and fanning herself and fiddling with the air-conditioning levers and talking and talking.

"Y'all will like California. You got to visit the parks they have over there. I've seen all the national parks out West. Yosemite, Sequoia, Yellowstone, the Grand Canyon, Death Valley. Once I went to visit the boiling mudpots, and a man standing only six feet away from me slips down the bank and falls right into them! The mud just steamed and boiled over him and he sank, they never found the body or nothing. But Hot Springs is different. The springs are natural but they're kind of domesticated, know what I'm saying? They're all surrounded by walkways and big hotels."

"It's coming up, Mama," Stanley said, peering over the front seat between Mrs. Doherty and his mother.

"We should be seeing that turn again any minute, Gertie," Mrs. Doherty confirmed.

Gert looked at her son in the rearview mirror. He had placed his baseball cap in the lap of his overalls, and his fine hair was sticking straight up like black cat fur. He had a dirt beard and the white sections of his cap were soiled to a rust red.

"Stanley, you look a mess," Gert told her son.

Stanley smiled in reply and delicately placed his hat back onto his head as he looked at his mother's hair. It lay every which way on her head like grass trampled by a wild animal.

Gert continued, "Anyone would think we left you to sleep out-side on the ground. I swear, Hope, all we did this morning was walk from the hotel to the car. You'd think we dressed him in dirty clothes every morning." Gert suddenly remembered Stanley had fallen asleep in his overalls the night before and *was* wearing dirty clothes.

"Gert, do you see that sign there?" Mrs. Doherty cried out. Gert forgot to turn on the blinker and veered sharply to the left. She was having trouble paying attention to her driving. She had missed the turnoff to Hot Springs twice, because whenever Mrs. Doherty stopped talking, Gert heard Buddy Shipley's voice fighting against hers in last night's argument.

"I thought you were going to do me up these shoes, Gertie." The shoes had snuggled against each other in Buddy's hand like two brown piglets.

"And what's wrong with them?"

Buddy held them up higher.

"Well, I'm sorry, they just wouldn't come clean and I ran out of polish a week ago."

"My mother blacked my daddy's shoes every night."

"Well, I'm not your mother. Your mother's another lady. She lives in another state. I'm your wife. You only have one mama and nobody's spoiled enough to need two."

Buddy had looked at Gert so forlornly, sitting down on the bed and depositing the empty shoes beside his narrow, boyish feet, that Gert had slammed the door and walked out to buy shoe polish.

"Gert, you can pull right over here and hook around to the left. There's a parking space to the side of that bank there."

It had been Mrs. Doherty's idea to spring Gert and Stanley from Little Rock for the day to go to Hot Springs. They had taken Mrs. Doherty's car, a new 1963 Plymouth with low fins and a pushbut-ton gearshift, and she was letting Gert drive to cheer her up.

Gert steered toward the curb to parallel park, and pushed a but-ton on the dashboard. The windshield wipers turned on. "Wrong gear," she said gaily, turning the wipers off and pushing another button. This time the car made a gentle sound like a refrigerator motor, and rolled forward in one deft motion onto its rectangle of asphalt.

"Well, now, I think I'll hire you as my chauffeur," said Mrs.

Doherty, unbuckling her seatbelt. "There's a hot water fountain on that big hill, but you don't want to climb all the way up there, it's not worth all that huffing and puffing on a hot day. There's a nice little walkway with water pools right up the street there that are every bit as good. I know Stanley will love Hot Springs." She turned around in her seat. "After we go see the spring we'll drive up the road to the I.Q. Zoo where chickens play the piano and a rabbit will take your photograph. They use some special way to teach animals there to do all kinds of things that lots of people can't learn. Then we'll go to the Alligator Farm and eat barbecue for dinner at Stubby's. You'll like that, won't you, honey?"

Stanley thought he might.

Gert reached behind the seat for her purse. "That sound OK to you, hun?"

"Yep."

Gert fumbled inside her purse for her compact, frowned into it, reached back into her purse for her mascara, eyeshadow, and lipstick, and painted on the face she had seen in *Seventeen* two weeks before and had been wearing since: green eyelids whiskered with mascara, tabby-orange rouge, and a thin, upturned mouth.

Gert held her face perfectly still and sat up to look in the rearview mirror. "It'll have to do," she said, sitting back down. She piled her makeup into the purse and, resting her hands on the steering wheel, told Mrs. Doherty, "I never thought I'd let him skip school. Aren't we wicked?"

"You like school?" Mrs. Doherty asked Stanley, fishing for her own purse. Mrs. Doherty was a large-boned lady with a long nose that dipped and widened at the end like a cow's. She was wearing a spotted black-and-white dress and was the first woman Stanley had seen close up who did not use lipstick. Her lips were wide and pale. She rented a room in the Little Colonel Hotel on a monthly basis, and when Stanley walked home from school, he usually went straight to Mrs. Doherty's, where he would find his mother whooping and laughing and talking in a loud voice alternating with furtive whispers.

"Nope," Stanley answered.

"Well, it's a good thing you aren't there then," Mrs. Doherty laughed. Mrs. Doherty often said she took great pleasure in the fact that she had never finished high school but had grown rich selling useless, outlandish clothes to college girls and bored society wives. She owned a clothing store two blocks from the hotel called Paraphernalia.

Mrs. Doherty and Gert slid out of their seats, opened the back doors, and tugged at the plastic jugs and water coolers piled in a barricade on either side of Stanley. When Stanley had crawled out of the car, Mrs. Doherty and Gert gently shut the Plymouth's doors and turned to walk toward the hill.

Mrs. Doherty insisted on taking an extra water cooler from Gert. "You're thin as a stick, gimme that thing." Stanley unhooked himself from the cooler as his mother let go of it, and he resettled his hand in hers.

"You know that awful sweater I showed you?" Mrs. Doherty continued. "Looked like it was made out of dyed purple chicken feathers? Mrs. La De Da Rollins bought it. 'That sweater is you,' I told her."

Gert answered, "They can't get him to read, but I didn't know how to read when I was six either. I was seven when I began first grade. I wanted to start him in kindergarten a year later so he wouldn't always be younger than everyone else, but Buddy said you can't tie a boy to your apron strings. So then I kept telling Buddy that as long as we were in Little Rock we should at least put Stanley in Our Lady, where he'd get more attention, but Buddy has this thing about the Pope an' all. Well, Stanley will come along."

Buddy Shipley rarely spoke directly to Stanley, but Stanley had been relieved to overhear him say that no kid of his girlfriend's was going to any Catholic school. Stanley had seen the pale, plaid-uniformed children lining up noiselessly outside Our Lady.

"I told Buddy all these moves aren't good for a little boy, and that maybe it's just as well he lost his job, that maybe he could find some other work and we could settle down a while. Whoosh! You should see the look Buddy gave me. He has his mind set on California."

After Buddy Shipley had been laid off from his job as an itinerant manager for the Little Colonel Hotel chain, he awoke one midnight in early May and reflected on the first dream he ever remembered remembering: Buddy and Gert and her son Stanley were riding in Buddy's old green convertible across a desert. Ahead of them, a road stretched and undulated like an electric eel. When Buddy looked carefully at the asphalt, he saw that the road was actually a bright, inky canal of water, and that the car was moving through it, wheelless, like a boat. The desert deepened in color and sprang up in front of Buddy and extended into an enormous arch. He recognized the arch as a picture of the Golden Gate Bridge he had seen in a *Life* in the hotel lobby.

All the rest of May, Buddy talked about the dream to Gert as if it were more real to him than his own family. He cut out the magazine picture and stuck it to the bathroom mirror. Buddy told Gert that everyone he knew who was anybody had moved to California. He said that by the year two thousand, half of California would be Southerners. San Francisco would be as flashy as Dallas.

He wrote an old navy friend in San Diego, who sent a letter saying that he could get Buddy a modest job as an undermanager in a fancy hotel, to commence in July. Gert understood that nothing she could do would prevent Buddy from leaving Arkansas for California. When she saw the state of California on the map, she thought it looked like a badly shaped pie crust, but finally she had given in. California was where men moved when they grew discontent with what they were, and although Gert worried about uprooting Stanley again, she felt the force of history was against her.

Stanley had moved five times in two years, as Buddy Shipley was transferred from one Little Colonel Hotel to another. Stanley had spoken with a subdued, mumbling drawl in Georgia and a rubbery twang when he lived in Montgomery, had resided long enough in Memphis to call it Mimphis, and immediately mastered a springy nasal accent in Little Rock. Some mornings when he woke up he did not know which manner of speech, accompanied by its own nuances of personality, would sail from his mouth when he dared to open it. When Mrs. Doherty talked in her soft New Orleans accent, Stanley felt himself swaying back and forth, as if cradled by swishing bathtub water. He vaguely recalled a time when his mother had talked the same way, before her accent had been filed down and rubbed smooth by constant moving. When Buddy had transferred a year ago to the Little Colonel in Miami, Stanley had begun to speak with a foreign inflection, like the Finnish man who permanently rented the General E. Lee suite in the left wing.

Stanley could not get past the *y* in his first name when his mother tried to show him how to write *Stanley Beaulieu* (she mentioned as other possible last names his father's surname, Ray, or Buddy's surname, Shipley, instead of her maiden name, but she never showed Stanley any of these others on paper). Stanley would stare distrustfully at the little *y* when he saw what a shady kind of vowel it was, capable of a forceful twangy sound but silent in "Stanley." He had heard his name pronounced Stayinly in Arkansas and Stanlah in Georgia, and listened to citified Miami people say Stan*lee,* as if only the last part of his name were recognizable. Inwardly he felt too indefinite and fragile to print his signature with a green-and-gold Dixon Ticonderoga pencil.

The tall man with the twisted leg was sitting so close to the spring that he seemed to be guarding it. But his face lit up when he saw Stanley, and he said, "Go ahayed and touch it and see how hawt it is." The man wore a visored red cap and had a toothless, lipless face that collapsed over his chin, and large ears that leaned forward, cupping the air. He rolled up his pants leg and showed Stanley the scar from a bullet wound he had gotten in World War I, and he listened politely as Mrs. Doherty told him the early history of Hot Springs while Gert sat staring vacantly in front of her, or glaring into her compact, or pushing back her cuticles.

As Stanley kneeled down to stick his hand in the bubbling water, Mrs. Doherty was saying, ". . . they came from everywhere in the old days during the wunner to take a cure and stayed in those hotels there, and you had to reserve a room to take a bath, and you could sit in the tub all day until you felt you were pure steam, just all wispy and vapory like a ghost. Once I fainted . . ."

Stanley dipped his fingertip in the water and then plunged in his hand. "Man, it's hawt!" Stanley shrieked, jerking back his arm and then sticking it in again.

The man finally stood, winking at Stanley and tipping his cap at Mrs. Doherty, and limped down the wide path. Stanley circled Mrs. Doherty and limped after him, surveying the ground for rare or unusually colorful or root beer bottle caps.

Gert watched Mrs. Doherty fold in three places in order to stoop and fill up a jug with spring water. When she had finished filling the fourth jug, Mrs. Doherty said, "You're really not supposed to do this here, you're supposed to use the hot water fountain, but who cares?"

"You know," said Gert, "now he's not working anymore, he's stopped calling me his wife in front of people. He introduces us as 'my girlfriend Gertie and her son.' Before that, we were always planning to marry and he promised to adopt Stanley and everything. But somehow we never got around to it, with all those moves. He hardly takes any interest in me and Stanley anymore. All he talks about nowadays is California. And Unemployment. You know he doesn't believe in Unemployment. So after he comes back from standing in line all day, he goes on and on telling me, 'I'm different, I earned it, I've been putting money into the till. Those other guys there are freeloading off the government, they've been living off that line most of their lives, but I've been working my whole life and I'm only taking back for a few months what I've been putting in all those years.'"

"Men get so hard to take when they can't work," Mrs. Doherty said, screwing the last water cooler shut. "You have to be an angel to put up with them. You should have seen him when I asked if you could work at the Paraphernalia. He stumped around the room like the carpets was full of bugs. He sure don't like me very much."

"That's not so, Hope. He doesn't have a thing against you. It's just that he doesn't like anybody at all anymore."

"I never did meet a husband who took after me," Mrs. Doherty laughed, unfolding herself and standing up. Mrs. Doherty had had a stream of boyfriends, but her own husband had left her twenty years ago, after three days of marriage. She had once told Gert that he took everything when he left, even her ring off the sink, and her bridal gown and white highheels. Gert had wondered what he had done with the dress. Sold it? Used it for his next wife? Slept beside it? Gert pictured a pale wedding gown lying specterlike on a dark bed next to a sleeping man.

"You know, Buddy would never run off and quit us. But sometimes it's, well, like everybody rotates around him, and he hardly notices me. But I just wouldn't have the courage to leave if things got bad. I been there once before, I can't even fall asleep at night if I'm left alone. But things won't get that bad. Buddy's a real find, I should know after Thomas Ray—Buddy doesn't drink or get rough or play around or anything. Oh Jesus, I don't know what I'm talking about."

"Looks like Stanley's going to have to help us carry these jugs." Mrs. Doherty placed the smaller ones in the cooler. "Well, you know how some men are? Living in the same house with you but not even there?"

Gert turned with wide eyes to Mrs. Doherty.

"They don't have to get up and leave you, because they're already gone."

Gert jumped up. "Where's Stanley?" The women looked around them, and then down the walkway, where they saw Stanley creeping behind the man who had been sitting by the spring.

"Stan-lee-uh!" Mrs. Doherty cupped her lips and hollered. Stanley turned around and came galloping back, his overall pockets jingling with bottle caps.

At the I.Q. Zoo, after Stanley played tic-tac-toe with a chicken and lost, he and his mother and Mrs. Doherty followed a family with an uncountable number of children into a dark room. The animal trainer took out a group of red, blue, and yellow macaws and directed them to a row of perches. Gert found herself watching the large family instead of the educated animals. There were over ten children, almost all boys, and a mother who looked twelve months pregnant holding a baby, and a lank man with a long face clutching two boys in one hand and a girl in the other. A row of boys lined up in front of him. They had various colors of hair, butterscotch and black and a brown midway in between, and reminded Gert of a crossbred litter of puppies. They pushed forward against one another to see the birds.

One macaw, whom the trainer had told to roller skate, was clutching two-wheeled weights in his claws and lifting them one at a time in determined, hulking steps across the stage, his movement the opposite of a skater's effortless glide. He reminded Gert of a man pushing a car.

Gert saw the pregnant woman tilt forward and whisper to the man, "Hun, it's so hot in here. I don't feel good at all."

But the man was mesmerized by a parrot strutting forward to shoot off a toy cannon. "It won't take long," he answered, looking down at the boys. "We paid so much, we better see it on out."

The woman stepped back and shifted her baby to her other arm.

Stanley jumped as the cannon went HUCK! and shot a ball into the crowd.

Stanley worked his way through the group of boys by the stage to get a closer look at the razorback hog that now paraded before them, waiting for directions. The boys moved over without noticing Stanley, their eyes fixed on the hog as he got ready to push a coal cart along a miniature railroad track.

"Hun, please, I really don't feel well." Stanley saw the boys' mother looking meaningfully at her husband. "I'm gonna take R.E. and go out and see if I can find a Coke somewhere."

The man let go of the little girl, then pulled a dollar bill out of his pocket and gave it to his wife. "OK, baby, I'll bring Penny and the boys out later myself and we'll look around for you." His wife backtracked across the room and went out the door, hoisting the baby to her shoulder.

The man reached down and took Stanley by the hand. At first Stanley was surprised, but then he let his hand stay in the long, moist fingers of the man. Stanley looked at his mother and Mrs. Doherty standing on the left side of the stage, but they did not seem to notice.

For the rest of the show, he clung to the man from one dark room to the other as they watched ducks play the banjo and chickens walk tight ropes. When the show was over, Stanley ambled through the brightly lit store still holding onto the man, who followed his string of children past Mrs. Doherty and Gert and the other family, out into the hot air of the street.

Gert looked at postcards while Mrs. Doherty paid the cashier to have her picture taken by a rabbit. The cashier aimed a box camera at Mrs. Doherty, and a black-and-white rabbit walked out of a cage and perched on a second camera connected to the first, aiming it at Mrs. Doherty's profile. He raised his paw and pulled a lever and the first camera let out a burst of light. The cashier pulled a square of film out of the camera, watched the rabbit climb back in his cage, and then peeled a strip of plastic off the film and handed the photograph to Mrs. Doherty.

"Look here, Gert," Mrs. Doherty called out. "The rabbit will take a picture of you getting your picture taken by a rabbit. We just have to do one all together."

Gert examined the photograph Mrs. Doherty held up in front of the postcards. "Oh, that's funny. Stanley, we've got to do that, too." Gert looked around but saw only a couple with three yellow-haired children lining up in front of the camera and no Stanley.

"Did Stanley come out of the room with us, Hope?" Gert walked through the store into the animal rooms, with visions of Stanley crying in some dark corner, lost. The cashier followed behind with Mrs. Doherty, turning on the lights. "He's not here!"

Gert slipped back through the store and rushed to the front door of the I.Q. Zoo. Stanley was nowhere in sight. She turned to the cashier and said, "Is there some door back here he could have gone out, or some place he could be hiding?"

"No, there's no doors. Why would he be hiding?" The cashier focused on Gert with a curious, accusatory expression.

Mrs. Doherty looked outside a second time. "There he is, right there."

Gert saw the pregnant woman walking toward the I.Q. Zoo and leading Stanley by the hand.

"Is he yours?" she called out. "My husband didn't realize he had the wrong little boy." The woman laughed. "He thought it was just another one of ours. We would have drove off if my girl Penny hadn't asked about him."

Mrs. Doherty answered with a bellowing laugh.

"Doesn't that beat all," said the woman. "As if we don't have too many already." Stanley let go of her hand and moved shyly over to Gert, pulling down his cap and looking into his pocket.

"Well, thanks for bringing him back," said Gert. She hoped she sounded calm and light-hearted like the woman, and that her voice did not betray the terror and hysteria and relief that were whirling inside her.

"You're welcome to have some of the other ones, too," said the woman as she walked away. "Take your pick."

Stanley saw four boys staring at him out of the car windows

while the man, who sat in the driver's seat, looked directly ahead as if he did not want to be noticed. Stanley stepped behind Mrs. Doherty until the car drove away. When the station wagon passed them, the woman leaned in front of her husband, pressing on the steering wheel so that the car honked three times to Stanley's mother and Mrs. Doherty.

Gert led Stanley back inside and he sat with his mother and Mrs. Doherty in front of the camera, posing for the rabbit. While Mrs. Doherty paid for the photograph, Gert looked through the postcards of Hot Springs. She picked out ten of them, saw that no one was paying attention to her, and slipped the postcards into her purse. Gert was surprised at herself, but then she also felt a pleasant spitefulness toward Hot Springs.

As she walked toward the exit, her purse seemed heavier and fuller.

"Whoosh," Mrs. Doherty said, once they were all three safely outside. "What a long day. I think we're going to have to skip the alligator farm for now and go right to Stubby's."

Gert turned toward her son. "You feel like eating, honey?"

Stanley nodded, and looked at the photograph in his hand: a black-haired boy stared back at him, wedged between his mother and Mrs. Doherty. Mrs. Doherty's head was turned toward the rabbit, her mouth open in mock surprise as the rabbit eyed her, seeming to ready the camera. Stanley's mother was looking down at the black-haired boy, with her hands grasping his shoulders like clothespins, as if she were afraid the next wind would blow him loose and carry him upward into the air.

Rick Bass

WILD HORSES

(from *The Paris Review*)

Karen was twenty-six. She had been engaged twice, married once. Her husband had run away with another woman after only six months. It still made her angry when she thought about it, which was not often.

The second man she had loved more, the most. He was the one she had been engaged to, but had not married. His name was Henry. He had drowned in the Mississippi the day before they were to be married. They never even found the body. He had a marker in the cemetery, but it was a sham. All her life, Karen had heard those stories about fiancés dying the day before the wedding; and then it had happened to her.

Henry and some of his friends, including his best friend, Sydney Bean, had been sitting up on the old railroad trestle, the old highway that ran so far and across that river, above the wide muddiness. Louisiana and trees on one side; Mississippi and trees, and some farms, on the other side—the place from which they had come. There had been a full moon and no wind, and they had been sitting above the water, maybe a hundred feet above it, laughing, and drinking Psychos from the Daiquiri World over in Delta, Louisiana. The Psychos contained rum and Coca-Cola and various fruit juices and blue food coloring. They came in styrofoam cups the size of small trash cans, so large they had to be held with both hands. They had had too many of them: two, maybe three apiece.

Henry had stood up, beaten his chest like Tarzan, shouted, and then dived in. It had taken him forever, just to hit the water; the

III

light from the moon was good, and they had been able to watch him, all the way down.

Sometimes Sydney Bean still came by to visit Karen. Sydney was gentle and sad, her own age, and he worked somewhere on a farm, out past Utica, back to the east, where he broke and sometimes trained horses.

Once a month—at the end of each month—Sydney would stay over on Karen's farm, and they would go into her big empty closet, and he would let her hit him: striking him with her fists, kicking him, kneeing him, slapping his face until his ears rang and his nose bled; slapping and swinging at him until she was crying and her hair was wild and in her eyes, and the palms of her hands hurt too much to hit him any more.

It built up, the ache and the anger in Karen; and then, when she hit Sydney, it went away for a while. He was a good friend. But the trouble was that it always came back.

Sometimes Sydney would try to help her in other ways. He would tell her that some day she was going to have to realize that Henry would not be coming back. Not ever—not in any form— but to remember what she had had, to keep *that* from going away.

Sydney would stand there, in the closet, and let her strike him. But the rules were strict: she had to keep her mouth closed. He would not let her call him names while she was hitting him.

Though she wanted to.

After it was over, and she was crying, more drained than she had felt since the last time, sobbing, her feelings laid bare, Sydney would help her up. He would take her into the bedroom and towel her forehead with a cool washcloth. Karen would be crying in a child's gulping sobs, and he would brush her hair, hold her hand, even hold her against him, and pat her back while she moaned.

Farm sounds would come from the field, and when she looked out the window, she might see her neighbor, old Dr. Lynly, the vet, driving along in his ancient blue truck, moving along the bayou, down along the trees, with his dog, Buster, running along- side, barking; herding the cows together for vaccinations.

"I can still feel the hurt," Karen would tell Sydney sometimes, when Sydney came over, not to be beaten up, but to cook supper for her, or to just sit on the back porch with her, and to watch the fields.

Sydney would nod whenever Karen said that she still hurt, and he would study his hands.

"I could have grabbed him," he'd say, and then look up and out at the field some more. "I keep thinking that one of these years, I'm going to get a second chance." Sydney would shake his head again. "I think I could have grabbed him," he'd say.

"Or you could have dived in after him," Karen would say, hopefully, wistfully. "Maybe you could have dived in after him."

Her voice would trail off, and her face would be flat and weary.

On these occasions, Sydney Bean wanted the beatings to come once a week, or even daily. But they hurt, too, almost as much as the loss of his friend, and he said nothing. He still felt as if he owed Henry something. He didn't know what.

Sometimes, when he was down on his knees, and Karen was kicking him or elbowing him, he felt close to it—and he almost felt angry at Karen—but he could never catch the shape of it, only the feeling.

He wanted to know what was owed, so he could go on.

On his own farm, there were cattle down in the fields, and they would get lost, separated from one another, and would low all through the night. It was a sound like soft thunder in the night, before the rain comes, and he liked it.

He raised the cattle, and trained horses too: he saddle-broke the young ones that had never been ridden before, the one- and two-year olds, the stallions, the wild mares. That pounding, and the evil, four-footed stamp-and-spin they went into when they could not shake him; when they began to do that, he knew he had them beaten. He charged two hundred fifty dollars a horse, and sometimes it took him a month.

Old Dr. Lynly needed a helper, but couldn't pay much, and Sydney, who had done some business with the vet, helped Karen get the job. She needed something to do besides sitting around on her back porch, waiting for the end of each month.

Dr. Lynly was older than Karen had thought he would be, when she met him up close. He had that look to him that told her it might be the last year of his life. It wasn't so much any illness or feebleness or disability. It was just a finished look.

He and Buster—an Airedale, six years old—lived within the city limits of Vicksburg, down below the battlefield, hidden in one of the ravines—his house was up on blocks, the yard flooded with almost every rain—and in his yard, in various corrals and pens, were chickens, ducks, goats, sheep, ponies, horses, cows, and an ostrich. It was illegal to keep them as pets, and the city newspaper editor was after him to get rid of them, but Dr. Lynly claimed they were all being treated by his tiny clinic.

"You're keeping these animals too long, Doc," the editor told him. Dr. Lynly would pretend to be senile, and would pretend to think the editor was asking for a prescription, and would begin quoting various and random chemical names.

The Airedale minded Dr. Lynly exquisitely. He brought the paper, the slippers, he left the room on command, and he brought the chickens' eggs, daily, into the kitchen, making several trips for his and Dr. Lynly's breakfast. Dr. Lynly would have six eggs, fried for himself, and Buster would get a dozen or so, broken into his bowl raw. Any extras went into the refrigerator for Dr. Lynly to take on his rounds, though he no longer had many; only the very oldest people, who remembered him, and the very poorest, who knew he worked for free. They knew he would charge them only for the medicine.

Buster's coat was glossy from the eggs, and burnished, black and tan. His eyes, deep in the curls, were bright, sometimes like the brightest things in the world. He watched Dr. Lynly all the time.

Sometimes Karen watched Dr. Lynly play with Buster, bending down and swatting him in the chest, slapping his shoulders. She had thought it would be mostly kittens and lambs. Mostly, though, he told her, it would be the horses.

The strongest creatures were the ones that got the sickest, and their pain was unspeakable when they finally did yield to it. On the rounds with Dr. Lynly, Karen forgot to think about Henry at all. Though she was horrified by the pain, and almost wished it were hers, bearing it rather than watching it, when the horses suffered.

Once, when Sydney was with her, he had reached out and taken her hand in his. When she looked down and saw it, she had at first been puzzled, not recognizing what it was, and then repulsed, as if it were a giant slug; and she threw Sydney's hand off hers quickly, and ran into her room.

Sydney stayed out on the porch. It was heavy blue twilight and all the cattle down in the fields were feeding.

"I'm sorry," he called out. "But I can't bring him back!" He waited for her to answer, but could only hear her sobs. It had been three years, he thought.

He knew he was wrong to have caught her off-balance like that, but he was tired of her unhappiness, and frustrated that he could do nothing to end it. The sounds of her crying carried, and the cows down in the fields began to move closer, with interest. The light had dimmed, there were only dark shadows and pale lights, and a low gold thumbnail of a moon—a wet moon—came up over the ragged tear of trees by the bayou.

The beauty of the evening, being on Karen's back porch and in her life, when it should have been Henry, flooded Sydney with a sudden guilt. He had been fighting it, and holding it back, constantly; and then, suddenly, the quietness of the evening, and the stillness, released it.

He heard himself saying a crazy thing.

"I pushed him off, you know," he said, loudly enough so she could hear. "I finished my drink, and put both hands on his skinny-ass little shoulders, and said, 'Take a deep breath, Henry.' I just pushed him off," said Sydney.

It felt good, making up the lie. He was surprised at the relief he felt; it was as if he had control of the situation. It was like when he was on the horses, breaking them, trying to stay on.

Presently, Karen came back out with a small blue pistol, a .38, and she went down the steps and out to where he was standing, and she put it next to his head.

"Let's get in the truck," she said.

He knew where they were going.

The river was about ten miles away, and they drove slowly. There was fog flowing across the low parts of the road and through the fields and meadows like smoke, coming from the woods, and he was thinking about how cold and hard the water would be when he finally hit.

He felt as if he were already falling towards it, the way it had taken Henry forever to fall. But he didn't say anything, and though it didn't feel right, he wondered if perhaps it was this simple, as if this was what was owed after all.

They drove on, past the blue fields and the great spills of fog.

The roofs of the hay barns were bright silver polished tin, under the little moon and stars. There were small lakes, cattle stock tanks, and steam rose from them.

They drove with the windows down; it was a hot night, full of flying bugs, and about two miles from the river, Karen told him to stop.

He pulled off to the side of the road, and wondered what she was going to do with his body. A cattle egret flew by, ghostly white and large, flying slowly, and Sydney was amazed that he had never recognized their beauty before, though he had seen millions. It flew right across their windshield, from across the road, and it startled both of them.

The radiator ticked.

"You didn't really push him off, did you?" Karen asked. She still had the pistol against his head, and had switched hands.

Like frost burning off the grass in a bright morning sun, there was in his mind a sudden, sugary, watery feeling—like something dissolving. She was not going to kill him after all.

"No," he said.

"But you could have saved him," she said, for the thousandth time.

"I could have reached out and grabbed him," Sydney agreed. He was going to live. He was going to get to keep feeling things, was going to get to keep seeing things.

He kept his hands in his lap, not wanting to alarm Karen, but his eyes moved all around as he looked for more egrets. He was eager to see another one.

Karen watched him for a while, still holding the pistol against him, and then turned it around and looked at the open barrel of it, cross-eyed, and held it there, right in her face, for several seconds. Then she reached out and put it in the glove box.

Sydney Bean was shuddering.

"Thank you," he said. "Thank you for not shooting yourself."

He put his head down on the steering wheel, in the moonlight, and shuddered again. There were crickets calling all around them. They sat like that for a long time, Sydney leaning against the wheel, and Karen sitting up straight, just looking out at the fields.

Then the cattle began to move up the hill towards them, thinking that Karen's old truck was the one that had come to feed them, and slowly, drifting up the hill from all over the fields, coming from out of the woods, and from their nearby resting spots on the sandbars along the little dry creek that ran down into the bayou —eventually, they all assembled around the truck, like schoolchildren.

They stood there in the moonlight, some with white faces like skulls, all about the same size, and chewed grass and watched the truck. One, bolder than the rest—a yearling black Angus—moved in close, bumped the grill of the truck with his nose, playing, and then leapt back again, scattering some of the others.

"How much would you say that one weighs?" Karen asked. "How much, Sydney?"

They drove the last two miles to the river slowly. It was about four A.M. The yearling cow was bleating and trying to break free; Sydney had tied him up with his belt, and with jumper cables and shoelaces, and an old shirt. His lip was bloody from where the calf had butted him.

But he had wrestled larger steers than that before.

They parked at the old bridge, the one across which the trains still ran. Farther downriver, they could see an occasional car, two round spots of headlight moving slowly and steadily across the new bridge, so far above the river, going very slowly. Sydney put his shoulders under the calf's belly and lifted it with his back and legs, and like a prisoner in the stock, he carried it out to the center of the bridge. Karen followed. It took about fifteen minutes to get there, and Sydney was trembling, dripping with sweat, when finally they gauged they had reached the middle. The deepest part.

They sat there, soothing the frightened calf, stroking its ears, patting its flanks, and waited for the sun to come up. When it did, pale orange behind the great steaminess of the trees and river below—the fog from the river and trees a gunmetal gray, the whole world washed in gray flatness, except for the fruit of the sun—they untied the calf, and pushed him over.

They watched him forever and forever, a black object and then a black spot against the great background of no-colored river, and then there was a tiny white splash, lost almost immediately in the river's current. Logs, which looked like twigs from up on the bridge, swept across the spot. Everything headed south, moving south, and there were no eddies, no pauses.

"I am halfway over him," Karen said.

And then, walking back, she said: "So that was really what it was like?"

She had a good appetite, and they stopped at the Waffle House and ate eggs and pancakes, and had sausage and biscuits and bacon and orange juice. She excused herself to go to the restroom, and when she came back out, her face was washed, her hair brushed and clean-looking. Sydney paid for the meal, and when they stepped outside, the morning was growing hot.

"I have to work today," Karen said, when they got back to her house. "We have to go see about a mule."

"Me, too," said Sydney. "I've got a stallion who thinks he's a bad-ass."

She studied him for a second, and felt like telling him to be careful, but didn't. Something was in her, a thing like hope stirring, and she felt guilty for it.

Sydney whistled, driving home, and tapped his hands on the steering wheel, though the radio did not work.

Dr. Lynly and Karen drove until the truck wouldn't go any farther, bogged down in the clay, and then they got out and walked. It was cool beneath all the big trees, and the forest seemed to be trying to press in on them. Dr. Lynly carried his heavy bag, stopping and switching arms frequently. Buster trotted slightly ahead, between the two of them, looking left and right, and up the road, and even up into the tops of the trees.

There was a sawmill, deep in the woods, where the Delta's farmland in the northern part of the county settled at the river and then went into dark mystery—hardwoods, and muddy roads, then no roads. The men at the sawmill used mules to drag their trees to the cutting. There had never been money for bulldozers, or even tractors. The woods were quiet, and foreboding; it seemed to be a place without sound or light.

When they got near the sawmill, they could hear the sound of axes. Four men, shirtless, in muddy boots with the laces undone, were working on the biggest tree Karen had ever seen. It was a tree too big for chain saws. Had any of the men owned one, the tree would have ruined the saw.

One of the men kept swinging at the tree—putting his back into it—with rhythmic, stroking cuts. The other three stepped back, hitched their pants, and wiped their faces with their forearms.

The fourth man stopped cutting finally. There was no fat on him and he was pale, even standing in the beam of sunlight that was coming down through an opening in the trees—and he looked old; fifty, maybe, or sixty. Some of his fingers were missing.

"The mule'll be back in a minute," he said. He wasn't even breathing hard. "He's gone to bring a load up out of the bottom." He pointed with his ax, down into the swamp.

"We'll just wait," said Dr. Lynly. He bent back and tried to look up at the top of the trees. "Y'all just go right ahead with your cutting."

But the pale muscled man was already swinging again, and the other three, with another tug at their beltless pants, joined in: an odd, pausing drumbeat, as four successive whacks hit the tree; then four more again; and then, almost immediately, the cadence stretching out, growing irregular, as the older man chopped faster.

All around them were the soft pittings, like hail, of tree chips, raining into the bushes. One of the chips hit Buster in the nose, and he rubbed it with his paw, and turned and looked up at Dr. Lynly.

They heard the mule before they saw him: he was groaning, like a person. He was coming up the hill that led out of the swamp; he was coming towards them.

They could see the tops of small trees and saplings shaking as he dragged his load through them. Then they could see the tops of his ears; then his huge head, and after that they saw his chest. Veins raced against the chestnut thickness of it.

Then the tops of his legs.

Then his knee. Karen stared at it and then she started to tremble. She sat down in the mud, and hugged herself—the men stopped swinging, for just a moment—and Dr. Lynly had to help her up.

It was the mule's right knee that was injured, and it had swollen to the size of a basketball. It buckled, with every step he took, pulling the sled up the slick and muddy hill, but he kept his footing and he did not stop. Flies buzzed around the knee, around the infections, where the loggers had pierced the skin with nails and the ends of their knives, trying to drain the pus. Dried blood ran down in streaks to the mule's hoof, to the mud.

The sawlogs on the back of the sled smelled good, fresh. They smelled like they were still alive.

Dr. Lynly walked over to the mule and touched the knee. The mule closed his eyes and trembled slightly, as Karen had done, or even as if in ecstasy, at the chance to rest. The three younger men, plus the sledder, gathered around.

"We can't stop workin' him," the sledder said. "We can't shoot him, either. We've got to keep him alive. He's all we've got. If he dies, it's us that'll have to pull them logs up here."

A cedar moth, from the woods, passed over the mule's ears, fluttering blindly. It rested on the mule's forehead briefly, and then flew off. The mule did not open his eyes. Dr. Lynly frowned and rubbed his chin. Karen felt faint again, and leaned against the mule's sweaty back to keep from falling.

"You sure you've got to keep working him?" Dr. Lynly asked.

"Yes, sir."

The pale logger was still swinging, tiny chips flying in batches.

Dr. Lynly opened his bag. He took out a needle and rag, and a bottle of alcohol. He cleaned the mule's infections. The mule drooled a little when the needle went in, but did not open his eyes. The needle was slender, and it bent and flexed, and slowly Dr. Lynly drained the fluid.

Karen held onto the mule's wet back and vomited into the mud, both her hands on the mule as if she were being arrested against the hood of a car, and her feet spread out wide. The men gripped their axes awkwardly.

Dr. Lynly gave one of them a large plastic jug of pills.

"These will kill his pain," he said. "The knee will get big again, though. I'll be back out, to drain it again." He handed Karen a clean rag from his satchel, and led her away from the mule, away from the mess.

One of the ax men carried their satchel all the way back to the truck. Dr. Lynly let Karen get up into the truck first, and then Buster; then the ax man rocked and shoved, pushing on the hood of the truck as the tires spun, and helped them back it out of the mud: their payment for healing the mule. A smell of burning rubber and smoke hung in the trees after they left.

They didn't talk much. Dr. Lynly was thinking about the pain killers, how for a moment, he had almost given the death pills instead.

Karen was thinking how she would not let him pay her for that day's work. Also she was thinking about Sydney Bean: she would sit on the porch with him again, and maybe drink a beer and watch the fields.

He was sitting on the back porch, when she got in; he was on the wooden bench next to the hammock, and he had a tray set up for her with a pitcher of cold orange juice. There was froth in the pitcher, a light creamy foaminess from where he had been stirring it, and the ice cubes were circling around. Beads of condensation slid down the pitcher, rolling slowly, then quickly, like tears. She could feel her heart giving. The field was rich summer green, and then, past the field, the dark line of trees. A long string of cattle egrets flew past, headed down to their rookery in the swamp.

Sydney poured her a small glass of orange juice. He had a metal pail of cold water and a clean washcloth. It was hot on the back porch, even for evening. He helped her get into the hammock; then he wrung the washcloth out and put it across her forehead, her eyes. Sydney smelled as if he had just gotten out of the shower, and he was wearing clean white duckcloth pants and a bright blue shirt.

She felt dizzy, and leaned back in the hammock. The washcloth over her eyes felt so good. She sipped the orange juice, not looking at it, and licked the light foam of it from her lips. Owls were beginning to call, down in the swamp.

She felt as if she were younger, going back to a place, some place she had not been in a long time but could remember fondly. It felt like she was in love. She knew that she could not be, but that was what it felt like.

Sydney sat behind her and rubbed her temples.

It grew dark, and the moon came up.

"It was a rough day," she said, around ten o'clock.

But he just kept rubbing.

Around eleven o'clock, she dozed off, and he woke her, helped her from the hammock, and led her inside, not turning on any lights, and helped her get in bed.

Then he went back outside, locking the door behind him. He sat on the porch a little longer, watching the moon, so high above him, and then he drove home, slowly, cautiously, as ever. Accidents were everywhere; they could happen at any time, from any direction.

Sydney moved carefully, and tried to look ahead and be ready for the next one.

He really wanted her. He wanted her in his life. Sydney didn't know if the guilt was there for that—the wanting—or because he was alive, still seeing things, still feeling. He wanted someone in his life, and it didn't seem right to feel guilty about it. But he did.

Sometimes, at night, he would hear the horses running, thundering across the hard summer-baked flatness of his pasture, running wild—and he would imagine they were laughing at him for wasting his time feeling guilty, but it was a feeling he could not shake, could not ride down, and his sleep was often poor and restless.

Sydney often wondered if horses were even meant to be ridden at all.

It was always such a struggle.

The thing about the broncs, he realized—and he never realized it until they were rolling on top of him in the dust, or rubbing him off against a tree, or against the side of a barn, trying to break his leg—was that if the horses didn't get broken, tamed, they'd get wilder. There was nothing as wild as a horse that had never been broken. It just got meaner, each day.

So he held on. He bucked and spun and arched and twisted, shooting up and down with the mad horses' leaps; and when the horse tried to hurt itself, by running straight into something—a fence, a barn, the lake—he stayed on.

If there was, once in a blue moon, a horse not only stronger, but more stubborn than he, then he would have to destroy it.

The cattle were easy to work with, they would do anything for food, and once one did it, they would all follow; but working with the horses made him think ahead, and sometimes he wondered, in streaks and bits of paranoia, if perhaps all the horses in the world did not have some battle against him, and were destined, all of them, to pass through his corrals, each one testing him before he was allowed to stop.

Because like all bronc-busters, that was what Sydney someday allowed himself to consider and savor, in moments of rest: the day when he could stop. A run of successes. A string of wins so satisfying and continuous that it would seem—even though he would be sore, and tired—that a horse would never beat him again, and he would be convinced of it, and then he could quit.

Mornings in summers past, Henry used to come over, and sit on the railing and watch. He had been an elementary school teacher, and frail, almost anemic, but he had loved to watch Sydney Bean ride the horses. He taught only a few classes in the summers, and he would sip coffee and grade a few papers while Sydney and the horse fought out in the center.

Sometimes Henry had set a broken bone for Sydney—Sydney had shown him how—and other times Sydney, if he was alone, would set his own bones, if he even bothered with them. Then he would wrap them up and keep riding. Dr. Lynly had set some of his bones, on the bad breaks.

Sydney was feeling old, since Henry had drowned. Not so much in the mornings, when everything was new and cool, and had promise; but in the evenings, he could feel the crooked shapes of his bones, within him. He would drink beers, and watch his horses, and other people's horses in his pasture, as they ran. The horses never seemed to feel old, not even in the evenings, and he was jealous of them, of their strength.

He called Karen one weekend. "Come out and watch me break horses," he said.

He was feeling particularly sore and tired. For some reason he wanted her to see that he could always do it, that the horses were always broken. He wanted her to see what it looked like, and how it always turned out.

"Oh, I don't know," she said, after she had considered it. "I'm just so *tired*." It was a bad and crooked road, bumpy, from her house to his, and it took nearly an hour to drive it.

"I'll come get you . . . ?" he said. He wanted to shake her. But he said nothing; he nodded, and then remembered he was on the phone and said, "I understand."

She did let him sit on the porch with her, whenever he drove over to her farm. She had to have someone.

"Do you want to hit me?" he asked one evening, almost hopefully.

But she just shook her head sadly.

He saw that she was getting comfortable with her sorrow, was settling down into it, like an old way of life, and he wanted to shock her out of it, but felt paralyzed and mute, like the dumbest of animals.

Sydney stared at his crooked hands, with the scars from the cuts, made over the years by the fencing tools. Silently, he cursed all the many things he did not know. He could lift bales of hay. He could string barbed-wire fences. He could lift things. That was all he knew. He wished he were a chemist, an electrician, a poet, or a preacher. The things he had—what little of them there were—wouldn't help her.

She had never thought to ask how drunk Henry had been. Sydney thought that made a difference: whether you jumped off the bridge with one beer in you, or two, or a six-pack, or with a sea of purple Psychos rolling around in your stomach—but she never asked.

He admired her confidence, and doubted his ability to be as strong, as stubborn. She never considered that it might have been her fault, or Henry's; that some little spat might have prompted it, or general disillusionment.

It was his fault, Sydney's square and simple, and she seemed comfortable, if not happy, with the fact.

Dr. Lynly treated horses, but he did not seem to love them, thought Karen.

"Stupid creatures," he would grumble, when they would not do as he wanted, when he was trying to doctor them. "Utter idiots." He and Buster and Karen would try to herd the horse into the trailer, or the corral, pulling on the reins and swatting the horse with green branches.

"Brickheads," Dr. Lynly would growl, pulling the reins and then walking around and slapping, feebly, the horse's flank. "Brickheads and fatheads." He had been loading horses for fifty years, and Karen would giggle, because the horses' stupidity always seemed to surprise, and then anger Dr. Lynly, and she thought it was sweet.

It was as if he had not yet really learned that that was how they always were.

But Karen had seen that right away. She knew that a lot of

girls, and women, were infatuated with horses, in love with them even, for their great size and strength, and for their wildness—but Karen, as she saw more and more of the sick horses, the ailing ones, the ones most people did not see regularly, knew that all horses were dumb, simple and trusting, and that even the smartest ones could be made to do as they were told.

And they could be so dumb, so loyal, and so oblivious to pain. It was as if—even if they could feel it—they could never, ever acknowledge it.

It was sweet, she thought, and dumb.

Karen let Sydney rub her temples and brush her hair. She would go into the bathroom, and wash it while he sat on the porch. He had taken up whittling; one of the stallions had broken Sydney's leg by throwing him into a fence and then trampling him, and the leg was in a heavy cast. So Sydney had decided to take a break for a few days.

He had bought a whittling kit at the hardware store, and was going to try hard to learn how to do it. There were instructions. The kit had a square, light piece of balsa wood, almost the weight of nothing, and a plain curved whittling knife. There was a dotted outline in the shape of a duck's head on the balsa wood that showed what the shape of his finished work would be.

After he learned to whittle, Sydney wanted to learn to play the harmonica. That was next, after whittling.

He would hear the water running, and hear Karen splashing, as she put her head under the faucet and rinsed.

She would come out in her robe, drying her hair, and then would let him sit in the hammock with her and brush her hair. It was September, and the cottonwoods were tinging, were making the skies hazy, soft and frozen. Nothing seemed to move.

Her hair came down to the middle of her back. She had stopped cutting it. The robe was old and worn, the color of an old blue dish. Something about the shampoo she used reminded him of apples. She wore moccasins that had a shearling lining in them, and Sydney and Karen would rock in the hammock, slightly. Sometimes Karen would get up and bring out two Cokes from the refrigerator, and they would drink those.

"Be sure to clean up those shavings when you go," she told him.

There were little balsa wood curls all over the porch. Her hair, almost dry, would be light and soft. "Be sure not to leave a mess when you go," she would say.

It would be dark then, Venus out beyond them.

"Yes," he said.

Before he left, she reached out from the hammock, and caught his hand. She squeezed it, and then let go.

He drove home slowly, thinking of Henry, and of how he had once taken Henry fishing for the first time. They had caught a catfish so large that it had scared Henry. They drank beers, and sat in the boat, and talked.

One of Sydney Bean's headlights faltered, on the drive home, then went out, and it took him an hour and a half to get home.

The days got cold and brittle. It was hard, working with the horses; Sydney's leg hurt all the time. Sometimes the horse would leap, and come down with all four hooves bunched in close together, and the pain and shock of it would travel all the way up Sydney's leg and into his shoulder, and down into his wrists: the break was in his ankle.

He was sleeping past sun-up, some days, and was being thrown, now, nearly every day; sometimes several times in the same day.

There was always a strong wind. Rains began to blow in. It was cool, getting cold, crisp as apples, and it was the weather that in the summer everyone said they would be looking forward to. One night there was a frost, and a full moon.

On her back porch, sitting in the hammock by herself with a heavy blanket around her, Karen saw a stray balsa shaving caught between the cracks of her porch floor. It was white, in the moonlight—the whole porch was—and the field was blue—the cattle stood out in the moonlight like blue statues—and she almost called Sydney.

She even went as far as to get up and call information, to find out his number; it was that close.

But then the silence and absence of a thing—she presumed it was Henry, but did not know for sure what it was—closed in around her, and the field beyond her porch, like the inside of her heart, seemed to be deathly still—and she did not call.

She thought angrily, I can love who I want to love. But she was angry at Sydney Bean, for having tried to pull her so far out, into a place where she did not want to go.

She fell asleep in the hammock, and dreamed that Dr. Lynly was trying to wake her up, and was taking her blood pressure, feeling her forehead, and, craziest of all, swatting at her with green branches.

She awoke from the dream, and decided to call him after all. Sydney answered the phone as if he, too, had been awake.

"Hello?" he said. She could tell by the true questioning in his voice that he did not get many phone calls.

"Hello," said Karen. "I just—wanted to call, and tell you hello." She paused; almost a falter. "And that I feel better. That I feel good, I mean. That's all."

"Well," said Sydney Bean, "well, good. I mean, great."

"That's all," said Karen. "Bye," she said.

"Good-bye," said Sydney.

On Thanksgiving Day, Karen and Dr. Lynly headed back out to the swamp, to check up on the loggers' mule. It was the hardest cold of the year, and there was bright ice on the bridges, and it was not thawing, even in the sun. The inside of Dr. Lynly's old truck was no warmer than the air outside. Buster, in his wooliness, lay across Karen to keep her warm.

They turned onto a gravel road, and started down into the swamp. Smoke, low and spreading, was all in the woods, like a fog. The men had little fires going all throughout the woods; they were each working on a different tree, and had small warming fires where they stood and shivered when resting.

Karen found herself looking for the pale ugly logger.

He was swinging the ax, but he only had one arm, he was swinging at the tree with one arm. The left arm was gone, and there was a sort of a sleeve over it, like a sock. The man was sweating, and a small boy stepped up and quickly toweled him dry each time the pale man stepped back to take a rest.

They stopped the truck and got out and walked up to him, and he stepped back—wet, already, again; the boy toweled him off, standing on a low stool and starting with the man's neck and shoulders, and then going down the great back—and the man told them that the mule was better but that if they wanted to see him, he was lower in the swamp.

They followed the little path towards the river. All around them were downed trees, and stumps, and stacks of logs, but the woods looked no different. The haze from the fires made it seem colder. Acorns popped under their feet.

About halfway down the road, they met the mule. He was coming back up towards them, and he was pulling a good load. A small boy was in front of him, holding out a carrot, only partially eaten. The mule's knee looked much better, though it was still a little swollen, and probably always would be.

The boy stopped, and let the mule take another bite of carrot, making him lean far forward in the trace. His great rubbery lips stretched and quavered, and then flapped, as he tried to get it, and then there was the crunch when he did.

They could smell the carrot as the mule ground it with his old teeth. It was a wild carrot, dug from the woods, and not very big, but it smelled good.

Karen had brought an apple and some sugar cubes, and she started forward to give them to the mule, but instead, handed them to the little boy, who ate the sugar cubes himself, and put the apple in his pocket.

The mule was wearing an old straw hat, and looked casual, out-of-place. The boy switched him, and he shut his eyes and started up; his chest swelled, tight and sweaty, to fit the dark soft stained leather harness, and the big load behind him started in motion, too.

Buster whined, as the mule went by.

It was spring again then, the month in which Henry had left them, and they were on the back porch. Karen had purchased a Clydesdale yearling, a great and huge animal, whose mane and fur she had shaved to keep it cool in the warming weather, and she had asked a little boy from a nearby farm with time on his hands to train it, in the afternoons. The horse was already gentled, but needed to be stronger. She was having the boy walk him around in the fields, pulling a makeshift sled of stones and tree stumps and old rotten bales of hay.

In the fall, when the Clydesdale was strong enough, she and Dr. Lynly were going to trailer it out to the swamp, and trade it for the mule.

Sydney Bean's leg had healed, been broken again, and was now healing once more. The stallion he was trying to break was showing signs of weakening. There was something in the whites of his eyes, Sydney thought, when he reared up, and he was not slamming himself into the barn—so it seemed to Sydney, anyway —with quite as much anger. Sydney thought that perhaps this coming summer would be the one in which he broke all of his horses, day after day, week after week.

They sat in the hammock and drank Cokes and nibbled radishes, celery, which Karen had washed and put on a little tray. They watched the boy, or one of his friends, his blue shirt a tiny spot against the treeline, as he followed the big dark form of the Clydesdale. The sky was a wide spread of crimson, all along the western trees, towards the river. They couldn't tell which of the local children it was, behind the big horse; it could have been any of them.

"I really miss him," said Sydney Bean. "I really hurt."

"I know," Karen said. She put her hand on Sydney's, and rested it there. "I will help you," she said.

Out in the field, a few cattle egrets fluttered and hopped behind the horse and boy. The great young draft horse lifted his thick legs high and free of the mud with each step, free from the mud made soft by the rains of spring, and slowly—they could tell—he was skidding the sled forward.

The egrets hopped and danced, following at a slight distance, but neither the boy nor the horse seemed to notice. They kept their heads down, and moved forward.

Kelly Cherry

WHERE SHE WAS

(from *The Virginia Quarterly Review*)

My mother was a child in Lockport, Louisiana, where there were six "good" houses distinguishable from the small row houses, each with a two-seated outhouse in the back yard, in which the unskilled workers, most of whom were Cajun, lived. To the east of the mill were houses for the sawyer and two mill officials; to the west, houses for the mill's bookkeeper, the commissary manager, and the filer, her father. Papa, she called him.

A wide veranda extended across the front of the house. Here my mother spent long hours in the lazy bench swing, saved from the fierce afternoon sun by a Confederate jessamine vine starred with small white fragrant flowers that relentlessly seduced big hairy black-and-yellow bumblebees and long-billed hummingbirds whose rapidly vibrating wings seemed an excessive labor on such days. Beneath the house, which was set high on pillars, was a cool, dark place hidden from view behind a skirt of green lattices, where her papa built shelves to store her mother's Mason jars of mayhaw jelly and mustard pickle and brown paper bags of sugar beets.

Inside the house, in the living room, were the phonograph and the piano, the Morris chair that was "Papa's chair," and several tall glass-enclosed bookcases containing, my mother remembered, illustrated editions of *Paradise Lost* and *Paradise Regained*, *A Child's Garden of Verse*, the family Bible, *Evangeline*, *Girl of the Limberlost*, complete sets of Scott, Hugo, and Dickens, and *The Princess and Curdie*, on the front of which was a picture of the princess in a gown of pale green silk that seemed to glow when she looked at it, like a will-o'-the-wisp.

She was a shy child, my mother, easily embarrassed, a perfectionist at five, but she was also inventive, able to entertain herself happily, and able to abandon herself to her imagination. On rainy days she read the Sears, Roebuck and Montgomery Ward catalogues or the French book her sister, studying library science at Carnegie Tech, sent her, with the nouns depicted in garments that suited their genders ("*la fenêtre*" wore a ruffled frock). She played her autoharp or copied music onto homemade manuscript paper, though she could not yet read the notes. She played with Isaac, the little black boy who helped her mother with her gardening, or Charlie Mattiza, whom she summoned by calling "Charlie Mattiza, Pigtail Squeezer!" from his yard.

The early evenings, the blue-to-lavender time between supper and bedtime, she spent on her papa's lap in the Morris chair, listening to phonograph records. His phonograph was his prize possession. It was the first one in Lockport. He had records of *Scheherazade*, *Night on Bald Mountain*, Weber's *Invitation to the Dance*, and overture to *Oberon*. (Later, he was to get Stravinsky's *Rites of Spring*, which he listened to over and over, until he felt he understood it.) She was her father's favorite, the two of them drawn powerfully to a world that did not even exist for the people around them, in Lockport, Louisiana, in the century's teens.

By the time my mother was in her seventies, living in England, she had come to believe that human beings were like cancer cells, destroying everything worthwhile—though she had her quarrels with nature too (eating, for example, was an essentially ugly act, whether performed by people or animals), and there were a few human achievements that conceivably validated our presence on earth (Bach's music). I think she felt that the life-processes had been devised purposely to humiliate her. She considered that sex was an invasion of privacy, sleeping was a waste of time, and having children was like signing a death-sentence for your dreams, whatever they might be. She told me these things while we were sitting in front of the television—the telly—flipping through the cable "videopaper" by remote control, to check out the temperature in Wisconsin, the exchange rate for dollars, the headlines. Emphysema and strokes had whittled her life down to the size of the screen. Despite my best intentions, I sometimes became irritated by her. I was at a point in my own life where what I wanted more than anything was to feel connected to other people, and I found it difficult not to feel bitter about a point of view that, I now saw, had to a great extent ghostwritten, as it were, my autobiography. For I was my mother's daughter, as she was her father's, and I had tried to be the reflection of her dreams that she wanted me to be —as she had tried to be her father's.

Sometimes her papa brought scraps of wood home from the sawmill for his youngest daughter to play with. As the saw-filer, it was his important job to keep razor-sharp the teeth of the whirling, circular saw that the sawyer, riding his carriage back and forth, thrust the logs into. Out came boards, and the curls and scraps and shavings he took home to my mother. She laid them out on the front lawn like the floor plan for a schoolhouse, assigning a subject to each "room," and wrote a textbook for each subject, using Calumet Baking Powder memo books, which were distributed free at the commissary, and elderberry ink. Requiring a pupil, she invited Elise Cheney to her schoolhouse—having decided that Elise, of all her acquaintants, was most in need of an education. After a few sessions of trying to teach Elise how to spell "chrysanthemum," she renounced her teaching career in disgust—my mother was impatient with dullards—and turned her attention to the seven Henderson children, whose names, for some reason, she felt compelled to remember in chronological order. Pumping her tree swing to the top of the great oak in the front yard, she sang loudly and mnemonically, for hours on end,

> Oh the buzzards they fly high down in Mobile
> (Lalla, Lillie, Georgia, Billy, Flossie, Edna, Beth).
> Oh the buzzards they fly high down in Mobile
> (Lalla, Lillie, Georgia, Billy, Flossie, Edna, Beth).
> Oh the buzzards they fly high
> And they puke right out the sky
> (Lalla, Lillie, Georgia, Billy, Flossie, Edna, Beth).

One summer they rented a house on Lake Prien, where her father fished for tarpon by day and was in demand as a dancing partner by night, when the grown-ups paired off to the strains of Strauss waltzes, starlit breezes blowing in through the open windows, billowing the muslin curtains. He was a handsome man, serious and loyal, permanently dazzled by his lively wife, a petite redhead he'd courted for a year in Mobile, wooing her with a bag of grapes in his bicycle basket.

My mother was going to be a beautiful woman, a finer version of the young Katharine Hepburn, but she didn't know it yet. She was the baby—a tall, skinny baby, she thought, while her mother and two sisters were visions of stylishness. This was the summer her middle sister, about to join the flapper generation, launched a campaign to persuade her parents to let her have her hair cut short. When tears and tantrums failed, she began to pin it up in large puffs that stuck out over her ears. These puffs were popular with her classmates and were called "cootie garages." Each day, the cootie garages grew a little larger—and finally, when her head began to look as though it had been screwed on with a giant wingnut, her parents said to her, "Please, go get your hair cut!"

My mother was still in her edenic chrysalis, fishing in doodlebug holes with balls of sand and spit stuck to the ends of broomstraws. She went fishing with her papa on his boat, *The Flick*, helping him to disentangle the propeller when it got caught in water hyacinths. The dreamy, wavy roots were like cilia or arms, holding up traffic. They passed the pirogues in which Cajun trappers push-poled their way through the bayous. Drying on the banks was the Spanish moss from which the Cajuns made their mattresses. Crawfish crept along the sandy bottom of the bayou, and water bugs skated on the surface. Cottonmouth moccasins slithered away in disdain. Hickory and hackberry, willow and cypress shut out the sun. Her papa pointed out birds that were like lost moments in the landscape, helping her to see what was almost hidden: white egrets, majestic as Doric columns, red-winged blackbirds, pelicans, and pink flamingos. This was my mother's world.

She had boyfriends. When she entered the consolidated school for Calcasieu Parish, at Westlake, which, like her pretend-school, had a different room and even a different teacher for each subject, she boarded the school bus at the commissary, always sitting next to Siebert Gandy, the sawyer's son, who never failed to save one of the choice end seats for her. From the two end seats, one could dangle one's legs out the rear of the van. On rainy days, the potholes filled up wonderfully with a red soupy mud that tickled one's toes.

Siebert was two years older than she was. He frequently handed her a five-cent bag of jawbreakers when she got on the bus. To cement their unspoken bond, my mother "published" a weekly newspaper, printed on wrapping paper from the butcher at the commissary. There was only one copy of each edition, which appeared at irregular intervals, and she delivered it surreptitiously to Siebert's front yard. After her family moved to Gulfport—the timber had been used up and oil had been discovered in the swamp and the mill closed down, scattering its employees—she received a letter from Siebert, whose family had moved to California, which began, "My dear little girl." She never got beyond the salutation. She burst into tears and handed the letter to her mother, who carried it off with her and never mentioned it again. So Siebert had loved her—but why had he waited until he was two thousand miles away to tell her? When she was in her seventies, living in England, she told me that she thought she really had loved Siebert. She never forgot him. He had been a part of the world that closed off after she left Lockport.

At first she loved Gulfport. They lived two blocks from the beach. She was growing up, and the freighters in the harbor, the sun flashing on the wide water that rolled across to Mexico, the white sand and palm trees and merchant seamen, all seemed like landmarks in her expanding horizon. But this new world was busy with other minds that had their own ideas about how things were to be done. She could no longer escape into private dreams, a secret music. A clamor began, and so did an unacknowledged rage at it—this infringement, this stupidity, this noise.

She did not let herself know how distressed she was. There was a glassed-in sleeping porch that became her bedroom; her middle sister was away at college, and her library-science sister had gotten a job in Tampa. It was a tiny, cramped porch, overlooking the back garden, and on the side, the alley that separated the lawn from the Everetts'. On the wall above her bed she pasted a picture she'd torn out of a magazine—white daisies, with yellow-button centers like butter in biscuits, on a field of green, a dark gray sky overhead like a monastery.

She was facing a whole new set of problems, worries she had

not realized came with growing up: how to make her stockings stay up (garters were not yet available; stockings were rolled at the top, and then the rolls were twisted and turned under; the other girls' stayed up, but hers slid down her thin legs and finished up around her ankles, so that she had to keep ducking behind oleander bushes on her way home to pull them back up); what to do if she met a boy on the way, God forbid; and, most of all, how to avoid being laughed at.

Despite the book of French nouns, she had gotten off to a bad start in French class in Gulfport. When she joined the class, skipping two grades, the students had already learned to answer the roll call by saying "Ici." She thought they were saying "Easy" and so when her name was called, she said "Easy." Everyone laughed. When she prepared her first assignment for English class, she thought her paper would look nice if she lined up the margins on the right side as well as on the left, which necessitated large gaps in the middle. The teacher held her paper up to the class as an example of how not to do homework.

That same English teacher terrified my mother by requiring every student, during senior year, to make a speech at morning assembly. My mother began to worry about her "Senior Speech" when she was still a sophomore. When senior Dwight Matthews walked out on the stage with his fiddle and said, "I shall let my violin speak for me," and then played "Souvenir," she fell in love with a forerunner of my father, and so my future began to be a possibility, an etiological ruck in the shimmery fabric of the universe.

My mother had inadvertently learned to read music back in Lockport when she'd entertained herself by copying the notes from her sister's piano étude books. The first time she attempted the violin, her fingers found their way by instinct to the right spots. Soon she was studying with Miss Morris at the Beulah Miles Conservatory of Music on East Beach. Miss Morris often carried her violin out to the end of the municipal pier in the evening to let the Gulf breezes play tunes on it. (She also recited poetry to the rising sun.)

My mother's violin was an old box that had belonged to her papa's father. Eventually, by winning the New Orleans *Times-Picayune*'s weekly essay contest, she saved up fifty dollars (though this took some time, as the prize for her essay on the Pascagoula Indians, for example, was fifty pounds of ice) and sent off to Montgomery Ward for a new violin, complete with case, bow, and a cake of genuine rosin (progress over her former sap-scraped-from-pine-bark).

Even with the new violin, there was time for boys. She and her best girl friend, Olive Shaw, used to go cruising, though this activity was not much more sexual than crabbing, which they also did a lot of. Olive had an old Dodge that Mr. Shaw had named Pheidippides, after the Greek athlete who'd run himself to death. Olive was only thirteen, but no one needed a license to drive in Mississippi. They liked to drive out to the Gulf Coast Military Academy to watch the cadets' parade and hear the band play "Oh, the Monkey Wrapped Its Tail around the Flagpole." She cannot have been as backward as she thought she was—when the marching was over, the boys gathered around the car, flirting like crazy.

But she knew nothing of sex, the mystery she and Olive were dying to solve. All the Zane Grey books ended with the hero kissing the heroine on the blue veins of her lily-white neck. My mother's neck was as brown as her cake of rosin, from her hours swimming in salt water and lying on the pier. She was not in danger of having her blue veins kissed—she examined her neck in the bathroom mirror, and not one blue vein showed under the light. Finally one of the cadets kissed her, after a movie date—on the mouth, not her neck. She worried that she might be going to have a baby, but her stomach stayed flat, and after a while she forgot to think about it.

Much social life revolved around church, which my mother nevertheless avoided as much as possible. When she did go— Sunday services were obligatory—she tried to act as if she were not related to her family. Her mother's mother's hymn-singing sounded rather like Miss Morris's violin-playing (off-key), and her own mama, perky in a new bonnet, seemed to become a stranger to her, as if she belonged to other people instead of to her own daughter—busying herself with the flowers at the altar, saying "Good morning!" and "Isn't it just a lovely day!" to all and sundry. My teen-aged mother cringed when her grandmother called across the street to her mama: "Hat-*tee*, when you come to lunch, bring the bowl of mayonnaise and the Book of Exodus!"

She survived these humiliations, and even her "Senior Speech" since she'd been lucky enough to be assigned a role in the school play. She had one line to speak: "I'm your little immortality," and after weeks of practice, she learned to say it loud enough to be heard by the audience. It came out "I'm your little immorality," but it satisfied the English teacher's requirement.

Her mama took her shopping in New Orleans for her graduation clothes: a green silk dress for Class Day, a white chiffon for graduation, and a pink organdy for the Senior Prom. But when the morning of the prom arrived, she still did not have a date. Her mama disappeared into the hallway to whisper into the telephone, and soon Alfred Purple, whose mother was, like my mother's mother, a member of the United Daughters of the Confederacy, called to ask my mother to go to the prom with him.

Alas, that night when Alfred called for my mother he had one foot done up in a wad of bandage, as if he had the gout. At the dance, they sat briefly on the sidelines; then my mother asked him to take her home. She hung the pink organdy prom dress on a satin-covered hanger. In two years, she would be one of the popular girls at LSU, dancing to all the latest tunes—but she had no way of knowing that that night. She was convinced Alfred had returned to the prom afterward, with both feet in working order. Anyway, she was done with high school. She was fifteen. This is a portrait of the girl who became my father's wife.

After my parents were married, and my mother was pregnant with my brother, they made a trip back from Baton Rouge to Gulfport. One day my mother and grandmother went for an afternoon outing in the Model-T Ford, my grandmother at the wheel. They drove past rice paddies and sugar cane fields, and cotton fields, the cotton bursting out in little white pincushions. As they scooted along the highway, relishing the breeze the car created for them, they chatted about love and marriage and impending babies. They stopped beside a deserted beach to eat the fried chicken wings and hard-boiled eggs that my grandmother had packed. From the car, the sparse dune grass seemed almost transparent in the haze of heat, like strands of blown glass. The gentle waves broke the water into smooth facets that flashed like the diamond on my grandmother's finger (my mother, a Depression bride, had only an inexpensive gold band). The salt in the air was so strong they said to each other that they could salt their hard-boiled eggs just by holding them out the window. My mother laughed. She felt so close to her mother, so free, now that she was grown up, about to have a baby, that she decided to ask her a question about sex. "Mama," she said, "isn't it supposed to be something people enjoy? Is something wrong with me?"

The gulls were diving off shore. My mother was aware of her heart beating like a metronome—she wished she could stop it, that determined, tactless beat. As soon as the question was out, she realized she had gone where you should never go—into your parents' bedroom. She blushed, thinking about the time she'd surprised her papa in the bathroom.

Her mother looked straight ahead, through the windshield, and drummed her fingers on the steering wheel. "Your father and I have always had a wonderful sexual relationship," she said firmly. "I'm sorry if it's not the same for you."

That was all. It was like a nail being driven in, boarding up a dark, hidden place. On Class Day, my mother's "gag" gift had been a hammer—because, as Bill Whittaker, the master of ceremonies, had explained, everyone knew my mother wanted something for her papa. She remembered how happy the little joke had made him as he sat in the school auditorium.

They fed the leftovers to the crying gulls. The sun was dropping in the west like an apple from a tree. On the way home, they talked about other things—her sisters, the apartment in Baton Rouge.

She had dropped out of graduate school to marry my father, at twenty. The apartment was in a building rented to faculty. My father taught violin and theory. In fact, my mother had been responsible for his coming to LSU: as the star violin pupil, she'd been asked to offer her opinion on the *vitae* the department had received. In those days, job applications were routinely accompanied by photographs. My mother instantly chose my father.

She was so pregnant—eight-and-a-half months, and it seemed to her that no one had ever been as pregnant as she. She felt like Alice after she'd bitten into the "Eat me" cake, grown too huge for the room. She thought she would never be pretty again—in less than a year, she'd become an old lady, almost a matron. Her dancing days were over. These were dull days. She had no friends, because any friendship one married woman had with another had to be shallow (you couldn't talk about your husband or your sex life or how much you hated having to cook three meals a day, or how you felt about anything). There was no money for movies or dresses—it was 1933, and only by the grace of Huey Long, who, demagogue though he might have been, saw to it that not a single LSU faculty member was laid off, the only university in the country that was true of, did they have any money at all (but often it was scrip). She couldn't have gotten into a new dress anyway, not any dress she'd want to get into.

She couldn't even practice—her stomach didn't give her arms enough mobility. When she did the laundry in the bathtub, scrubbing shorts and socks on a grooved aluminum washboard, she felt so solidly planted on the tile floor that she envisioned getting up again as an uprooting.

In bed, she lay with her back to my father, facing the wall. Such long sticky nights, and then the barest increase in comfort with the coming of winter—but the emotional temperature in the room remained high. My mother did not understand what had happened to her, how just by loving music and my father she'd become enmeshed in misery, in a spartan orange-crate apartment, in a life that was devoid of the beautiful epiphanies of her childhood.

But she was too well trained to inflict her depression on my father. There were no tears—she was not one for self-pity. Even on Christmas morning, which felt as foreign to her as Europe, as exotic as Catholicism or snow, because this was the first Christmas she had not spent with her family, she made the bed and fixed my father's breakfast, no lying in or moping around. The tree reached almost to the ceiling, and the lights, which she had tediously tested one by one, were all shining. On top of the tree stood a gold star that lasted through the years until I got married, and my parents began to dispense, a little bit at a time, with the ceremonies and symbols Christmas had acquired for them.

She and my father were awkward with each other that morning, addressing each other with a formal politeness better suited to guests. It seemed to them that every small choice they made was setting a precedent for Christmases to come—and also represented a rupture from their pasts. They ate pain-du, day-old bread fried in egg yolk and sugar, a Cajun variant of French toast. My mother drank cocoa and my father drank coffee—choices that later became habits and eventually defining characteristics. In the early morning light, which temporarily softened the drab apartment, lending an impressionistic reticence to the sharp edges of the furniture, the scratchy upholstery, they sat self-consciously on the floor by the tree. My father kissed my mother and placed in her hands the present he had bought for her with a kind of desperate good will, searching all over New Orleans for something that would make her happy again, glad to be married to him. When he had bought it, leaning over the glass counter in Maison Blanche on a fall day that was hot even for Louisiana, conferring with the sales clerk while sweat ran down the inside of his shirt sleeves under his suit jacket, he had seen my mother gesturing gracefully with the little evening bag in her left hand like a corsage of sequins, her beautiful smiling face a sonata on a blessedly cool evening.

It was red. It seemed to slide under your fingers, the hundreds of tiny, shiny sequins as tremulous as water. It was as flirtatious as a handkerchief, as reserved as a private home. When my mother took it out of its box, the tears she'd been hiding from my father were released—they fell from her eyes like more sequins, silvery ones. She knew how she was hurting him, but there was nothing she could do about it. She tried to explain how ugly the evening bag made her feel, but the more she tried to explain herself, the more she seemed to be accusing him.

She ran to the bathroom, sobbing, where she could be alone. The red evening bag lay half in its box, half out, like a heart at the center of the burst of white tissue paper. My father's present waited under the tree. He went into the kitchen and sat at the formica table, drinking another cup of coffee. There were tears in his eyes too, behind his glasses. He blew his nose. He was drinking his coffee from a pale green cup with a vee-shape, a brand of kitchenware that was omnipresent at the time. He felt wounded and frustrated and angry, and sad, and confused, and disgusted.

When I was seventeen, I took a train by myself from Virginia to New Mexico, having transferred for my sophomore year to the New Mexico Institute of Mining and Technology. On the way out there I stopped over in Gulfport to visit with my mother's mother,

Grandma Little. She was at the station to hug me hello. She was wearing white open-eyelet shoes and a lavender print and a pale pink straw bonnet, and when she smiled her face turned a pretty shade of rose as if she were a bouquet all by herself. "You may call me Hattie now," she offered, meaning that if I was grown up enough to make a trip like this alone, I was grown up enough to be treated like an equal. She was eighty-two.

She was standing in front of the chest of drawers in the hallway, watching herself in the mirror as she took off the bonnet. Partly because her name was Hattie, she always wore hats—and also because they kept the sun off her face. She showed me where I could put my suitcase.

She still lived in the old house just a couple of blocks from the beach. The house had thick stone walls to keep the heat in in winter and the coolness in in summer. She had made up a bed for me on the sleeping porch, and when I woke up the next morning the first thing I saw was a blue jay in the pecan tree. The second thing was Grandma Little brushing her long white hair. It fell almost to her waist, even pulled over her head from the back as she brushed the underside, and made me think of a bridal veil. She had been a widow for eight years. After she put her hair up, we ate breakfast in the kitchen. I had never been alone with her before. The day in front of us seemed as long as a railroad track.

She drew a map for me, and I walked down to the beach. The sun on the water was as bright and sharp as knife blades. By the time I got back to the house, in the midafternoon, clouds had rolled in—they arrived on time, I learned, like a train, every day at this time of year, and it rained for an hour, and then the sun came out again, as nonchalant as if it had never been supplanted.

Grandma Little had her feet propped on a footstool Grandpa had made for her for Christmas one year. She was sitting in a deep, wide armchair. I sat on the couch, and she told me about my mother. The light in the room grew heavier and slowly sank out of sight. I turned on the floor lamp.

"When we moved to Lockport," she said, "your mother was five. Up until then, we had been living in Lake Charles. Your mother had to leave her rabbits behind, and she was very upset about that. She loved those rabbits. She always preferred animals to people. When she was *very* little, and we had company to dinner, she used to hide under the table, where no one could see her eat. She insisted that I hand her a bowl of oatmeal—that was all she would eat—under the tablecloth. Well, when we first moved to Lockport, she decided she was going to learn how to be sociable, and on her first day of school, she came home with all her classmates. She had told them it was her birthday. My goodness, I don't know how many children there were! I didn't want to embarrass her by telling them that it wasn't her birthday, but of course there was no ice cream or cake in the house. Why would there be? And we made our own ice cream in those days, don'tcha know. So I gave each of them a banana and a glass of lemonade and they all sang 'Happy Birthday' to your mother, and I think she felt very pleased with herself about what a grand occasion it was."

I blinked back tears. I was seventeen and homesick.

"Oh, yes," she said, "your mother was a handful, strong-willed and skittish."

Grandma Little had gotten quite stocky, and she had to work to get out of the enveloping armchair, but she refused to let me help her, saying it was better for her to make the effort. Finally she was standing in front of me, her hands on her hips, head cocked to one side. "Dinner is ready," she announced.

We ate chicken spaghetti off the Spode plates in the dining room. As we ate, it seemed to me that the room filled up with the ghosts of children. The air shimmered with their small shapes. Elise Cheney and Charlie Mattiza stood at the back of the room, and all seven Hendersons (Lalla, Lillie, Georgia, Billy, Flossie, Edna, Beth). Isaac was there with his trowel, almost as big as he was. Siebert Gandy came with a bag of jawbreakers, his birthday present for my mother. Then things got mixed up and others crowded in—Olive Shaw, Dwight Matthews, the cadets. They were all so young that even I felt old. They were almost as young as the century had been. They seemed to be playing, or dancing in slow motion, and laughing—I could almost hear their laughter, as if it were an overtone, the music behind the music. Their faces were as translucent as wind.

I washed the dishes while Grandma Little went on ahead to bed. She got up at four every morning, to do the cleaning and most of the cooking while it was still cool. The hot, soapy water on my hands felt like a reprieve from a disembodied existence I was both tempted by and frightened of. I dried the dishes and returned them to their shelf on the china closet in the dining room. I remembered my mother's saying how she had found a secluded glen on the high ground on the far side of the narrow footbridge that crossed the swamp at the west end of Lockport, near, it seemed to her, where the sun went down. It was a circular clearing completely enclosed by leafy shade trees. Here she could lie on the grass, surrounded by wild violets and forget-me-nots and dandelions, and watch the clouds of yellow butterflies that drifted across the sky above her. As she lay there, she heard a symphony she had never heard before. It was not on any of her papa's records. It seemed to come from inside her head, and yet she didn't know how it could, since she couldn't write music. When she was in her seventies, living in England, she was to say, "I wished I could have written it down, because I wanted so much to remember it. It was the most beautiful symphony I have ever heard. After that first time, I spent many afternoons in the glen. No one ever disturbed me there. Nobody ever knew where I was."

Mark Richard

STRAYS

(from *Esquire*)

At night stray dogs come up underneath our house to lick our leaking pipes. Beneath my brother and my's room we hear them coughing and growling, scratching their ratted backs against the boards beneath our beds. We lie awake listening, my brother thinking of names to name the one he is setting out to catch. Salute and Topboy are high on his list.

I tell my brother these dogs are wild and cowering. A bare-heeled stomp on the floor off our beds sends them scuttling spine-bowed out the crawl space beneath our open window. Sometimes when my brother is quick he leans out and touches one slipping away.

Our father has meant to put the screens back on the windows for spring. He has even hauled them out of the storage shed and stacked them in the drive. He lays them one by one over sawhorses to tack in the frames tighter and weave patches against mosquitoes. This is what he means to do, but our mother that morning pulls all the preserves off the shelves onto the floor, sticks my brother and my's Easter Sunday drawings in her mouth, and leaves the house on through the fields cleared the week before for corn.

Uncle Trash is our nearest relative with a car, and our mother has a good half-day head start on our father when Uncle Trash arrives. Uncle Trash runs his car up the drive in a big speed splitting all the screens stacked there from their frames. There is an exploded chicken in the grill of Uncle Trash's car. They don't even turn it off as Uncle Trash slides out and our father gets behind the wheel, backing back over the screens, setting out in search of our mother.

Uncle Trash finds out that he has left his bottle under the seat of his car. He goes in our kitchen pulling out all the shelves our mother missed. Then he is in the towel box in the hall, looking, pulling out stuff in stacks. He is in our parents' room opening short doors. He is in the storage shed opening and sniffing a Mason jar of gasoline for the power mower. Uncle Trash comes up and asks, Which way is it to town for a drink? I point up the road and he sets off saying, Don't y'all burn the house down.

My brother and I hang out in the side yard doing handstands until dark. We catch handfuls of lightning bugs and smear bright yellow on our shirts. It is late. I wash our feet and put us to bed. We wait for somebody to come back home but nobody ever does. Lucky for me when my brother begins to whine for our mother the stray dogs show up under the house and he starts making up lists of new names for them, soothing himself to sleep.

Hungry, we wake up to something sounding in the kitchen not like our mother fixing us anything to eat. It is Uncle Trash throwing up and spitting blood into the pump-handled sink. I ask him did he have an accident and he sends my brother upstairs for Merthiolate and Q-Tips. His face is angled out from his head on one side, so that sided eye is shut. His good eye waters wiggling loose teeth with cut-up fingers. Uncle Trash says he had an accident all right. He says he was up in a card game and then he was real up in a card game, so up he bet his car, accidentally forgetting that our father had driven off with it in search of our mother. Uncle Trash said the man who won the card game went ahead and beat up Uncle Trash on purpose anyway.

All day Uncle Trash sleeps in our parents' room. We can hear him snoring from the front yard where my brother and I dig in the dirt with spoons making roadbeds and highways for my tin-metal trucks. In the evening Uncle Trash comes down in one of our father's shirts, dirty, but cleaner than the one he had gotten beat up in. We then have banana sandwiches for supper and Uncle Trash asks do we have a deck of cards in the house. He says he wants to see do his tooth-cut fingers still flex enough to work. I have to tell him how our mother disallows all card playing in the house but that my brother has a pack of Old Maid somewhere in the toy box. While my brother goes out to look I brag at how I always beat him out, leaving him the Old Maid, and Uncle Trash says, Oh yeah? and digs around in his pocket for a nickel he puts on the table. He says we'll play a nickel a game and I go into my brother and my's room to get the Band-Aid box of nickels and dimes I sometimes short from the collection plate on Sunday.

Uncle Trash is making painful faces, flexing his red-painted fingers around the Old Maid deck of circus-star cards, but he still shuffles, cuts, and deals a three-way hand one-handed, and not much longer I lose my Band-Aid box of money and all the tin-metal trucks of mine out in the front yard. He makes me go out and get them and put them on his side of the table. My brother loses a set of bowling pins and a stuffed beagle. In two more hands we stack up our winter boots and coats with hoods on Uncle Trash's side of the table. In the last hand my brother and I step out of our shorts and underdrawers while Uncle Trash smiles and says, And now, gentlemen, if you please, the shirts off y'all's backs.

Uncle Trash rakes everything my brother and I own into the pillowcases off our beds and says let that be a lesson to me. He is off through the front porch leaving us buck naked across the table, his last words as he goes up the road shoulder-slinging his loot, Don't y'all burn the house down.

I am burning hot at Uncle Trash, then I am burning hot at our father for leaving us with him to look for our mother, and then I am burning hot at my mother for running off through the fields leaving me with my brother, and then I am burning hot at my brother who is starting to cry. There is only one thing left to do and that is to take all we still have left that we own and throw it at my brother, and I do, and Old Maid cards explode on his face setting him off on a really good red-face howl.

I tell my brother that making so much noise will keep the stray dogs away and he believes it, and then I start to believe it when it gets later than usual, past the crickets and into a long moon over the trees, but they finally do come after my brother finally falls asleep, so I just wait until I know there are several beneath the bed boards scratching their rat-matted backs and growling, and I stomp on the floor, what is my favorite part about the dogs, watching them scatter in a hundred directions and then seeing them one by one collect in a pack at the edge of the field near the trees.

In the morning right off I recognize the bicycle coming wobble-wheeling into the front yard. It's the one the boy outside Cuts uses to run lunches and ice water to the pulpwood truck Mr. Cuts has working cut-over timber on the edge of town. The colored boy that usually drives it snaps bottle caps off his fingers at my brother and I when we go to Cuts with our mother to make groceries. We have to wait outside by the kerosene pump, out by the papered-over lean-to shed, the pop-crate place where the men sit around and Uncle Trash does his card work now. White people generally don't go into Cuts unless they have to buy on credit.

We at school know Mr. and Mrs. Cuts come from a family that eats children. There is a red metal tree with plastic wrapped toys in the window and a long candy counter case inside to lure you in. Mr. and Mrs. Cuts have no children of their own. They ate them during a hard winter and salted the rest down for sandwiches the colored boy runs out to the pulpwood crew at noon. I count colored children going in to buy some candy to see how many make it back out, but generally our mother is ready to go home way before I can tell. Our credit at Cuts is short.

The front tire catches in one of our tin-metal truck's underground tunnel tracks and Uncle Trash takes a spill. The cut crate bolted to the bicycle handlebars spills out brown paper packages sealed with electrical tape into the yard along with a case of Champale and a box of cigars. Uncle Trash is down where he falls. He lays asleep all day under the tree in the yard moving just to crawl back into the wandering shade.

We have for supper sirloins, Champale, and cigars. Uncle Trash teaches how to cross our legs up on the table after dinner but says he'll go ahead and leave my brother and my's cigars unlit. There is no outlook for our toys and my Band-Aid can of nickels and dimes, checking all the packages, even checking twice again the cut crate bolted on the front of the bicycle. Uncle Trash shows us a headstand on the table drinking a bottle of Champale, then he stands in the sink and sings "Gather My Far-flung Thoughts Together." My brother and I chomp our cigars and clap, but in our hearts we are low and lonesome.

Don't y'all burn down the house, says Uncle Trash pedaling out the yard to Cuts. My brother leans out our window with a rope coil and scraps strung on strings. He is in a greasy-finger sleep when the strings slither like white snakes off our bed and over the sill into the fields out back.

There's July corn and no word from our parents. Uncle Trash doesn't remember the Fourth of July or the Fourth of July parade. Uncle Trash bunches cattails in the fenders of his bicycle and clips our Old Maid cards in the spokes and follows the fire engine through town with my brother and I in the front cut-out crate throwing penny candy to the crowds. What are you trying to be, the colored men at Cuts ask us when we end up there. I spot a tin-metal truck of mine broken by the Cuts' front step. Foolish, says Uncle Trash.

Uncle Trash doesn't remember winning Mrs. Cuts in a game for a day to come out and clean the house and us in the bargain. She pushes the furniture around with a broom and calls us abominations. There's a bucket of soap to wash our heads and a jar of sour-smelling cream for our infected bites. Fleas from under the house and mosquitoes through the windows. The screens are rusty squares in the driveway dirt. Uncle Trash leaves her his razor opened as long as my arm. She comes after my brother and I with it to cut our hair, she says. We know better. My brother dives under the house and I am up a tree. Uncle Trash doesn't remember July, but when we tell him about it he says he thinks July was probably a good idea at the time.

It is August with the brown twisted corn in the fields next to the house. There is word from our parents. They are in the state capital. One of them has been in jail. I try to decide which. Uncle Trash is still promising screens. We get from Cuts bug spray instead.

I wake up in the middle of a night. My brother floats through the window. Out in the yard he and a stray have each other on the end of a rope. He reels her in and I make the tackle. Already I feel the fleas leave her rag-matted coat and crawl over my arms and up my neck. We spray her down with a whole can of bug spray until her coat lathers like soap. My brother gets some matches to burn a tick like a grape out of her ear. The touch of the match covers her like a blue-flame sweater. She's a fireball shooting beneath the house. By the time Uncle Trash and the rest of town get there the fire warden says the house is Fully Involved.

In the morning our parents drive past where our house used to be. They go by again until they recognize the yard. Uncle Trash is trying to bring my brother out of the trance he is in by showing him how some card tricks work on the left-standing steps of the stoop. Uncle Trash shows Jack-Away, Queen in the Whorehouse, and No Money Down. Our father says for Uncle Trash to stand up so he can knock him down. Uncle Trash says he deserves that one. Our father knocks him down again and tells him not to get up. If you get up I'll kill you, our father says.

Uncle Trash crawls on all fours across our yard out to the road. Goodbye, Uncle Trash, I say. Goodbye, men, Uncle Trash says. Don't y'all burn the house down, he says and I say, We won't.

During the knocking down nobody notices our mother. She is a flat-footed running rustle through the corn all burned up by the summer sun.

James Gordon Bennett

PACIFIC THEATER

(from *The Virginia Quarterly Review*)

I'm on the phone in my father's bedroom trying to keep my voice down. My sister has decided at the last minute not to fly up.

"You'll be all right," she says. "Just talk to him for a change."

I pick up the brass Oriental calendar from my father's dresser. It's made from an artillery shell. "The man's been in three wars," I say. "Guess how many war stories he ever told me?"

"What about that one where he parachuted into a dump?" my sister says.

"That was only jump school. And I practically had to hound him to death just to get it." It's a two-thousand-year calendar and I set the disk on my mother's birthday. "Anyway, I was twelve then. What chance am I supposed to have at thirty?"

"Didn't he land on an old hospital bed or something?" my sister says.

"He got lockjaw from the rusty springs. He only told me it because he thought it was funny."

My sister laughs. "Dad would, wouldn't he?"

"And he hasn't changed one iota."

"Well, hound him then."

I unwrap the phone cord from my finger. "Besides, it's depressing around here. She's turned the place into Pier One, for Christ's sake."

Sing, the woman my father's been living with, is Vietnamese.

"Wait'll you taste her tempura," my sister says. "She cooks with chopsticks. It's amazing."

It's dark in the room, and I suddenly notice something curious about my father's bed. Like a backed-up wave the blanket bulges above the headboard.

"He hurt his back playing racquetball," my sister explains. "Some chiropractor recommended it."

I ease down gingerly on the mattress. "Dad on a waterbed," I say. "What next?"

What next, as it turns out, is a six-course meal of authentic Vietnamese cuisine. Sing has spent the afternoon in the kitchen hunched over a steaming wok. Each vegetable comes wrapped in a thin sheet of dark green seaweed. Piled atop a hot plate on the table, strips of beef simmer in soy sauce while all around me metal dishes brim with exotic concoctions.

My father, meanwhile, acts as if the feast were only the most common daily fare for him. Nor does Sing give any indication of having slaved for hours for her guest's benefit. She only smiles shyly when I deem to compliment the moist lotus roots of her parboiled poon dip.

Still, there's no mistaking my father's pride in the shipshapeness of his redecorated quarters.

"I'd like to propose a toast," he says after lighting the candles.

Even in his sixties, my father's still a handsome man. The racquetball no doubt helps, but more than this, he seems happier than I ever remember him being with us.

"To my bride."

It's not the pickled egg that drops my jaw, and it's a moment before I hear any more of the toast. My heart's pounding in my ears.

"We decided not to live in sin any longer," my father is saying, still holding his glass out to Sing. "It's been long enough."

Now we're both staring at the ridiculously bashful woman seated between us.

"How long?" I manage to blurt out at last. "I mean, how long ago did you get married?"

When my father confesses that it's been nearly two years, I have trouble concentrating. Even though I should have seen it coming. They weren't exactly living as brother and sister. But it's hard not to feel a little provoked. Wasn't *I* the one who drove 1500 miles in a VW with a broken floor heater? Where's my toast? Only it isn't sympathy I see in my father's face. Or even gratitude for his dutiful son. It's bliss. Second-time-around bliss that has nothing, absolutely nothing to do with me.

"Well, " I offer weakly, and Sing bows her head at her new stepson. "All the best."

I know that he doesn't intend to be callous. It's just his way. And that my own thin skin could use a little thickening. Besides, it's typical. My father doesn't know the meaning of brood. I'm my mother's son.

For dessert, there's a small glutinous rice cake that's filled with sweet bean paste. A tradition at Oriental weddings, the happy groom remarks.

Afterward, when Sing refuses to let me help with the dishes, I drift dumbly down the hall to the phone.

"There you have it," I break the news to my sister. "So how's it feel to be Number One stepdaughter?"

"I've known for a while."

I want to take a hat pin to the waterbed or at least kick over one of the Chinese goddess lamps. "Well, look who else is turning inscrutable on me."

"I didn't have the guts to tell you."

Her stereo's on, and I can hear a Jackson Browne album.

"You just sucker me up here, then cancel your reservation."

"That's not true. I honestly planned to come."

"Right. But there you are and here I am."

My sister is quiet for a moment. "She's not that young, you know. She's at least fifty."

"They all look alike to me."

"You should try to talk to her. Really. Her English isn't that bad."

"I don't have anything to say to the woman. And I've got even less to say to her husband."

"Look, if it's any consolation, I was upset too. It just took—"

"Time. But now you're over it, right?"

My sister's breath whistles in the phone. "Well," she says wearily, "maybe we should just call it a night."

We both listen to the chorus of "Doctor, My Eyes" for a minute and then politely agree to say goodbye.

In the hall, Sing has hung several framed scrolls commemorating my father's long military career. He retired with two stars, and I study the picture of him in starched khakis and pith helmet presenting a silver bowl to some generalissimo. There's a pained expression on his face. It was about the same time my mother threatened to bring the kids home if he didn't swing a stateside assignment. She was tired of mosquito nets and water buffalos and military compounds surrounded by nine-foot walls.

As soon as Sing sees me, she pads into the kitchen for some hung yun char (almond tea) and farr shung tong (peanut brittle). She's been playing cards with my father. Along with ballroom dancing they take courses in bridge at the community college.

"A little colder than you're used to," my father says. He pretends to study his hand.

"Much colder."

It's the first time we've been alone together, and we're both eager for Sing to get back.

"What're you fixing now?" my father calls out to her.

But she only answers in Vietnamese.

"You put a pound a year on and it adds up," he says, tapping the deck on the folding table.

"Like everything," I say.

He gives me a fishy look and yawns. "So what do you hear from your sister? I'm sorry we missed her."

"Oh, we keep in touch. She brings me up to date."

I sit down on the rattan chair and watch him go through the cable stations with the remote control.

"The numbers come on at eight," he says. "The jackpot's up to twelve million."

Sing carries a tea tray in, and I can smell the almond.

"Your father," she says. "He always play the same numbers."

"You pick any six between zero and forty," he says. "We box them for a buck."

"Once your father get four," Sing says. She sets the peanut brittle out on my mother's china. "Closest he come."

"And what'd you get for that?" I ask her.

"Eighty bucks," my father says. "About a month's worth of tickets."

Sing wags her head. "Your father like to gamble all his money away. I tell him to buy present instead."

My father checks his watch. "It gets the adrenalin going."

I think of something I might have said to my sister. But then there's a lot I might have said if she'd been around. In any event, I've got my own little surprise for the newlyweds. I'm heading back tomorrow.

"Peter very lucky," Sing says. Her brother works in the city. "Only one missing two times already."

My father stoops in front of the set to adjust the picture. Someone in a tuxedo is explaining how "tonight's numbers" will be drawn.

"In morning," Sing says to me, "Peter come to see you. He very eager to meet your father's son."

"Well . . ."

But we all stop to watch a ping-pong ball get sucked up through a clear plastic cylinder.

"Good start," my father says as the number is turned towards the camera.

"Not us," Sing says.

We wait out the other numbers.

"Peter and Esther have a six-year-old," my father says, turning the sound off. "You won't believe the kid's English. She's always correcting her parents."

Sing is smiling proudly. "Once she stay with your father and me. She not want to come home again."

"Where'd her parents go?" I ask.

"Nowhere," my father says. "They just wanted some time to themselves. Peter's an interesting character. He taught himself computers. Three years ago he's driving a taxi in the city. Now he's pulling down twice my retirement."

Like his sister, he was born in Saigon, where their father had been a successful manufacturer.

"The Vietnamese businessman's worse than your Japanese," my father says. "They're nonstop. They don't know when to quit."

I ask Sing what kind of business her father had been in, but we've been talking too fast for her.

"He was back and forth to Taiwan," my father says. "Until Uncle Ho took a bead on him."

Sing doesn't stop smiling, and so it's a minute before I realize what my father has just said.

"He was shot down?" I say.

My father cups his hand like a plane nose diving. "On his way to his shoe factory."

Sing cracks a piece of peanut brittle between her teeth and blushes. It's the first time I've seen her eat anything. She can't weigh a hundred pounds.

My father gets up to peer out the window at the gray sky. "Supposed to get some snow tonight."

"You like more tea?" Sing asks me. "Very good for hair." She smiles crookedly at my father. "See what happen. He not listen."

It's the mother's side determines, of course, but I don't say anything.

Sing stacks our plates. She'll handwash them in the kitchen sink despite the automatic dishwasher.

"What's on the tube tonight?" my father asks as soon as Sing comes back with the kettle. Whenever she's out of the room we struggle to make conversation.

"Your father like his TV," Sing says. "All the time he watching the news."

"I switch around," my father says. He holds up the remote control. "You can see how they twist the same story. It's whatever they want it to come out."

I think of how I would have caught my sister's eye.

"At least with Cronkite," he says, "you felt the guy had a little more to him."

Sing has fixed a darker tea for herself. She studies the guide for something that might interest my father.

"Didn't Peter Jennings adopt a Vietnamese kid?" I say. "I thought I read that somewhere."

My father only stares stonily at the commercial.

"It wouldn't surprise me in the least," he says.

I follow Sing back into the kitchen, and she smiles at me quizzically.

"I thought I'd have some Coke," I say.

She rinses a clean glass from the shelf and dries it with a paper towel.

"Your father fall asleep now," she says, twisting the cap from the liter bottle. "Sometime he feel a little sore."

"He ought to quit that ridiculous racquetball," I say, but it's more for my benefit than hers.

She sets the bottle back on the counter. Nothing in the house is allowed long out of its place. "He take his medicine," she says, rubbing her hands together as if to point out where it hurts. "Only his fingers not change."

"His fingers?" I say. "I don't understand."

"Your father not going to say," and she giggles as if at a promise not to tell. "He just go to sleep and wake up better."

Her broken English requires a fierce concentration and I focus cross-eyed on her lips.

In the living room, my father sleeps with his chin on his chest. His hands, crossed peacefully on his stomach, rise and fall with his faint breathing. And for the first time I see that his thumbs are gnarled and swollen.

I tiptoe back down the hall looking for Sing. I want to ask her about tomorrow. But she's not in the kitchen or the dining room. I don't think to knock on my father's bedroom door but as soon as I push it open, Sing, bent over at the waist, looks upside down at me, her shiny black hair nearly touching the straw mat.

"Christ, I'm sorry."

She's holding my mother's sterling silver hair brush.

"You use phone," she says, apologizing for me. "Other one wake up your father."

She tries to move past me but I block the door with my arm.

"It's your house now," I say. "I should knock."

With the brush behind her back, she covers her mouth with her other hand. "Your father wake up in maybe half hour."

I nod. "I'll make a quick call then." And I lower my arm. "I'm charging them to my own number."

But she only smiles, easing the door shut after her.

My sister, pulled from her shower, nevertheless listens patiently.

"I think it's all the serenity getting to me," I tell her. "Dad sits around like Gautama or something. I mean, it's the Inn of the Sixth Happiness up here."

"They get along," my sister reflects.

"And Mom and Dad didn't," I say. "That the subtext?"

"You were there."

"That's right. And now I'm here. But the real question's where you are."

"Dad's not going to change, you know. He's an old soldier, and he's never going to put you at ease. That's not a heart behind the medals; that's a sandbag. Now, that what you want to hear?"

"You're saying he's just going to fade away."

"Honey, you might as well dig a great big fox hole and jump in. Dad's Dad. He was that way with Mom. He was that way with me. Why should he be any different with you?"

"What about Sing?"

"I don't know," my sister says, exhausted. "Maybe it helps not to speak the same language."

In the morning, a bright white glare illuminates my bedroom like a floodlight. It's been years since I've seen snow, and raising the bamboo shades, I wipe my sleeve across the glass. Everything is either white or black. My father's lot slopes down steeply to a small frozen creek which separates his property from his closest neighbor's. My mother hated the claustrophobia of wherry housing and insisted in retirement on a big backyard.

On my bedstand, there's a covered cup of tea and two almond cookies. I dip my finger in and it's still warm.

Sing's in the kitchen making pancakes, which incredibly she flips with chopsticks.

"Your father outside," she says.

She turns her back to me to adjust the gas on the stove. Her straight black hair is streaked with gray and I think that my sister might be right. Although younger than my father, she's hardly a young woman. And then I wonder how long they must have known each other. There's always been a large Asian community in the area, and I'd just assumed that they met here. But then I've never really gotten the chronology straight. The few times my father's ever written or called, Sing was only his "housekeeper."

"How many for you?" Sing asks. The warming plate is stacked high with pancakes.

"A couple's fine."

She pours a tall glass of orange juice. "Your father think you too skinny. I tell him because you don't have wife."

She's surprisingly more familiar with me this morning. And I wonder just how genuine the wallflower routine is. For one thing, I can't imagine my father thinking twice about my weight. Never mind a wife.

"What's he doing out there?"

Sing wipes the kitchen window with a dish towel and taps on the glass.

"He like to shovel it," she says.

My father signals that he's almost done.

"It runs in the family," I say.

At the garage door, I watch him hike the shovel briskly over his shoulder, his breath steaming in the frigid air.

"Breakfast," I shout.

But there's only a small patch to go and he raises his gloved hand without looking up.

On the other side of the car, stacked against one wall of the stucco garage are several boxes with "Trophies" printed in Magic Marker across them. I pry open the lid on the top one and pull out a brass plaque with my father's name on it. It's for some tournament three years ago in Las Vegas.

"Your father not let me bring them in house," Sing says when I ask her about the boxes.

"He was really in Nevada just to play racquetball?"

"Last time to Canada. Your father senior champion."

"You're kidding."

"Have to be sixty years old," she says proudly. "'Golden Masters.' Your father win all time."

In the dining room, I sit at the table until I hear my father stamping his boots on the porch. I feel like telling him that I'd almost forgotten to mention the Publisher's Clearing House contest I won last month. Half a million dollars a year for the rest of my life. By the time he sits down at the table, his ears red-tipped and his face beaming robustly, I'm frustrated enough to empty my pancakes in his lap.

"I thought I'd head back tomorrow," I say finally, setting my knife on the edge of my plate. "Maybe stop by and see my runaway sister."

My father stirs his coffee. Sing has given him a large soup spoon which he grips awkwardly.

"Sorry to hear it," he says. "We had some things planned."

"Tomorrow?" Sing asks my father. "He go home?"

"Sounds like it," he says.

"Oh, no," Sing says to me sadly.

My father folds the corners of his paper napkin into an origami stork. "You're not exactly driving a snow plow."

"I'll take it easy," I say.

But we all turn at the sound of a car in the driveway. Sing stands up and quietly lifts her chair back under the table.

"Sounds like Peter," she says.

"Sounds like a damn tank," my father says.

We don't bother with our coats. Although Peter appears at least as old as his sister, his wife, Esther, looks younger than me. Their daughter, Roberta, hugs Sing about the waist.

"You'll put that thing out of alignment," my father scolds his brother-in-law.

The car, a bright red Mercedes, is laden down with chains on all four tires.

"This deep," Peter says, patting his ankle to show how much snow has fallen on the freeway.

My father looks over at me. "There you go."

Esther and Sing collect grocery bags from the trunk of the car and carry them into the kitchen. Roberta trails after them with a Cabbage Patch doll balanced on her shoulder. Only Sing, the first to get her green card, has yet to adopt an American name.

At the door, Peter peels off his galoshes. He's dressed up: a pin-striped suit and black wingtips. And I wonder how much of this is for me.

In the living room, my father turns a football game on but keeps the volume low. He's obviously heard his brother-in-law's stories before. And Peter is a talker even though his English isn't much better than Sing's.

Although the women stay in the kitchen, Sing is her usual atten-tive self. Every five minutes she emerges to check our glasses or to carry out another snack tray. I never hear a peep from the child.

By halftime, my father is out cold on the couch. And I discover that Peter (who, innocent of any intrigue, answers all my questions candidly) has known him even longer than Sing.

"So you two go back a ways together?" I say but rephrase it when he only smiles blankly. "You've been friends for what? Since before Roberta was born?"

"Yes, yes," he says happily. "Your father my commanding officer. All through war."

But I'm thinking of Europe and that he can't have been old enough. Then I understand that he means Vietnam.

"You were with his battalion then?" My heart is racing. Because it all makes its crazy sense now. My father had volunteered a second combat tour. Despite my mother's long-distance tirades and suspicions.

"Yes, yes," Peter says solemnly. "Your father very great man."

There's no point in calling my sister. I know what she'd say. She's known for quite a while. And, besides, Mom's been dead and buried a long time now.

My father hasn't budged at the end of the couch. He looks like a crafty barn owl with his chin tucked against his chest. And I'm reminded of how he always used to fall asleep while we watched "The Big Picture" together on Saturday afternoons. It wouldn't surprise me if he asked Peter out here on purpose. But as I stare at his painfully swollen hands I can't help wishing that they were mine and not his to suffer.

Peter, meanwhile, watches with a foreigner's fascination the parade of high-school bands that march with military precision across the football field. Sing, clearly happy with the miraculous assembly of her new family in one place, comes in to set a bowl of pretzels down like an offering on the table before me.

Even though I try, it's impossible to hate her. To believe she's anything more than what she is: a Vietnamese immigrant by way of Saigon by way of some idiot war by way of New Jersey. Safe here in America with her arthritic, racquetball-playing ex-general and his sullen son.

I borrow my father's boots from the hall closet and sneak out of the house through the garage. The snow's already crusty on top, and in the backyard, I can see where my father must have put his tomato plants in this year. The row of sticks barely pokes through the drift of snow along the basement wall. No matter where we were stationed or how little soil my father had to work with, he always seemed to have tomatoes picked and ripening on the kitchen windowsill.

Down closer to the creek I find the apple tree Sing had told me about. It's a strange looking hybrid, its branches gnarled from various graftings. I can't quite picture the thing in bloom, but in the summer, my stepmother assures me, it will produce half a dozen different kinds of apples. She'd shown my father how to band the limbs together, and next season he wants to put in a whole orchard of them.

I'll hang around maybe a day or two longer. Who knows? Maybe Roberta's my half sister. It wouldn't surprise me in the least. Yet I noticed that the six numbers on my father's lottery ticket were our birthdays, my mother's included. I'd have thought he forgot all that. The way only great men can. But when I turn back towards the house, I look up to see everyone smiling down at me from the big picture window of the living room. Peter is waving, his diminutive wife next to him, while at their feet their daughter presses her small, flat face to the glass. And on either side of them, like happy temple dogs, stand Sing and her bridge partner. An all-American family, I think, and struggling back up the embankment, try to keep from slipping in my father's unlaced combat boots.

Frank Manley

THE RAIN OF TERROR

(from *The Southern Review*)

"My name is Oletta Crews."

It sounded like a public announcement.

"This is James Terry Crews, my husband." She indicated the old man on the sofa beside her. He was dressed in khaki trousers and six-inch work boots. The woman had on a print dress, a bold floral pattern like slashes. She wore no shoes.

James Terry Crews gestured silently, acknowledging himself.

"Don't act like an idiot," Oletta Crews said, and the man dropped his hand.

"Just sit there." She turned away from him.

"This is James Terry Crews, my husband." She spoke in a powerful voice, lifted like a singer's from her diaphragm. "He's retired. We're both retired," she added significantly. "Him from work and me from housework. I got a bad heart, and I'm stout besides. You can see that. Doctor says I'm hundreds of pounds overweight, shortening my life with every bite of food I take. But what if I didn't. You think that'd help?"

She leaned forward and spoke confidentially. "There's more dies of hunger than does of the other."

She leaned back and gestured toward her husband again. "He helps me," she said. "He does what he needs to."

James Terry Crews sat beside her and stared straight ahead. He looked afraid.

"Listen to me," Oletta Crews said.

James Terry Crews started to get up, but she held out a hand and restrained him.

"Sit there," she ordered.

"Listen," she said. "I live here alone all by myself, a poor old woman, except for him. He lives here, too. Both together."

There were one or two aluminum windows, an aluminum door, a dinette set, strings of laundry overhead, a scattering of shoes and other debris on the floor, aluminum cans, some in plastic sacks, some loose, piled in the corner. The feeling was that of a cave or a nest—the secret bestial place.

"This is a trailer, you notice that?"

James Terry Crews corrected her. "Mobile home."

"Same damn thing." She was suddenly angry. "I told you that. Pay attention."

James Terry Crews ignored her. "Trailer's something you trail after you," he explained. "That's what it means, trailer. You hitch it on the back of a car and hit the trail."

"And mobile home's mobile," Oletta Crews shouted. "That means it moves."

It seemed like an argument they had had before, the lines already memorized, the positions taken not only well known but entrenched and fortified.

"Tell them about the rain of terror."

"The rain of terror," Oletta Crews said, repeating the words, savoring them. She turned to James Terry Crews. "They don't want to hear about mobile homes. They want to hear about the rain of terror." She bugged her eyes as she said *the rain of terror*. The effect was not comic. Her eyes were filled with something other than fear.

"It was at night."

"Two nights ago." James Terry Crews sounded incredulous.

"It was two nights ago," Oletta Crews said. "And it was dark. James Terry was already home soaking wet from the weeds where he'd been and changed his clothes already to dry them. He was picking aluminum cans. I'm too stout to get out and help or else I'd be there driving the truck, but I can't even drive no more. It's bad on my heart, and the pedals are too close anyway. They're all underfoot. It's hell to be old." She leaned forward. "If I was you, I'd die before I got there." She laughed silently, baring her gums.

"I used to be a house painter," James Terry Crews announced suddenly. "Twenty-eight years and every day sober on the job."

"That don't matter," Oletta Crews shouted. "They don't want to hear about that. You're retired. He sells aluminum cans," she explained. "That's what he does now. They got a yard in town buys them. Beer cans and such as that."

"I didn't always do it," James Terry Crews said. "I used to paint with the best of them."

"That was then. This is now. I'm telling this," Oletta Crews said, picking up where she had left off. "He came in sopping wet from the rain of terror where he been out in the weeds all day looking for beer cans, and I told him what I saw on TV so he don't fall too far behind. And he was changing his socks. I can close my eyes and still see him sitting right there." She pointed across the room at an overstuffed chair that matched the sofa. The arms were shiny and greasy with wear. The seat was piled high with clothes, the upper layers of which had toppled over onto the floor. "Sitting in that chair right there changing his socks, when I heard this knocking at the door."

"What did you think?"

"I thought, Who's that?"

"Me, too," James Terry Crews said. "I thought, Who's that?"

"I thought, Who's that knocking on the door in the dark? I knew it wasn't nobody I knew. His children are gone, and I don't have none, and all my kinfolks are dead before me."

"Tell them about the news."

"I don't generally watch the news if I can help it," Oletta Crews said. "But this night was special. The good Lord led me to it this night. It's like I almost heard this voice said, 'Don't touch the TV. I got something on the news.' I was too tired to get up, and it said, 'Don't do it then. I got something better for you to do than get up and change the channel. I got something to show you right here on this one you're watching.' It's like I almost heard this voice beside the still waters, leading me on in the valley of the shadow of death where I fear no evil for thou art with me. Thy rod and staff they comfort me."

"And you were afraid."

"Of course I was afraid after hearing what I heard and knowing it was some kind of message delivered on TV special for me. Of course I was afraid. Who wouldn't be? I knew he'd protect me like he done. That's why I'm alive and the other one's dead because I could walk through the valley of the shadow of death and fear no evil. So the answer is no. No, I wasn't afraid. But I *was* interested. When I heard how he escaped from the work camp and killed two men, and it wasn't more than five miles down the road and was coming this way, I wasn't afraid, but I *was* interested."

"She heard the knock," James Terry Crews explained.

"I heard the knock and wondered, Who is it? But I already knew. I said, 'It's him.'"

"And I said, 'Who?'"

"Let me tell it," Oletta Crews shouted. "You weren't even there when it happened. I'm telling it. Listen," she said. "This is how it happened. I heard the knock, and I said, 'It's him,' and James Terry looked up from his sock and said, 'Who you mean?' and I said, 'The one on TV when you wasn't here escaped from the work camp and killed two men. It's him at the door,' and he put on his sock," indicating her husband, "and said, 'What you want to do?' And I said, 'Go get it. He might have some money hid.'"

"And I said, 'Money? What you mean money?'"

"Where he hid it after he stole it," Oletta Crews said. "I thought he might have some, and I said, 'Let him in. He might have some money hid.' And James Terry went to the door, one shoe on and one in his hand, and it was him. I was sitting right here where I always sit on this side of the sofa, and I saw him standing in the door soaking wet where it was raining outside in the dark as far as the eye could see. Looked like silver knives. And he said, 'Can I come in? I'm awful wet.' And I yelled, 'I can see you are, honey. Let him in, James Terry. Let him in to get dry.' And he came in, and I said, 'Get him a towel.' And James Terry got him a towel and sat down and put on his shoe. And I said to him, 'I know who you are.'"

"She knew who he was."

"I told him I saw his picture on TV, and I knew who he was, thanks to God, and what he was there for."

"What was that?" James Terry Crews asked.

"You were there. Don't ask things you already know. He was there to rob us. He came there to rob us."

"Your life was in danger."

"My life was in danger. As soon as I saw him, I knew I might not live."

She paused, staring at something in the distance.

"Go on."

"I told him his name. I said, 'You're Q. B. Farris, escaped from the work camp.' And he said, 'Yes, ma'am. I can't fool you, I can see that.' And I said, 'That's right. There's many a one better than you tried all my life, and they didn't do it so why should you?' And he laughed. He was good-hearted. I can say that for him. He might have been mean, but he was good-hearted. He didn't care."

"I liked him," James Terry Crews said.

"Then he said, 'You know who I am? You know what I done?' And I said, 'Some. I know the most recent.' And I told him he killed two men. And he said that was exaggerated. And I said, 'It's on TV.' And he said he didn't care. It was exaggerated. And I said, 'Don't kill me. I'm just a poor old woman. It won't help to kill me. I don't know where your money's hid.' And I saw him looking at James Terry where he just finished putting on his shoe, and I knew what he was thinking. I said, 'Don't kill him either. He got to help me. I'm retired.' And he laughed like he done and said, 'What you retired from, momma?' And I said, 'Don't call me momma. I ain't your momma. I ain't nobody's momma.' And he said, 'You look like you ought to be. You got a kind face and a big bosom.' And I thought then, He's going to rape me. Been in prison with men too long."

"His name was Duke," James Terry Crews explained.

"Q. B. Farris. He said his name was Duke. He said, 'Call me Duke. I don't know who Q. B. is.'"

"And I said, 'What's the Q. B. stand for?'" James Terry Crews said. "And you know what he said? He said, 'Queer Bastard.' I didn't know what to make of that."

"Except he wasn't queer," Oletta Crews said. "Else he wouldn't have wanted to rape me."

"Unless he was both."

"I'm telling this," Oletta Crews shouted. "We already agreed on that." She looked straight ahead. "That's the kind of person he was, full of useless jokes like that. He didn't care. You know what he said when I said don't kill me? He said, 'I wouldn't kill you or him either, momma. I got a momma of my own.'"

"What did you think about that?"

"I thought, Well where is she? I said, 'You say you got a momma, where is she?' I figured she might have the money. And he said, 'Oconee, Tennessee—in the graveyard,' and looked at me and laughed. And I said, 'You laughing because she's dead or you laughing because you broke her heart?' That straightened him out. He quit laughing and said, 'Neither one. I loved my momma. She's the only one I trust.' And I said, 'I reckon. I'd trust her too, state she's in now.' That's when he hit me."

"He hit you?" James Terry Crews glanced at her, then turned away.

"He tried to," Oletta Crews said. "Then he looked at me and said, 'She died when I was still in prison. I never got to go to the funeral because it was out of state.' Said if it'd been in the state, they'd have let him, but she was buried in Tennessee, and that's a whole other system. And I thought, So what? She wouldn't know if you were there or not—chained like a wild dog at a funeral. 'They all die. That's a common fact,' I told him. 'She'd have died if you were in jail or not.' And he said it wasn't the dying he minded. It was they wouldn't let him out to be there. That's what he hated. And that's when he told me about the nine years. He said, 'I ain't been my own man in nine years and nine more to go.' And I thought, Whose fault is that? Don't come crying on my shoulder. You should have thought about that when you decided what you wanted to be."

"What do you mean?"

"What do I mean? I mean a robber—steals money and hides it somewhere. And I said, 'Your momma's house still standing? That where you going?' And he said no, he liked it here. And I said, 'I don't got no money. You might want to go and get yours.' And he said, 'Mine?' like he didn't know what I was talking about. He said, 'I don't got no money. What are you talking about?' And I said, 'That money you got hid you come out of jail to get.' And he said, 'I don't got no money hid. I come out because I couldn't stand to stay in,' and laughed like he done so I knew he was lying. I said, 'Where's your home at in Oconee? You from town?' I figured that's where he hid the money. And he said, 'Oconee? I ain't from Oconee. I'm from right here.' He was born and raised in this county. Reason his momma died in Oconee, she was living with her sister, and they buried her there. That's when I knew he had it on him. All the money he stole and buried, it was right there beside me. Only difference was he had it, not me, and he was fixing to leave if he could."

"I didn't know what that meant," James Terry Crews explained, "but she said it was stolen already and buried nine years, and besides they're all dead anyway. . . ."

"I said I'd tell it," Oletta Crews said, each word heavy with its own weight.

James Terry Crews did not look at her. He did not answer.

"And that's when he said, 'How about some supper?' He was looking at me. And I said, 'You talking to me?' And he said, 'I was. I ain't now,' and laughed like it was some kind of joke. He said, 'You look like you might be hungry. How about you and me eating something?' And I said, 'I ain't hungry.' And he said, 'Well then why don't you rustle up something for me?' And I said, 'I don't cook. I'm retired.' And he said, 'Retired? What are you retired from?' And I said, 'The human race.' That took him back. And he said, 'Lord God, I thought you had to be dead for that.' And I said, 'Some do. Your momma maybe.' And he said, 'Don't talk about my momma. She's some kind of saint in heaven when you rot in hell.' And I said, 'I don't believe in saints.' And he said he didn't care, he knew her, I didn't, and he started doing these things on his head like he was beating up on himself. And I said, 'What's that?'"

She turned to her husband. "Show how he done."

James Terry Crews looked surprised. he took off his glasses and slapped at his forehead, then at his ears. First with one hand, then with the other.

"I saw Duke do that," Oletta Crews said. "I said, 'What you do that for?' And he said it was something he learned in prison. Means you're sorry for what you done. And I said, 'What for?' And he said, 'Whatever. It works for all.'"

"I thought he was crazy," James Terry Crews said.

"Me too. I figured he was going to kill us both or else stay there and keep us for ransom."

"What she means is hostages."

"That's right. Stay with us here till he was safe and then kill us as soon as he walked out that door going to California."

"She wants to die in California," James Terry Crews explained.

"That's right. I'm a poor old woman. That's my only hope, to see California and die happy there. That's all I want."

"That's all she wants."

"They got the Pacific Ocean out there. I got a picture in the bathroom from *National Geographic*. You ever see that one on California? That picture I got's the best one in it. I see that picture, I get all smooth inside. The jitters fall off like leaves off a tree. Shows the ocean and the sun going down, smooth and calm as far as the eye can see. Another thing—it don't ever rain. There ain't no rain of terror out there. Nature is mild. They got orange trees, bloom all year, and you want an orange, you pick it yourself."

"They got retirement," James Terry Crews said.

Oletta Crews turned and stared at him. James Terry Crews fell silent.

"What he was saying is they take care of you out there even if you don't got no children."

"I got a daughter."

"There ain't no minimum social security," Oletta Crews said. "No matter how much you made, they fix it up so you live like a prince. It ain't like here. They care about you in California. All it takes is getting out there. You got a bus ticket to California, you got a ticket to the Garden of Eden. It's like what they call your Heart's Desire. 'Lay up for yourselves treasure in heaven, where neither moth nor rust doth corrupt, and where thieves do not break through nor steal. For where your treasure is, there will be your heart also.'"

"They know all that," James Terry Crews said. "Tell them what happened."

"That's what I'm trying to do. He was going to California, and we stopped him, that's all." Oletta Crews stopped suddenly as though slamming a door. "We already told the police."

"That was yesterday. This is today," her husband explained.

"What do I care? I'm old." She paused. "I said, 'Fix your own supper. I'm too old.'"

"I fixed it for him."

"He fixed it."

"I told him I'd fix it. I said, 'I generally fix the meals around here.'"

"And he said, 'You know how to cook?'" Oletta Crews turned to her husband. "I'm telling this."

James Terry Crews stared straight ahead as in an old photograph. He gave no sign of having heard. He looked as though he might have been dead the last twenty or thirty years.

"All right," Oletta Crews said, leaning forward. "Listen to this. Duke said, 'You know how to cook?' like he was surprised at a man cooking. And I said, 'How you think you ate in prison?' And he said 'With my hands.' And I said, 'What?' And he said, 'I ate with my hands. Haw haw.' And I said, 'I thought you might have used a spoon.' That straightened him up. And then I said, 'He learned in the army,'" meaning James Terry Crews. "He was in the Second World War and cooked for generals when he wasn't killing folks."

"I cooked for General Eisenhower." The memory seemed to stir the ashes in James Terry Crews. "I cooked steaks and eggs for breakfast, and he drank whiskey. He didn't touch a drop of coffee. He said, 'I'll have whiskey, Cookie. You got some bourbon?' And I said, 'Damn right. I'll make it myself.' I didn't even know what I was talking about. He was the most famous man in the world. This was overseas in France."

"They don't want to hear about that," Oletta Crews shouted. "That's too long ago, and he's dead anyway. They want to hear about Q. B. Farris."

"He's dead, too."

"He died more recent."

James Terry Crews turned away.

"Now, where was I?" Oletta Crews asked.

"Cooking supper," James Terry Crews replied.

"You were out cooking supper. I was entertaining him. I asked what he robbed to get in the work camp for eighteen years. I figured it must have been a bank. And he said, 'Robbed? Who told you that?' And I said, 'I don't need nobody to tell me nothing. I can figure it out by myself.' And he said, 'Then in that case you tell me.' And I said, 'A bank. I figure you for robbing a bank.' And he looked up quick under his hair. Had this hair over his eyes. And that's when it came to me. If he robbed a bank, there must have been a lot of money. Where was the suitcase? I said, 'You got a car?' And he said, 'Not yet. I'm fixing to.' And I said, 'How'd you get here then?' And he said, 'Through the woods. I walked.' And that's when I knew he had it on him, thousands of dollars wrapped up in plastic inside his pocket. And I said, 'You going to California?' And he said, 'Not if I can stay with you, momma. I love you too much to go off and leave you.'"

"Then we ate supper," James Terry Crews said, "and I told him about the army. He said it sounded a lot like prison, and I told him he was wrong about that. 'There's a world of difference between them,' I said."

"They just talked about this and that," Oletta Crews said. "Most of it him and the other one. I didn't listen. I was thinking about what comes next. And then I asked him, 'Are we prisoners?' And he said, 'Not any more than I am.' And I said, 'What's that supposed to mean?'"

"That was what you might call a threat," James Terry Crews explained.

"A threat?"

"Meaning we were hostages."

"That's right," Oletta Crews said. "We were hostages. It was a threat."

"Then we finished supper."

"We finished supper," Oletta Crews said. "And he said, 'Here, let me help you.' And I said, 'Help what?' And he said, 'Clean up. Don't you clean up the dishes? You let them stay dirty or you got dogs?' And I said, 'Dogs? What dogs got to do with it?' And he said, 'A joke.' He was joking. He was a jokey fellow, he said. That's one thing I got to get used to. And I said, 'What for?' And he said, 'What for? To understand what I'm saying. That's what for. To get the good out of me.' And I said, 'I don't see nothing funny about dogs.' And he said he meant lick the dishes. Clean them that way. And I said, 'James Terry does the dishes. And besides that I never had a dog in my life. Dogs unclean. It says in the Bible.' Then I told him, 'They don't have dogs in California.' And he looked surprised at that and said, 'California? You ever been out to California?' And I said, 'Not yet. I'm fixing to.'"

"As soon as she can sell this place," James Terry Crews explained. "She's been talking about it ever since she retired. 'Going to California,' I told him. 'That's where she wants to go and die happy.'"

"And he laughed at that," Oletta Crews shouted. "I said, 'What are you laughing at? That some kind of joke like dogs?' And he said, 'No ma'am. I was thinking about dying happy.' That struck him funny. He said, 'I can't figure that one out.' And I didn't even look at him. I told my husband, I said, 'You better clean up the dishes before he calls in some dogs to do it.' And he laughed and made like he was going to hug me, but I flung him off. And he said, 'That's why I like you, momma. You're so fast and full of jokes.'"

"Then we went and washed the dishes," James Terry Crews said. "He called me dad."

"Same way he called me momma," Oletta Crews shouted. "He didn't mean it. I told him, 'I ain't your momma. Your momma's dead. I wouldn't have a son in the work camp.' And he said, 'It'd break your heart. It'd break your heart, wouldn't it, momma?' And I told him it'd kill me for sure if I had a child and he ended up in the work camp for eighteen years. And he said, 'Nine'—like he was setting me straight. He laughed and said, 'I stayed for nine. I ain't fixing to stay for the rest. That way I'm ahead.' He didn't care."

"Tell them about the dictionary."

Oletta Crews reached under the sofa and pulled out a book. The covers were torn off, the pages dirty and dog-eared. She held it up for inspection.

"This is the dictionary," Oletta Crews announced. It was like an exhibit, a piece of evidence. "I was reading it."

"Reads it all day, that and the Bible, when she ain't watching television," James Terry Crews explained. "That's what she does. She does that to pass the time."

"It's all in there, everything you need to know," Oletta Crews said. "One's the head and the other's the heart. I got something to figure out, I read the dictionary till I find what it is."

"The Bible's the heart," James Terry Crews explained. "She reads it to ease her heart."

"When it gets too full," Oletta Crews said. "When I get to suffering too much. It puts my weary heart to rest. But I couldn't find it. It was there, but I couldn't find it."

"Find what?"

Oletta Crews looked at her husband as though she could not believe he was stupid enough to have asked such a question.

"What comes next," she said. "And then it came to me. I was in the bathroom, and I heard them washing dishes and talking like bees in the wall, and I was looking out at the ocean, that picture I told you about of the water. And that's when it came to me."

"That's when she decided," James Terry Crews explained.

"I didn't decide. Something told me."

"Something told her."

"Like a voice in California. I got up and flushed the toilet and went back and sat down and turned it over in my mind."

Oletta Crews held up her hand. "Listen to me," she said. "This is the main part. I knew what he was fixing to do, and he knew I knew. He already killed two men to get here. I heard that where God led me this far on TV, and now he was telling me what to do next."

"God," James Terry Crews explained. It was like nailing a pelt on a wall. "The voice she heard. It was God."

Oletta Crews looked at him with contempt. "They know that. Who else got a voice? Of course it was God. Speaks in your heart just like he led me on TV to know who it was came to the door in the rain of terror. And he opened it," indicating her husband, "and I looked out and knew who it was like in a mirror he looked so familiar."

"You were afraid."

"Yes."

"You killed him because you were afraid."

"Yes." And then, "I didn't kill him."

"I killed him."

"Don't listen to him," Oletta Crews shouted. "Listen to me. He don't know nothing."

"I don't know nothing."

"He just did it. I heard the voice."

"She heard the voice. I'm the one murdered him."

"It wasn't a murder. Police say that. Police say, 'You shoot who- ever you want to, lady, breaks in your house and keeps you hos- tage.'"

"Damn right, wouldn't you? She was afraid he might kill her."

"And I was afraid he might kill him, too," Oletta Crews said, indicating her husband. "I need him to help me. Besides I heard the voice. It spoke in my heart." She stopped as though reflecting. "'You can't serve two masters.' That's what it said. 'No man can serve two masters: for either he will hate the one, and love the other; or else he will hold to the one and despise the other.' "

"That's right. Then what?"

"I thought how to do it."

"How to kill him."

"I thought of ways of how to do it. Like roach tablets. Putting them in his grits at breakfast. And then I thought, What if they don't work? What if they just work on roaches? Then I thought of rat poison. But what if he tastes it? Drano. That's too strong. Lysol and Clorox. He might have to drink a gallon. Poison is out."

"I told her about the nail."

"That was later, when he went to bed."

"You were still thinking about it."

"Not that way I wasn't."

"In the ear . . ." James Terry Crews began.

"Let me tell it," Oletta Crews shouted. "I'm telling this. It was all over by then. I already figured it out. He said, 'What about a nail?' And I said, 'A nail?' And he said, 'I read about it in the paper.' "

"No, I didn't. It was in the *Police Gazette*. In the Charlotte, North Carolina, bus station. I was there waiting, and I went to the newsstand and picked up the magazines like you do, looking for pictures. . . ."

"They got pictures of half-naked women where they been raped in the *Police Gazette*," Oletta Crews said. "That's what he was looking at."

"No I wasn't. I was just looking, waiting for the time to pass till I got my bus, and I picked up the *Police Gazette*, and the first thing I turned to, that was it. Nail Murder. All about how this farmer in Kansas and this girlfriend he got killed her husband by driving a thirty-penny nail in his ear." James Terry Crews glared about him in triumph. "They killed him by driving a nail in his ear." He leaned forward. "You know why they did that?"

"So it wouldn't be a wound," Oletta Crews shouted. "They know that. The nail went in, and they wiped up the blood and burned the rag and called the doctor and said, 'He rose up in the bed and shouted and fell over dead.' And the doctor didn't even look in the ear. Said, 'Must have been a heart attack.' And they almost got away with it except for the farmer. He went crazy and confessed it all. Otherwise, they'd have joined the farms, his and the one she got from the murder, and made a million dollars by now selling it off for shopping centers."

"You ever hear anything like that?" James Terry Crews said proudly. "That's what you call a perfect crime except he went crazy."

"That's where he went wrong," Oletta Crews said. "That's why it ain't perfect. So I told him the nail was out." She lowered her voice. "I even thought of cutting his throat. Waiting till he was asleep and then creep in the light at the end of the hall shining in so we could see the vein in his neck beating and then pull the razor across it. But what if it's too deep? What if the gristle is too hard to cut through? I ain't that strong, and I knew he couldn't do it," indicating her husband. "He can talk about nails all he wants to, but I knew he couldn't even hold it still. He's too soft. He might look at him and feel sorry for him. I couldn't chance it. I didn't want Duke getting up, throat flapping open from ear to ear where I cut at it and him not dead. Ain't no telling what he might do bleeding like that, bubbling and shouting. He'd kill me for sure. That's when I knew James Terry would have to shoot him."

"I had to. You heard her."

"Hold on," Oletta Crews shouted. "Don't rush ahead. They ain't finished the dishes yet. I got out of the bathroom, and they came in and sat down, and James Terry said, 'Duke's been telling me about all the good times they had in the work camp. He liked it there.' And I said, 'If he liked it so much, why didn't he stay? Why come around here bothering us?' And then Duke says, 'What's on TV?' And I say, 'Nothing.' And he says, 'They got Monday Night Football.' And I say, 'I don't watch it. I don't know the rules.' And he says, 'What about you, old dad?' speaking to my husband, James Terry Crews."

" 'I don't watch it either,' I said. And he said, 'Why not? You don't know the rules?' And I said, 'I know them. I just don't watch it.' " He glanced at his wife. "It's too rough."

"That's right," Oletta Crews said. "I told him that game's all right for the work camp. I said, 'Rough men done worse than that to each other every day of their lives, but it ain't all right for women and children. It's too rough. Besides which,' I told him, 'it ain't Monday night.' And he said, 'Not Monday?' And I said, 'That's right. Yesterday was Monday. This is Tuesday.' And he laughed and said, 'Lord God,' and grinned like he just ate something he shouldn't."

"He had this kind of shit-eating grin," James Terry Crews explained.

"It was attractive, I don't mean that," Oletta Crews said, "but it's like he been eating something he shouldn't. And he said, 'I can keep up with it in the work camp. It's when I get out, that's when I lose track.' And I said, 'How many times you get out?' And he said every chance he got. That and Monday Night Football's his only pleasure, he said. That and beating up on folks to get in the work camp in the first place. 'And grinning,' I said. 'You left out grinning.' And he laughed and said, 'That's right, momma. That's the only pleasure I got, that and being here with you. What about going to bed?' And I thought, This is when the raping commences. And I said, 'Not me. I don't go to bed and get raped.' And you know what he did? He laughed. He fell on the floor like he couldn't stand up and kicked his feet in the air pretending. Looked like the devil come up through the floor from hell. And he said, 'Momma, you ever think you going to get raped, you know what I'd do?' But I didn't answer. I was too ashamed. And he laughed and said he'd stay up instead. 'I'd stay up all night before I'd go to bed and get raped,' and so on like that. But I didn't look at him. I heard him scrabbling around down there, but I didn't dare cast my eyes on him to see what nasty thing he was doing."

"He was getting up," James Terry Crews explained.

"I didn't want to see what it was for fear it might be something I didn't want to see. That's how he was. He didn't care. Then I felt him lean over me, grinning and mocking, and say what he meant was for me to go to one bed and him to another and sleep this time if that was all right with me. And that's when I knew there wasn't no way. Even if I could have saved him before, I knew I couldn't after that. I was a prisoner in my own house."

"He trusted us," James Terry Crews explained. "He said, 'I sleep light, but I trust you anyway, old dad. I know you don't want me to go back to the work camp for nine more years.' And he said to Mrs. Crews, 'Wake me for breakfast, you hear me, momma? Don't let me oversleep my welcome. I'm just going to rest a minute.

Then I'm going to have to leave you, much as you hate to see me go.'"

"And I thought, To California. He's going to California without me," Oletta Crews shouted, "and leave me alone and take all the money. And that's when I told James Terry to kill him. I said, 'Go get your gun.'"

"I got this single-barrel shotgun," James Terry Crews said. "First gun I ever owned."

"They don't want to hear about that."

But James Terry Crews turned on her. "Let me talk," he said. "This is interesting. I got that gun in Fayetteville when I was a boy. Walked in and slapped down seven dollars and said, 'I'll take that Stevens single-barrel,' and Mr. Robert reached up and got it out of the cradle. Had this cradle made out of deer hoofs, and he said, 'This squirrel gun?' And I said, 'Squirrel gun? I could bring you down with it if I had some buckshot.' That's the way I was then. I didn't take no smart talk from nobody. I said, 'This gun cost too much to waste on squirrels.' And he said, 'What you fixing to shoot with it, if you don't shoot me?' And I said, 'I don't know,' like I was still thinking about it. I said, 'I ain't made up my mind yet.' And then I said, 'Give me some buckshot' and looked right at him. That got his attention. Buckshot'll blow a hole in a man big as a melon. I was a man when I was fourteen, when I first went to work for the sawmill. I worked there till I hurt myself and moved to Atlanta and got married and went to painting. But I kept that gun. I had others, but it was my favorite. It reminded me."

"That's beside the point," Oletta Crews said. "The point is I could say, 'Go in there and do it,' and James Terry would go in there, and I'd feel it shake where he shot at him—once, twice, three times maybe—in the head or in the back, wherever it hit him. But what then? He was laying in my bed, and he'd bleed on it and ruin the mattress."

"Not to mention the shot," James Terry Crews said. "She didn't even think about that. I had to tell her. I said, 'Blood ain't nothing. Blood washes off. But buckshot—buckshot'll blow a hole in a man as big as a melon right through him and the mattress both. Might even blow a hole in the floor.'" His face lit up. "I ever tell you about the time we were moving, and there was a copperhead in the house, and I had the gun, but the shells were packed up somewhere in boxes?"

"Don't be an idiot."

"I shot a hole in the floor," James Terry Crews shouted, hurrying to finish while he still had the chance. "I found the shells and shot the floor clean out. Snake with it." He looked at his wife. "Ever see buckshot hit a melon?"

"Hush up," Oletta Crews said. "You're talking too much."

James Terry Crews said, "It explodes. You can't even find the pieces. It just lifts and disappears. Same way with heads."

"I knew I'd smell it," Oletta Crews said. "Whenever I put my face to it, I knew I'd smell it in my sleep no matter how good I washed it. The police would come and take off the body, but they'd leave all the blood in the mattress and on the sheets and on the rug across the floor where it runs out when they carry him off, and I'd have to clean it up. He can't clean," indicating her husband. "All he can do is paint."

"I say paint it. If it's dirty enough to wash it, it's dirty enough to paint it, I say."

"Only trouble is you can't paint sheets and mattresses where all the blood ran out." She leaned forward and spoke confidentially. "If it wasn't drinking, it was talking. All his life. He'd get to painting a house and talk himself right off the job. Couldn't even climb the ladder or mix the paint, he talked so much. Folks don't like that. They run him off. And it wasn't even drinking sometimes. It's what he calls high spirits."

James Terry Crews looked at her balefully. "High spirits," he said.

"Besides which I thought of something else," Oletta Crews said, rocking forward again. "What about Q. B. Farris?" She bugged her eyes as someone else might simulate fright. "Where was his gun? And then I thought about the money. What if he had it in his pocket and James Terry shot it all full of holes? Would they still take it? What do they do with money like that?"

"They don't do nothing," James Terry Crews replied. "Because it blows away just like a melon. If he had that money in his pocket, you couldn't even find the pieces."

"That's what I thought. Besides which he can't even see in the daytime let alone in the dark at night. He might point it at his head and hit the wrong place, where the money is, and just wound him, and he'd come crawling out at me."

"That's why I picked up two other loads," James Terry Crews explained. "In case I missed. I ain't never shot a man before."

"He said he might miss the first but not the second. But I told him, 'No. It's too dangerous. There's some other way.' And he said, 'I can't think of it.' And I said, 'I know. I wasn't expecting you to. Give me a minute.'" She paused and then spoke in an altered voice. "'Even though I walk through the valley of the shadow of death, I fear no evil, for thou art with me.' And then it said, 'It ain't your death. That's why it's a shadow. If it was your death, it'd be real. But killing him's only a shadow.' And as soon as I heard that, I knew who it was, and all my fear fell off me like sweat, and I dried up, it's like I was reborn. I knew what was promised. And I said to James Terry, 'Let it go. Don't shoot him now. Wait till later.' And he said, 'When?' And I said, 'When he's fixing to kill us.'"

"And I said, 'What if it's too late? What if he beats me to it?' And she said, 'Then you don't have to worry. You'll already be dead by then.' That don't make no sense to me."

"And I said, 'It won't come to that. Just get it loaded. I'll give you a sign—like this.'" She winked her eye and waved her hand.

"And I said, 'What if I'm tying my shoe and don't see you do it?'" James Terry Crews said. "'What if I get up and go to the bathroom?'"

"We heard him rattling around in there," Oletta Crews said. "And I said, 'Get ready. He's fixing to kill us.' And James Terry said, 'What do I do?' And I said, 'Sit here.'" She patted the cushion beside her. "'Sit down here and hide the gun under the sofa where you can get at it.'"

"And I said, 'That's too slow. He'll shoot us both before I get to it.' And she said, 'That's good. In that case you don't got nothing to worry about.'"

"All my fear dried up like sweat."

"And I cocked it and put it under the sofa. There ain't no safety on a single-barrel Stevens," James Terry Crews started to say, but his wife interrupted him.

"They don't want to hear about that. We were sitting on the sofa waiting."

"Not me. I was thinking about what if he kills me. That worried me. I knew what she said, but it still worried me."

"And always will," Oletta Crews said. "That's what's wrong with you." She paused suddenly. "We heard him stirring and singing, and then he came in tucking James Terry's shirt in his pants where he hid the gun and stopped and fell back all of a sudden like he was surprised and said, 'I didn't see you sitting there. You almost scared me to death sitting there side by side. You know what you look like?' But I ignored him. And he said, 'Two cats. You look like two cats lined up waiting for dinner. Ever see that?'—grinning and laughing to show he was lying. He tried to hug me, but I pushed him off. And then he said, 'I got to go, much as I hate to leave you, momma.'"

"And I said, 'Why don't you stay then? What's your hurry?'" James Terry Crews said. "I didn't mind him so much. He wasn't too bad except he might kill us. He had a good heart. Then I saw her look at me, and I felt my bowels tighten up. They were feeling loose. . . ."

Oletta Crews ignored him. "And then Duke said, 'I'd sure like to stay, old dad. It feels just like home.' And I said, 'Home? It ain't your home. I don't want children. I never had them.' And he laughed at that and said, 'I know. I'd have guessed it at how you kept your figure even if you hadn't told me about it. You sure look good for a woman your age'—laughing and grinning so I didn't know if he meant it or not. And I tried to hit him. I said, 'Go on. Don't talk like that, my husband sitting right here beside me.'"

"And I said, 'Don't mind me. I think she's pretty good-looking myself.'"

"And then he said, 'They'll be along directly looking for me. Don't tell them I been here. I'd rather be dead than go back to the work camp the rest of my life. How would you like it?' And I said, 'I wouldn't. But I wouldn't deserve to.' That straightened him up. And he said, 'Well, I got to go. Much obliged for the company. It ain't often I get to have such high old times.'"

"And I said, 'Me neither,'" James Terry Crews said. "'I enjoyed it,' I said. 'Come back. You ever get where they ain't looking for you, come back. You know where it's at. Come back and stay. We'd like to have you. You're good company.'"

"I didn't say nothing," Oletta Crews said. "And he said, 'How about you? You want me to come back too, momma?' And I said, 'I won't be here. I'm fixing to go to California.' Then he got serious all of a sudden. His face fell, and he looked old. He said, 'I sure do wish you luck,' reaching over to shake James Terry by the hand. And he said to me, 'I know how you feel wanting to go someplace like that, even if it's only to go there and die. That's one thing I learned in the work camp.'"

"Then he slapped me on the shoulder," James Terry Crews said, "and hugged me like that and backed off and said, 'I might buy this place myself if I had the time.'"

"That's how I knew he had the money," Oletta Crews said. "He wasn't lying."

"He'd have done it if he had the time."

"And the money," Oletta Crews said. "That's when I told him I might see him out there. And he said, 'Where?' And I said, 'California.' And he grinned and said, 'You might do it.' Then he looked at me. He looked me right in the eye and said, 'I'll see you in California, momma.' And I knew then I was right. He's fixing to walk right out that door and shut it behind him and stomp his feet down the steps like he's going somewhere and then creep back when we're sitting here side by side on the sofa thinking he's gone now, the danger is over, our lives are safe in our own hands again, praising God and weeping for joy we ain't dead, he didn't kill us, when all of a sudden the door flings open, and there he is standing there grinning and laughing like a devil from hell because it's a joke, don't you see, pretending to leave and then coming back and shooting us both right on the sofa side by side, one after the other —bang, bang, bang—till it wasn't even a sofa no more, just a hole in the floor and us in it, bits and pieces mixed with the stuffing."

"That's a shotgun," James Terry Crews explained. "You're talking about a twelve-gauge shotgun."

"That was his plan," Oletta Crews said. "I saw it as clear as I'm seeing you, and I knew I was right. It's just like him, I thought to myself—kill us like we were some kind of joke. You ain't got no will if you're a hostage. It's like you get tired. You can't even move. You got to sit there and wait."

"Unless you kill him first. That's right, ain't it, Letta?"

"It's like you can't move. You ain't got no will of your own."

"That's what I mean. That's why I killed him. No matter how good a heart he had, he was conceited."

"Listen to this," Oletta Crews shouted. She held up her hand again. "I said, 'Ain't you scared?' And he said, 'What for?' I didn't know if he was joking or not. I said, 'There's a posse of police out there waiting.' And he said, 'What for?' like he didn't know what I was talking about and went to the door and stuck his head out like he was trying to see who was out there. And I said, 'Because you don't care. You joke too much. You ain't serious.'"

"He was conceited. I could see that."

"I made the sign. And James Terry reached under and got the shotgun, and Duke turned around and looked at James Terry, and James Terry looked at Duke, and then his head lifted off. If it weren't for the roaring in my ears and the light and the smoke and the shaking on the sofa beside me where James Terry shot it off, I'd have thought it busted or something, like a balloon. One minute it was Duke Farris, the next minute it was gone like it went out the door. It was still raining, and I thought to myself, It ain't there. It ain't out there. You can look all you want to, but there ain't even bits and pieces. It lifted clean off. That head exploded."

She paused. "I was glad the door was open. That way it went right out. It didn't blow a hole in the wall, and there wasn't nothing left to clean up. I said, 'Here. Help me up.' But he didn't move. I got up and went over there, and you know what he had in his pockets? A ring snap off an aluminum can. He didn't even have a wallet. If he was hit by a car on the highway and killed on the spot, you wouldn't have even known who he was. I searched everywhere, and I told my husband, I said, 'James Terry, I can't find the money.' I couldn't believe it. And he said, 'What money?' He didn't even know what I was talking about. And I said, 'That money he's going to California with. The money he hid and come out to dig up.' And James Terry said, 'Where is it?' And I said, 'I don't know. You shot him too soon.'"

"He didn't even have a gun," James Terry Crews explained.

"He didn't have nothing except a ring snap off an aluminum can," Oletta Crews said. "But how was I to know that? The police said, 'Don't worry. You shot him on your own property.' And I said, 'My own property? I shot him in my own house. How was

I to know?' And they said, 'No way. He might have had a gun to kill you.'"

"That's probably even my ring snap off an aluminum can," James Terry Crews said. "He had on my trousers. There wasn't nothing in his at all."

"Police said it was self-defense," Oletta Crews continued. "Said, 'You killed him to save yourself. That's only natural.'"

"Ain't a jury in the land convict you of that."

"I couldn't move it," Oletta Crews said. "I sat down on the floor beside it and tried to push it out with my feet. I wanted to close the door. It was still raining. I said to James Terry, 'I can't move it by myself. Get up and help.' And he got up. Then I saw him lift an arm and start to drag him out. A leg slid by me and then a foot, and then I was free. The door was open, and I looked out and saw the rain. The floodlight was still on. It went out in the yard like a room and lit up the rain. I could see it coming down like knives. It was all silver, and in the tree, it was all silver like ice—like the whole world turned to ice. And James Terry started to come in, and I said, 'Get the light.' And he got the light, and it was dark. It was dark out there as far as the eye could see, and I could still hear it raining. It was like it was moving, like a great wind lifting and heaving. And I said to James Terry, 'Close the door. Close the door on it.' And he closed the door."

"He wasn't so bad," James Terry Crews said as though in eulogy. "I don't care what they say he done. He had a good heart. Lots of folks rob banks got better hearts than the people that own them. He was what you might call a godsend. I thought that. I thought to myself, Q. B. Farris—Duke, you're what you might call some kind of godsend."

"We were hostages," Oletta Crews shouted. "He took our will."

"I mean before that."

"There wasn't no before that. As soon as he came and knocked at that door, he took our will."

"I mean when we were doing the dishes. I thought to myself, He's some kind of a godsend. I wouldn't be here laughing and talking and cutting the fool if he wasn't here. I'm grateful to him. I'm grateful he's here. He reminded me of when I was working." He paused. "Robbing banks. . . . Robbing banks ain't so bad. I might have done that myself if I hadn't got hurt and moved to

Atlanta and got married. It's a whole other way of doing—a whole other kind of life."

"Listen to me," Oletta Crews shouted. "I know about godsend. As soon as I heard that knock on the door, I felt it knocking in my heart, and I said to myself, It's God knocking at the door of my heart, asking me to open up and let him come in and change me, change my whole life." She paused. "There's a better place than this, and I thought I was going. But I know better now, even if he don't," indicating James Terry Crews. She lowered her voice, increasing its intensity. It sounded like someone else speaking inside her: " 'For even Satan disguises himself as an angel of light. His end shall be according to his deeds.' And his shows that," Oletta Crews said, "when James Terry shot him and there wasn't no money."

"And no gun."

"And nothing to show except mockery. All my hopes mocked and bleeding half in and half out the door where I couldn't even shut it myself, and he dragged it out where it'd been killed, I felt like something inside me was dead."

"Me, too. It felt like something inside me was dead too. I didn't know what it was."

"I did. I sat on the floor where I'd been looking for money and thought to myself, 'You can't serve two masters.' Satan appeared as an angel of light and killed all my hopes, took my will and killed all my hopes. But I'm still alive. I ain't dead, and I ain't changed. I'm just like I was."

Kurt Rheinheimer

HOMES

(from *Southern Magazine*)

"Let me put it to you this way," Tommy says to the husband, reaching up to put a hand on the man's big soft shoulder. "I'd never in this life put you in anything I wouldn't live in myself." Tommy glances at the wife when he says *in this life,* making sure she sees his spiritual side. "My family's lived in a home almost identical to this one for over two years," Tommy goes on, taking his hand from the shoulder and looking the husband in the eye, "and we haven't had any call to move. Come to think of it, I'd love for you folks to come by and visit us sometime. Just look over the home and get a sense of the real pleasures of mobile home living. We've got the room, the comfort, the furniture, the *safety* we need. I know when your family comes along safety will be an even greater consideration than it is now." He steers them around to the side of the trailer. "See these?" he says, pointing at the side of the unit. Then he looks up into the hot, clouded sky, as if searching for rain. "These are steel bands—made of the same metal that goes into skyscrapers and jet aircraft. And each Greenpath home is steel-banded to its foundation in four separate locations." He gestures upward over the top of the unit, guiding their eyes over the first of the bands and then allowing them to glance down at the others.

With safety taken care of, and the wife kind of patting the husband's arm—he is brushing her away subtly while he pretends to inspect the trailer's construction—Tommy knows he's close. "Listen," he says suddenly and just a little too loudly, projecting an air of importance and consequence, "this is not the kind of thing you jump right into." He smiles as he makes eye contact with each of them. Then he speaks quietly. "It's not quite like deciding between a Big Mac and a Quarter Pounder, is it?" He smiles broadly, forcing them to do the same. "So let's go back to the office, have a Dr Pepper, and sit down and talk about it." He watches them as he mentions Dr Pepper. Older couples you use coffee. Younger ones that look like they have a little money, you use something light like 7-Up. These couples—he works in construction and she works in a laundromat and says she does some ironing—you go with Dr Pepper. He leads them back around the side of the unit and across the rock lot of Greenpath Homes. Out front the big banner is almost still in the air. YOUR GREENPATH HOME: $149 A MONTH AND NO MONEY DOWN, it says in huge green letters on a white background. Tommy hesitates as he starts to ask the husband if maybe they didn't know each other in high school. His fear is that the man never made it that far. He starts more cautiously. "Don't I know you from someplace, Bob?" he says when they are halfway to the office. "Softball maybe, or church, or maybe Clarion High?" The husband, who has said nothing since giving his name and talking about his job, looks fully at Tommy for the first time.

"High school maybe," he says. "When'd you get out?"

"Been out five years," Tommy says, holding up his right hand to show off the ring.

"I was two years ahead of you," Bob says, "but maybe I do remember you. You ever have Fisher for English?"

Tommy sees his opening. "Twice," he says, with no recollection of anyone named Fisher. "Flunked my butt hard the first time, and I just barely made it through the second time."

Bob laughs out loud, looking at his wife for verification of this evidence of his intelligence. She returns his smile, apparently glad that he is perking up a little. "He was tough," Bob says, "but I got out of there in one go-round."

Inside the office—a lux double-wide with Astro-turfed steps and deep carpet everywhere except in the kitchen—Tommy guides them toward the soft drink machine. "Mountain Dew, Pepsi, Grape, Orange, 7-Up, Dr Pepper," Tommy announces as they reach the machine, as if he is about to treat them to a gourmet meal. They both ask for Dr Peppers and Tommy pops hers open first. Bob makes a half-move toward his own pocket, and Tommy waves him off grandly. "Are you kidding?" he says in great mock offense. "These here are Greenpath quarters." He grips Bob's elbow briefly as he hands him the can. Then Tommy pops open his own, takes a long swig, and leads them down the hall to his office. Once they've got the safety worry out of the way and a Dr Pepper in their hands, and Tommy can see that the wife wants it, there's no way he can lose it. Candy from a baby, he tells Ellis and Tucker and the others when they ask him how he keeps turning them over. Instinct, he tells them. Then he feels like he's been bragging and won't say anything. But Tommy Conners sold his first Green-path home before he was out of high school. He looked at his home town, saw four thousand people, a bottling plant, two bars, a rubber belt factory, and the Greenpath dealership, and decided the only thing he'd touch was Greenpath. The town is just off the interstate, though it built itself up around the old north-south two-lane and is twenty-five miles outside of the city.

In the office, Tommy sits Bob and Shirley down, looks them in the eye, and asks them point-blank what they have in the bank. No problem at all, he tells them when they answer. No problem at all. He gets out his calculator, asking what they might be able to get from their parents. They look at each other and come up with a total of two hundred dollars. Great, Tommy tells them. Fantastic. He plays at the calculator—pretending to work hard at an acceptable figure—and then looks up at them triumphantly. "Three-fifty," he says. "I can put you in that beauty with the rust appliances —this year's model—for three-fifty down and one-eighty-nine a month."

"But the no money down?" Bob says.

Tommy didn't expect that. He already went over the banner with them. He tells everybody about that right away—that it's only one or two used units and there are even better deals on new units.

"You're right, Bob," Tommy says. "You're absolutely right. And there are two of those units out there we can put you in without you giving me so much as a dime. That blue one we looked at first, and a one-bedroomer back at the edge of the lot there." He stands, as if he'll run them out there right now to show them.

"No, no," Shirley says. "We understand." She turns to her husband. "We'd be dumb to get a little one when all it takes is three-fifty to get in a new big one." She says this in a semi-whisper, as if Tommy's not supposed to hear it.

Bob shrugs in apparent agreement.

"Smart girl you married there, Bob," Tommy says, and gets out the paperwork. They're nailed. His second sale of the day and seventh of the week. The quarterly sales prize for the region—a week in the Bahamas—is long since in the bag. No way anyone can catch him. No way anyone east of the Mississippi River can catch him.

The main reason Tommy likes church picnics is that Paula, his wife, is the best-looking girl there by far, and the only one who dresses like you're supposed to for a church function. Today, on a coolish day for summer, she has on a baby-blue cotton dress with a row of little yellow and white daisies across the top, which runs across her chest about halfway between her breasts and her throat. The dress has a sort of starched look to it—it is firm and pure to Tommy's eye—and over it she is wearing a little white jacket that has the same look. The jacket is cut short—not even to her waist—and, in combination with the dress, it makes Paula look strong and innocent and good, which is what Tommy wants to see in her. She looks like Easter to him as she moves easily among people, talking about the weather and her children, who are with her mother. Paula is so pretty and perfect in the sun that Tommy feels a real ache of some kind. It is not quite a sexual feeling, or even quite love—it is more a vision of wifely perfection and Paula's fulfillment of it. Tommy moves through the crowd with almost equal ease as he watches her. He talks about sports with men who are nearly all fifteen or so years older than he is, and takes the time to watch Paula, seeing her as exactly what a woman at a church picnic should look like and act like.

At the picnic there is a lot of chicken and potato salad and baked beans. In the glen near the little creek that runs through the church property, there are fifteen or so picnic tables scattered out, all covered with white paper tablecloths that stand out brilliantly on the new green grass that the grounds committee put in the spring before last. Sometimes Tommy and Paula sit together at these picnics, and sometimes they don't, preferring to spread themselves out and let themselves be seen and talked to by more people. They are, because of their youth and good looks and poise, the darlings of the older church people who stand with big bellies and broadening hips and talk about how young and lucky the Connerses are.

Today, midway through the picnic, as Tommy is talking about the ever-increasing size of the guards in pro basketball, there is a sudden shower. The water falls in fat drops onto the white tablecloths and into the tubs of potato salad, and washes some of the barbecue sauce off the chicken. At the first drops, the women stand from the tables almost in unison, gathering bowls and trays and running in a waddly, bent-over mass toward the main building, making noises that sound almost like clucks as they worry over their shoes, their hair, and their food. The men, with no food to protect, are more leisurely—a few standing to look at the clouds and others continuing conversations as they head in. By the time the women have gotten everything inside and the men are approaching the building, the rain stops as suddenly as it began, leaving behind a brief rainbow, a truncated picnic, and greatly increased humidity. People will now wander between tables inside and outside, going one place for food and another for conversation.

Paula is among the first women to come back outside. As if by magic, or perhaps youth, she is much less affected by the weather than the older women. Her hair, arranged in soft dark curls around her face, has not been mussed, and her dress and jacket have somehow repelled the drops, or perhaps absorbed them without evidence. She steps out into the renewed sunshine and looks directly at Tommy, who is talking to his old junior high school basketball coach, Buddy Hansen. Tommy is trying, for the tenth time, to talk him out of buying a mobile home. The Coach, who is perhaps Tommy's best friend, has been talking for months about selling his house and moving into a trailer. As Paula comes near them, Tommy can almost feel her will and power to separate the two men —can nearly smell her wish that Tommy not have anything to do with the Coach. And the Coach himself, who wanted Tommy to go on from high school and play college ball instead of marrying Paula, seems to feel it too, and begins to edge away from Tommy.

He says he ought to go find his own wife and see how upset she is with him for eating too much.

"You look gorgeous, Paula," the Coach says when she is still fifteen feet away and he is already leaving. "Just gorgeous." It is as if he is twenty-three and she is forty-six, instead of the other way around, so boyish and proper is his approach and retreat.

"Well, thank you, Buddy," Paula says, stepping carefully over a muddy spot.

"Catch up with you on the flip side," Tommy says to the Coach.

"Right," the Coach says.

Paula slides her pale, bare arm in under the tan linen sleeve of Tommy's jacket. She leads him out toward the end of the new grass, out toward the little creek that runs into town. They played along the creek as children. And though they did so separately, their families like to tell stories about them playing there together and getting to know each other, and being perfect for each other even at that age. The creek is narrow and meandering, set down into a four-foot-wide gorge where the water moves gently over small rocks.

"I was talking to your daddy inside," Paula says as they walk. Tommy is immediately irritated for two reasons. One is that, since she is walking him away from the picnic, he knows she wants to talk about something. Moving out of the apartment maybe. Or his job. Ever since the Bahamas trip, she has been asking about moving. She saw a huge bug one day and spent the rest of the trip worrying she'd see another one. Since then, she's been telling Tommy they should have cashed in the trip money and saved it for a house. This threatens Tommy in a way he's not sure he understands. He wants to know what she thinks about things, but he does not like it when she disagrees with what he has already decided is the best thing for the family. She wants a house with flat ground and a big yard, so Annie can learn to walk—so they can have a real life—and can't they afford it with all the money he's making now? Tommy yelled at her when she said that, telling her she'd be the first to know when they could afford the kind of house they wanted. Second to know, she corrected, and Tommy stopped talking to her.

The second thing that bothers Tommy about the walk and talk is that he did not know his parents were at the picnic. They had said they were going to stay home and work in the garden. But Tommy does not say anything about either of those things. He allows his arm to be held and his pace to be dictated by his pretty wife.

"And he agrees with me, Tommy, on how you're getting shorted, on how you're shorting yourself. I didn't say a word to him, and he just started telling me how he thought you are so much better than just selling mobile homes. He said real homes. Or maybe even commercial real estate, Tommy. Commercial real estate. In town."

Tommy can feel heat at his neck and under his arms. He almost never yells at Paula when he is angry but has gone as long as two days without saying anything to her except what has to be said to make sure the children get taken care of. "I think that may happen sometime," he says softly. "I think I may still have a few things to learn from Porterfield and a few of the others."

"And he said he didn't see any reason you couldn't run your own business too, Tommy," Paula says, as if he hadn't spoken. "With as good as you are with the paperwork and the deals, you'd be a natural."

"Those are things that everybody at Greenpath does," he says.

"How come everyone didn't go to the Bahamas then?" she says, with a hint of a whine in her voice. "I think he's right, Tommy. I think you should just quit, but you're too scared. We have money in the bank, and you'd find something fast—I bet they'd come looking for you once the word got out."

Tommy decides this is too much to respond to. He has been working since he was fourteen and has never left a job without having the next one to go to. When he has thought about quitting, it has been to go to school, to take a few business courses. But Paula never mentions school because she is afraid he'll listen to the Coach and enroll full time someplace and play basketball. Once, the Coach said to Tommy that if Paula were forced to choose between Tommy having another woman on the side and Tommy playing college basketball, she'd take the other woman on the side.

"Well, I can see there's no getting anywhere with you right now," Paula says into his thoughts, and pulls at his arm to turn them back toward the church.

They walk in silence for a distance and then she lets go of his arm. "I don't mean to push, Tommy," she says. "It's just that you don't know how good you are. You should hear people talk about you."

Tommy has heard people talk about him since the seventh grade, when he could first hold a basketball behind his knees, drop it, clap his hands in front of his legs, and then catch the basketball before it hit the floor. He has never understood how it has ever helped him to have people talk about him, so he has listened less and less over the years. "You certainly look pretty today," he says to Paula as she walks ahead of him to go into the church. She smiles quickly back over her shoulder but doesn't say anything else to him.

At the apartment on a Tuesday afternoon, Tommy and the Coach are carrying a big, blond wood-framed mirror up the steps to go into the dining room. The mirror is as wide as a table, and like so many of the other pieces of furniture in the apartment, it just sort of came to be Tommy's. His mother bought it to go in her dining room, and when it didn't match the wood in her table closely enough, she gave it to Tommy instead of going through the trouble of taking it back. "Who needs a mirror to watch themselves eat anyway?" she asked Tommy. He thinks it will work well in his dining room, which is really a little dinette off the kitchen. People have told Tommy that for somebody twenty-five years old —especially a guy—he has a great sense of furniture and how it fits in a room. The Coach shakes his head over Tommy and furniture, saying that if he didn't know better, he'd think Tommy had some fag blood in him or something.

Paula is away on a bus trip with a group to see the amazing frescos in two little churches in North Carolina. She read about them in the newspaper—they're supposed to be as pretty as Michelangelo's and are drawing hundreds of thousands of people to a place that's only 175 miles from where they live, and so she wanted to see them. Tommy told her if they turned out to be as pretty as she thought, then he and the kids would drive down with her and they could make a Sunday trip out of it.

The Coach is now a guidance counselor at the junior high school where Tommy Conners was the best basketball player in the twenty-two-year history of the school. The Coach used to get Tommy out of classes, buy him beer, even set him up with easy high school girls, starting when Tommy was in the eighth grade.

The Coach said Tommy was going to be all-state in high school, but two things happened. One Tommy could have told him— Tommy stopped growing at just over five foot seven, two inches taller than his father. And the other was that Tommy met Paula— actually sort of discovered Paula—when he was in the tenth grade and she was in the ninth. He decided he needed to work, and didn't have all the time it took for basketball. The Coach did nothing short of blow up over that, asking Tommy who the hell he thought he was to pour all that basketball talent down the toilet for some girl. After maybe a month, he calmed down, and has kept up with Tommy ever since. He still tells Tommy two or three times a year that they ought to get in touch with North Carolina and see if Tommy could get in. Tommy laughs, and the Coach tells him he has the quickest hands he's ever seen in his life—that Tommy wouldn't have to score a single damn point to be an all-star.

"What are you going to do with this mother?" the Coach says when they are most of the way up the metal stairway between the two sets of apartment buildings.

"You mean the mirror?" Tommy says.

"You know what the hell I mean," the Coach says. Tommy has been trying for a long time to get the Coach to cut down on the crude language—as a way of getting Paula to ease up on him a little.

"Mom was going to put it in her dining room so I thought about trying that," Tommy says as they flatten the big mirror over the turn in the stairwell up to the third floor.

"Doris wouldn't even think about where to put a mirror," the Coach says. "I bought one right after we got married, to go in the bedroom, and she freaked. Literally." He laughs. "It's been in the garage for fifteen years. I think the damn dog peeing on it once in a while is the only use it gets. Another reason I need to sell the damn house. We live in two rooms, keep all the junk in the basement and the attic, and never even look at it. It's a waste of space for two people with no kids anymore." The Coach's daughters both got married right out of high school and moved into the city.

Tommy decides not to say anything to the Coach about wanting to buy a mobile home. Tommy has told him a dozen times it's a bad idea, but the Coach sticks with it, as if it's because that's what Tommy sells. Tommy puts his end of the mirror down so he can open 306. He hates the apartment as much as Paula does. The door is metal—a thin, hollow-sounding metal just like the stairs, except the stairs are sort of corrugated, and the door is painted white so it kind of looks like wood. The whole apartment sounds tinny and hollow to Tommy, sort of like a trailer, and he wouldn't live in one of those if they paid him. What Paula hates most is being up on the third floor with the kids. Benji is really pretty much O.K.— he is almost six now and has never fallen in the two years they've been there. But Annie is different. She is fourteen months, and just starting to walk, and Paula is afraid she'll fall.

"In here," Tommy says to the Coach, walking backwards into the dinette. The apartment smells like plastic, and Tommy has never been able to figure out why.

"When are you going to buy a house, Tommy?" the Coach says, as if he is thinking about the smell too. "Or at least a trailer."

"Next time I win the sales contest," Tommy says, just realizing it as he says it. "Next time I win, I'm not taking the trip. I'm taking the money and looking for a house down near Cauthen."

"Cauthen?" The Coach is sitting at the dining room table now. It is just big enough for Tommy and his family, and when somebody comes for dinner, they have to bring in the coffee table and let the kids eat off that.

"Yeah," Tommy says. He is tapping at the wall to find a stud. "Paula likes it over that way."

"Paula Schmaula," the Coach says with a long resigned breath. His jealousy of her seems to be getting stronger as his own marriage gets worse and worse and he doesn't have any kids to coach anymore. It's as if he got stalled out with Tommy—as if Tommy was his big hope for somebody he had coached to go on to be a star in high school, college, and maybe even the pros. But when Tommy met Paula and stopped growing, the Coach stopped growing too. Within two years after Tommy left junior high, the Coach moved into an office and started getting fat. Right now, he is signed out from school on an appointment with a consulting psychologist.

"She has a sister over that way," Tommy says. He's always been real calm and even with the Coach over Paula. There's no real reason to be angry with the Coach about it—it's just a little frustrating that he doesn't have any more to do than to hang around, now that Tommy doesn't need girls or beer or basketball coaching anymore.

"So what is it with the mirror in here?" the Coach says, as if to change the subject. "You going to watch yourself eat?" Tommy laughs and says that's just what his mother said.

"Smart woman, your mom," the Coach says. "If I'd've been two or three years older, you never know." The Coach says that about Tommy's mother almost every time she comes up in a conversation. She is a softly overweight woman of forty-nine. She is still attractive, maybe especially to men like the Coach.

"Does this sound like a stud to you, Coach?" Tommy says as he taps on the wall with the back end of a screwdriver.

"Not till your voice gets a little deeper it don't," the Coach says, and laughs.

Tommy goes into the kitchen and gets a big nail out of his tool drawer. "I should use one of those toggle bolt things," he says to the Coach when he comes back in, "but I don't have any."

"You got any beer, Tommy?"

"Coach, it's two o'clock in the afternoon. Aren't you working?"

"Hell yes I'm working," the Coach says in mock offense as he spreads his beefy arms over the table. "I'm counseling one of my old students in how to hang a mongo mirror in his dining room so his kids can see what great table manners the old man has."

Tommy starts driving the nail while the Coach is still talking. It feels good and strong going in—he's hit the stud dead square, he decides. He tilts the mirror away from the table and looks at the wire that runs across the back. It is hooked at either side with a little eye-screw. Tommy gives each screw a pull to make sure they're tight. Then he stands by his end of the mirror with a hand on his hip, as if he's asking the Coach whether he's going to help or not.

"What about you, Hotshot?" the Coach says as he stands up. "Aren't *you* working?"

"Coach, the people I work with don't leave for the day at three-thirty. That's about when they start to show up."

They hang the mirror but then take it back down because Tommy left too much nail sticking out and so the angle away from the wall is too severe. Tommy hits it four or five times and they hang it again and then sit down at the table to admire it.

"You going to give me a beer or not?" the Coach says.

"You forget where the refrigerator is?" Tommy says in the same mock-irritated tone the Coach used and that they have used with each other most of the time since Tommy was an eighth-grade gunner who scored twenty-five points a game and who didn't pass off to the guys he didn't like.

The Coach pulls the tab on his beer and says "Bussssssssch," like he always says when he opens any beer, no matter what brand, and just as he is about to finish his word the mirror crashes off the wall and onto the floor next to them. It doesn't break immediately when it hits the floor—it falls sort of straight down—but, after it does hit, it falls into the back of the chair on that side of the table and big pieces of glass fall—almost in slow motion—onto the dinette floor. The Coach reached for the mirror about the time it hit the chair. He and Tommy stand up—Tommy was across the table from where the mirror hit—and then the Coach says, "Hell, Tommy, if you'd've been over here, you'd've caught the damn thing. No way those hands would have missed it."

Tommy doesn't say anything. He glances at the nail—he drove it in too far, he decides—and goes to get the broom and the trash can. They pick up the pieces, and Tommy wants to blame the Coach, but knows he can't. By the time they've finished cleaning up, the Coach is ready for another beer. He goes and gets it and sits back down at the table. Tommy says he's going back to work.

At the door, Tommy pauses to say something else to the Coach about going back to work, but then decides not to. The Coach tells him to keep selling all those hillbillies all those trailers they can't afford. Tommy doesn't say anything to that and looks past the Coach at the empty mirror frame. The Coach looks back over his shoulder, following Tommy's line of sight, and then tells Tommy if they'd hung it in the bedroom where it belongs, then it never would have broken. He laughs, and takes a sip of beer.

A few days later Tommy is standing with Van Ellis at the Coke machine at the office. Everybody else is at lunch. Tommy is there because he just closed a sale (a brand-new double-wide to a middle-age couple he never thought would buy) and because his car is in the shop for a tune-up and oil change. Ellis is there because he likes to sit in the office next to Tommy's so he can listen to Tommy

and how he does it—how he tells people the walls in the trailers are soundproof, for instance. "You know," Tommy always tells
them, "the kids don't need to hear quite everything now, do they?"
Then the couple laughs and Tommy laughs and he has another
sale. Tommy has known for a long time that Ellis listens to him
and lives with mild dread that one day Ellis will pick that time to
sneeze or cough and send the sound right through. Right now,
though, Ellis is congratulating him.

"It's balls," he's saying. "Everybody around here thinks of you
as Mr. Churchpew himself, but what it really is is looking like
that and then pulling off the stuff you do." Ellis looks down at
Tommy with what appears to be a combination of admiration and
jealousy. Ellis is in his early forties, tall, and his gut seems to get
bigger by the week. He has been a steady, unspectacular mobile
home salesman since he left high school—for most of that time
with Greenpath. He is one of the reasons Tommy thinks about
leaving—he doesn't like to picture himself as someone forty-five
years old, fat, and selling mobile homes.

"You know I could whisper over here and blow your sale," Ellis
is saying. "And you know they could check into the construction
bull you sling. And you know you could hit Porterfield after a bad
night with one of those wild-ass financing deals you pull. But no,
you're Tommy Conners and you just grab it by the balls, smile that
little choirboy smile, and pull it right the hell off every time." Ellis
hits Tommy, just a little too hard, on the shoulder.

Tommy smiles and puts coins in the machine. "What'll it be,
Van My Man?" he says. "Drinks are on me."

"Hell," Ellis says. "I'm going to lunch." He turns, pushes the
door hard enough that it bumps against the side of the trailer, and
heads out to his car. Tommy goes back to his office and figures his
commission on his calculator. It comes out exactly the same as it
did in his head. This will be the fourth sale he hasn't told Paula
about. Of the last ten, he's mentioned only six. This seems to have
had the dual effect of making her talk less about his getting a new
job—maybe because six sales over that long is a bit of a slump for
Tommy—and of allowing Tommy to put some money in reserve,
maybe against the day when he does go in and talk to Porterfield.

He tells himself that the thing that has put him even close to
thinking about leaving is not Paula at all, or even the message from

his father, which was never delivered directly to Tommy. Instead, it is what happened to a seventh-grade classmate named Aaron Hutchins. Aaron Hutchins was the biggest nerd ever to hit the seventh grade, and he never changed a bit all the way through high school. The only thing that changed was that his face got worse for a while, then a little better, and then he went away to college. Now he's been back from college for just over three years, and he's making a giant fortune in telephone services and equipment. It irritates Tommy that he doesn't even understand exactly what Aaron does to make all that money. Just that the big phone company got broken up, and then optical cable came along, and then cellular phones, and Aaron Hutchins got up from his computer and his acne medication long enough to step into the right place at the right time. Tommy looks out his office door into Porterfield's office, where there is a computer terminal on the desk. Tommy has never seen Porterfield use it, but he's heard it has all the inventory in it—you just punch up a button or two, and a whole description of every trailer in the region lights up on the screen. Then you push another little button and the whole thing comes out on a piece of paper. As Ellis' car rolls off the lot, Tommy goes into the office to look at the computer more closely. He has a feeling that if he knew how to use it he could make more money out on the lot, and if somebody as goofy as Aaron Hutchins can make money with one, then Tommy Conners ought to be able to make a lot more. Porterfield has been talking about getting terminals for all of them, but then he's also talked about company cars, matching jackets, and a retirement plan, too. The machine just sits there— like it belongs in a hospital or someplace—but Tommy has the odd feeling that it is keeping an eye on him. He goes back to his own office to check in with two couples who are ready to close and whose financing he has already arranged.

He reaches the husband of the first couple, who says he has decided to stay in the apartment a while longer. "Hoo-wee," Tommy says into the phone. "An apartment is money down the tubes. *Straight* down the toilet." Tommy knows as he says this that he is reacting too strongly. Any other day he would compliment the man on his thought and decision-making, and *then* start slowly on the rent/toilet number. "What the hell," the man tells Tommy. "It's my money, right?" And he hangs up the phone. Tommy holds the receiver and looks at it for a moment before he hangs it up. He starts to dial the man's number again and then stops, asking himself silently why he was tempted to call again when it didn't have a chance to do anything but make the guy even angrier.

While he is dialing the wife of the other couple, he hears a car roll onto the lot. He puts the phone down, thankful for a face-to-face customer. But it's not a customer. It's Porterfield. Tommy watches him from the front window of the trailer. He gets out of his car—a new, black Chevrolet—and adjusts himself at the crotch as he starts for the trailer. He is just over fifty and has been sell-ing since he was nineteen. He owns stock in Greenpath, and, like the ministers who ask for money on TV, he genuinely believes he is helping a lot of people by putting them into Greenpath mobile homes. And so Tommy has come to admire him, and to learn from him. Things like how to be as sincere as all get out with your customers and still make money for yourself.

"Yo Tommy," Porterfield calls as he comes in, as if to see if Tommy's there.

"Yo," Tommy calls back.

"You got the fort, huh?" Porterfield says. They have not had a secretary for almost a month, since the last one walked out.

"I guess," Tommy says. "No big raids going on right now though." Tommy is sitting at his desk looking at his hands. He is thinking, for a reason he doesn't know, that if his hands were big-ger, maybe he really would have pushed the basketball and given college ball a try.

"Come on down here," Porterfield calls out to him.

Tommy goes down the hall to the office with the computer. Porterfield tells him to sit down. Then he rubs his hands together a moment and looks up at Tommy.

"You know what this business needs, Tommy?" he says.

Tommy says no, he doesn't.

"More like you," Porterfield says immediately. "Two more like you, and we'd blow the roof off headquarters, Tommy. You realize we have the second-smallest territory, for population I mean, in the company? And the third-highest sales? That's fifty-eight terri-tories in eleven states, Tommy." Tommy has heard all of this many times. "Where can I get more like you, Tommy, do you know?"

Tommy shrugs, smiling off to one side.

"I mean it. Even *one* more like you. I send these guys down to damn Houston for all that training, and they come back hungover and gung ho for three days and that's it." He takes a little cigar—a Garcia Y Vega that Tommy likes the smell of—out of his pocket and looks at it for a few seconds. He looks over it at Tommy and then back at the cigar. "And what if you left, kid?" He looks hard at Tommy, as if trying to gauge his reaction. "Where would I be then?"

Tommy shrugs again, wanting the conversation to go away. "Nobody's irreplaceable," he says. "They break the records whether it's Babe Ruth or Greenpath Homes."

Porterfield smiles as he lights his cigar. "And you know what else?" he says. "It's not just every record getting broken, but every man having a price." He smiles at Tommy again. "So I'm prepared to do two things for you, Mr. Conners. To put you in charge of the rest of these bozos for another grand a year, and to add another percentage point to your commission. Make that three things. You tell me today, and I'll make it effective today."

Tommy moves his hand back over his hair and makes a little whistly noise as he blows out some air. "That's heavy stuff," he says. "And real flattering." He stands up. "Do I get to think about it till five?"

"You can think about it till eleven-fifty-nine," Porterfield says. "Or on into tomorrow, but it's midnight tonight if you want it to show up in your next check."

Tommy starts out of the office. Once he is back at his own desk, he hears cars on the lot. He goes to his window and sees that one is Van Ellis back already and the other is the Coach, here again, Tommy assumes, to renew his pitch that Tommy sell him a home. Tommy thinks for one second about the two-year-old dented double-wide at the back edge of the lot and how pleased the Coach would be with it—for a month or so. Then he opens his desk drawer. He takes out his calculator and a half-eaten pack of cinnamon Life Savers. He takes the little glass-framed family portrait off the top of his desk, and sticks it in the inside pocket of his jacket, and then goes out to meet the Coach. The heat has built up on the lot, as it does when you have that much shiny tin in one place. The Coach waves at Tommy from across the lot and Tommy waves back, genuinely pleased to see the Coach. Tommy meets him mid-lot and puts his arm up over the pudgy shoulders of the first person who ever told him he was a star. The shoulders are thick and maneuverable under Tommy's arm; they seem to carry within them the soft, mushy feel of the Coach's life. At the car, Tommy deposits the Coach on the passenger side, and, as he goes around to get in and drive them off the lot, he is thinking about how long it will take him to get both their lives back to where they're supposed to be.

Mary Ward Brown

IT WASN'T ALL DANCING

(from *Grand Street*)

In the morning a strange black girl in white uniform stood by Rose Merriweather's bed. Even her shoes and stockings were white. Like a fly in a bucket of buttermilk, Rose's mother would have said years ago. Rose's mother had been a St. Clair of Mobile, who had married a Pardue from the Canebrake, a family just as good or better.

"I'm Rose Pardue, of Rosemont," Rose had introduced herself as a girl. It had been her open-sesame all over the Black Belt of Alabama. She fixed her once-famous eyes on the girl by her bed.

"Who are you, may I ask?"

"Your new nurse," the girl said pleasantly.

Rose pushed herself up on the pillow. The girl had a confident smile, quick eyes, small hard-muscled body.

"What became of the other one?" Rose asked.

"Your daughter let her go." The girl picked up a Kleenex from the rug, dropped it into the wastebasket Rose had missed.

Rose sighed. No sooner did she become used to one than Catherine fired her or she quit.

"Help me to the bathroom, please," she said.

This trip was the hardest of the day, since her muscles and joints had stiffened while she slept; but the girl was strong, steady, and kept her mouth shut. Once inside, Rose held on to the safety rail put up when she broke her hip.

"You can step out and shut the door now," she said.

The girl didn't move. "Your daughter said to don't never leave you."

"My daughter's not here, though, is she?" Rose raised one eyebrow and wiggled it, an old trick of hers. She was a beauty, people had said in her day, but also fun. In demand every minute. Her father, a tease, had called her the "Sigma Chi Sweetie," though her hair wasn't gold, her eyes not the blue of the song, and her beaux mostly SAEs and Phi Delta Thetas. Her eyes had been dark and mysterious." Like sapphires, she'd been told.

The girl turned and went out, closing the door behind her. Straight face. No smile.

Back in bed, a cup of steaming coffee in her hand, Rose watched her new companion transfer a small Spode coffeepot from tray to bedside table. The pot was from a breakfast set Rose had forgotten she ever owned.

Nervy of the girl to get it out, though, she thought. And what if she broke it? Well, Catherine wouldn't want those dishes anyway, just because they'd been hers. Might as well use and enjoy them.

"What's your name, new nurse?" she asked.

"Etta. Etta Mae Jones." Slight pause. "You ready for some breakfast?"

Rose had already placed herself for the day. This was her own tester bed in her own house—hers and Allen's, though Allen had been dead for years now. Some days she thought she was back in the country, back in the home of her childhood, in spite of the fact that she knew very well that house was no longer even in the family. At other times, her problem was worse. She'd wake up to find several days had gone by without her knowing anything about it. There would be Monday and Tuesday, then nothing at all until Friday. Wednesday and Thursday would be wiped out completely.

The doctor wouldn't tell her what was wrong with her, if he knew, except that he thought it was age-related. "How old did you say you were?" he would ask, a sudden twinkle in his eyes.

She would look at him, as over the edge of a fan. "I didn't say," she would tell him.

She'd get a new pill of a different color. "Don't worry, sweetheart. You're all right. You could outlive us all."

The tray Etta brought was set with more Spode, and good silver. There was orange juice in a pressed glass tumbler, a soft-boiled egg with toast and crisp bacon. Everything just right, as in the days of trained servants, and Rose was suddenly hungry. Starving.

"Very good!" she said, when Etta came back for the well-cleaned tray. "Thank you." She pointed to the egg cup. "I haven't seen one of these in years. I'm surprised you knew what it was."

Etta looked at her directly. "Mrs. Fitzhugh Greene, that I stayed with so long, wouldn't have her egg no other way," she said.

"But where'd you *find* all these dishes?"

"You don't know?" Tiny night lights seemed to come on in the dark of Etta's eyes. Her face lit up. "You got a jewelry store, right there in your kitchen. All kinds of stuff up in them cabinets. I been with rich folks before, but they didn't have what you got."

Rose had stopped breathing to listen, her mouth half open. "It's old stuff too, some of it," she said. "Handed down in the family. It couldn't be replaced at any price, ever. Besides the sentimental value . . . Did my daughter tell you?"

Across a gulf of sudden silence, they looked at each other. Only their eyes seemed involved.

"You thinking about do I steal," Etta said, unexpectedly.

Rose's mouth went dry. She had no idea what to say.

"You don't have to worry, Mrs. Merriweather." Etta flashed out the words like a switchblade. "I don't take nothing. And on top of that, you don't have nothing I want."

She picked up the tray without rattling a dish, but her mouth was set, her eyes wide open. Holding the tray up protectively, she gave the door to the hall, which stood halfway open, a jab of the hip like a boxer's punch. Without looking back, she sailed out of sight.

Heavens above! Rose thought. How did that come about? And what if she quit? Rose was ready to explain, apologize, beg if necessary. Anything not to lose her.

Down the hall, pots and pans began to rattle. Water ran through pipes. A dishwasher was turned on. When Etta came back, the expression she'd worn from the room had been erased. She picked up a nightgown as if nothing had happened.

So talent was touchy, Rose thought; and now black was touchy too, it seemed.

At last she got up the nerve to ask, "Etta, if there's nothing here that you want, what *do* you want in this world?"

"Nothing in nobody's house," said Etta, her interest obviously leftover and cold by now. Her attention was on all the pill bottles, empty glasses, and neglected laundry scattered about.

"That girl left this place in a mess," she said.

Later in the day, as part of the routine, Rose sat up in a chair. Once settled, she turned her face toward the window. It was October and the leaves outside, though doomed, were still on the trees. Through blue autumn haze, the sky was like the tinted windshield of a car. She sat for a while without speaking, a far-centered look in her eyes.

"You think I'm rich, Etta?" she said at last, her voice like that of an old blues singer, saying a few words on the side. "To tell you the truth, I don't have any money. I've lived so long, I'm sure it's all gone. Catherine hasn't said so yet, but I expect to hear it any day. What will become of me then, I don't know."

Etta didn't waste any time. Empty pill bottles clattered into wastebaskets. Old magazines and newspapers were stacked up and carried out. Nightgowns were checked, refolded, and put back in the drawer. While Etta worked, they talked.

"You don't have no other chirren, just that one girl?"

"That's all. I didn't want any more at the time. My husband did, but I didn't. I should have tried for a boy at least, to carry on the name. What about you?"

"I don't have none at all."

"You didn't want any either?"

"Not unless I was settled down—good husband and all."

"You're not married?"

"That's right."

"No boyfriend?"

"Oh, yeah. I got one of those."

Rose drew a quick half-breath. "I don't guess you could say 'yes, ma'am,' could you? Would that set back the whole Movement?"

The silence that followed was dense with resistance.

"Ah, well," said Rose. "Forget it."

Rose bathed herself sitting up in a chair. In a fresh gown, she watched Etta take away the pan of water and clean up the spills. A bed bath would have been easier on both, but would have cost Rose independence. When Etta had combed and brushed what was left of her hair, she asked for a mirror.

"Time to view the ruins," she said.

Once a day, in a silver mirror with her initials on the back, she looked at herself. As if to hide nothing, she no longer put on makeup. Her hair was drawn back in a thin ponytail. Her face had changed even in shape, had seemed to let go and fall, settling down along the jaw line and pulling everything with it. When she turned her head to the side, she saw jowls. Beneath her chin, loose skin hung like an old stretched sweater. Her eyes, above depressing gray circles, looked out as from a scene of disaster. The eyes themselves, once large and arresting, had shrunk and faded but were still familiar, her lifelong eyes. Her nose too, though thinner and sharper, was the same. Otherwise no trace remained of the vivid girl or dark-haired matron she had been.

All in all, what she saw was a stranger, as much male as female, in whom she was disappearing day by day.

She handed back the mirror in silence.

"You know something?" One morning Rose fixed her eyes on Etta, who was dusting a carved chest of drawers. "The name 'Etta' doesn't suit you. I don't care for that name at all. What if I call you something else, something cute, like *Mari*etta? Or *Henri*etta?"

Etta shook her head as if humoring a child. "Don't make no nevermind to me."

"You could call me 'Miss Rose.'"

Etta straightened up and turned the dust rag over in her hand. "Naw, I just call you Mrs. Merriweather right on," she said. "That other stuff all over with now."

On the mantel a clock began to strike, its measured strokes tamping down a silence that seemed about to fill the room. Rose drew a deep breath.

"I see," she said. "Then you be *Henri*etta. *Mari*etta won't do, with *Mrs. Merri*weather. Too many *M*s."

Each day brought new questions and answers.

"How come your phone don't never ring?"

"Out of sight, out of mind, I guess," Rose said, in a moment. "Also, most of my old buddies don't have phones where they are. . . . My daughter calls up sometimes, doesn't she?"

"Yeah, but she times it to when you be sleep, look like."

"That figures."

"You got two grands. They don't never call?"

"Oh, no. They were turned against me years ago, Henrietta. I could be dead, as far as they're concerned."

As if targeted, their questions and answers moved past ever-decreasing circles of facts.

"You had just that one husband?"

"Yes, just Allen. A lovely man, a cotton broker." Rose gave a deep sigh. "He deserved better than he got from me. For years I was nothing but a butterfly, just here, there, yonder. A husband and child were the least of my worries. Something finally brought me down, but it was a long time coming, I'm afraid."

Henrietta had stopped pushing the dust mop to listen. She looked at Rose. "You must have kept the house nice, though, and all like that, didn't you?"

"Well, I had a full-time cook and a housemaid. But to answer your question, yes. I did keep it nice. I had a flair for decorating —a 'touch,' people said; and I had something to work with. Furniture from my side of the family, and a collection of silver from Allen's. Big tureens on trays, wine coolers, a writing set. Even a pair of silver peacocks." She smiled, remembering. "The house was lovely, if I do say so, and I looked after it religiously. We polished that silver till it all but put your eyes out. My mother used to say, 'Before you sit down to read your Bible, sweep your front porch.'"

Henrietta was grinning. "Where your Bible at now?" she asked.

"Well, where do you want it? Out by my bed for show?"

Henrietta looked down at the mop, moved it absently back and forth. "You pleasured your husband at night, didn't you?"

"Pleasured him?" Rose was taken by surprise. "I guess I did, sometimes."

"You didn't cheat on him, did you?"

She had flirted, Rose thought, with too many; but it was only a game. To test her powers, she supposed. Once, though, it hadn't been flirting, and it hadn't been a game. She didn't answer the question. "I was wild enough, Lord knows," she said, instead. "I was what they called 'fast' back then, a 'fast girl.' Always restless until . . ."

"Unh-uh!" Henrietta interrupted. "Now I know what you was. A flapper!"

Rose laughed. She laughed often now, she'd noticed, and it

made her feel good again. At times, almost happy. Dear, sweet Jesus, she thought in the afterglow, please let her stay. Just let her stay till it's over.

The next day she asked for her lap desk and wrote a note to Catherine. "Dear daughter: I like the new nurse you got me very much. She's the best one I've had so far. Please don't let her go without my consent. I'm doing fine now and don't need a thing. Lots of love, Mama." Her writing was large and shaky, but as carefully legible as a second-grade child's.

Then, without warning, she lost a few days. It was like falling asleep at a concert, except that when she woke up the concert was over and everyone had gone.

All but life itself had been stripped away from her. She had no self and no name. Through mental fog she thought of as hell, she had to get back to the bed in which she lay. Across the room, a chest of drawers appeared like someone from the past, someone she ought to know, saying expectantly, "You know *me*!" She knew nothing. She might have just been born. A blue velvet rocker, with a bathrobe on the back, drew the same kind of blank. Though she shut her eyes tight, tears seeped out and rolled down.

"Look at choo!" The voice was familiar, but she couldn't place it. A hand took hold of hers.

Holding to the hand, Rose opened her eyes. "Oh, God," she said. "God . . ."

The black girl smiled. "You better call on somebody knows you, hadn't you?"

In a flash, the name was back. Henrietta!

"Like who?" Rose said weakly, trying to smile in return. "Who would you suggest?"

Henrietta brought a bowl of homemade soup, a glass of milk, and toast made in the oven. Strengthened, propped up on pillows, Rose waited to hear what had gone on during what she would call, when feeling good, her "temporary demise."

"Your daughter been here," Henrietta said at last. She was sitting in a chair beside the bed.

"Oh? And what did she 'llow?"

"She 'llowed as how we better stop having these spells, or she have to make a change-up."

"Change-up?" Rose looked hard at Henrietta, then lowered her eyes. "Did she say what was wrong with me?"

"It's nothing to say, like I tell you. You comes and goes, and that's it. When you wake up you fine, so quit worrying. Your new style magazine just come. Want to see it?"

"No, thank you."

Henrietta sat on a straight, cane-bottomed chair, a braided wool pad on the seat. Idly, she smoothed the uniform over one compact thigh, then the other. At last she broke the silence. "Your daughter's not good-looking like you was, is she?"

Rose looked up quickly. "What makes you think *I* was good-looking?"

"Because you still got them ways. Airish. And your picture bees out, in different rooms."

"It could be my fault she's not more attractive," Rose said. "I was no mother, to anybody. I was out being the belle of the ball myself. I went off and left her with any black woman who'd sleep on a cot in her room. She has every reason to feel the way she does toward me."

The clock struck seven. It was dark outside. Henrietta got up and drew the curtains, then came back to sit by Rose's bed.

"Some chirren come up worse than that," she said, "and don't blame nobody. Besides, she don't have to be stout, and all like that. You didn't give her them weak-sighted eyes. You don't even wear no glasses."

"Do you know what she remembers most about me, as a child?" Rose fixed her eyes on Henrietta. "A few smells, she says. Gardenias from my corsages. Hot cheese in the canapés I served at parties." She looked down. "Chanel Number Five as I went out the door, then alcohol and cigarettes when I came in her room late at night . . ."

Both were silent, thinking.

Henrietta sighed. "She got a pretty face, though. She could get her some contacts, and fix herself up if she wanted to. Unless she don't care. She got a nice husband, like she is."

"Oh, yes. She's a good wife and mother. Very domestic, wonderful cook. Everything I wasn't."

"You fault yourself too much, Mrs. Merriweather. You all right —a nice lady. Everybody make mistakes in life. You ought to see some I have stayed with. Complaining every minute, couldn't please them for nothing. Your folks just don't know how to preciate you."

"You didn't know me when I was young, though, Henrietta. 'Spoiled' is not the word."

In the matte blackness of her face, Henrietta's eyes began to twinkle. "You had lots of slaves back then?" she asked.

Rose's eyes twinkled dimly in return. "Ho, ho," she said.

She wasn't feeling jolly underneath. The threat of a "change-up" was still in her mind, like the threat of death itself. Both would be coming soon, she knew. Just not tomorrow or the next day, she hoped.

Breakfast was cantaloupe, cheese grits, little sausages, and biscuits. Why so special? Rose wondered. She took her time and enjoyed it all, good food on a pretty tray, thanks in part to Mrs. Fitzhugh Greene, the *late* Mrs. Fitzhugh Greene. "I was with her till she passed," said Henrietta.

As she leaned over to pour a second cup of coffee, Henrietta delivered the news she'd held back overnight.

"She thinking about selling some stuff out the parlor."

Rose was holding the cup in her hand. She set it carefully back on the table by her bed. "What stuff?"

"Furniture. Mirrors."

Rose waited. "No silver?"

"Just furniture, far as I know, and big gold mirrors. Antique lady coming tomorrow. Not to buy, just look."

Rose said nothing. While Henrietta got things ready for her bath—clean gown, towels, bar of English soap—she stared out the window.

"That's Pardue furniture," she said, at last. "My grandfather Pardue lived on a plantation and had twelve children. He had that sofa and chairs made in North Carolina for his wife. They shipped it down by boat, my father said." She paused. "As a child, I loved to sit on that sofa and feel the velvet with my hands. I thought all velvet was that faded blue color."

Henrietta brought a pan of hot water and a fresh bath rag. She tested the water with her fingers and flipped them dry over the pan, not touching Rose's towels.

"Tomorrow, you say?" Rose asked. "Could we keep my door shut? I don't want to see her unless I have to."

"You don't have to do nothing. That's how come I'm here."

For the rest of the day Rose was quiet. All afternoon she lay in the darkening room without turning on a reading light. She couldn't eat her supper when it came.

At bedtime Henrietta brought a cup of Ovaltine and sat down by the bed. "Everything going to be all right," she said, like a spoken lullaby. "She won't do it less she have to, she say. Your money getting low."

"I know," Rose said. "Now run on to bed and let me think."

After breakfast, with Henrietta still in the kitchen, Rose propped herself up in bed without help. When Henrietta came back, she was waiting.

"You know what comes next, don't you?" she asked.

"I'm fixing to cook us some collards. That's what come next. Frost done fell on them now, and they'll be *good*."

"I'll wake up in the nursing home, and you'll be looking for a job."

Henrietta bent down to pick up a pair of bedroom slippers. She placed them neatly by the bed, toes pointing under the mahogany frame.

"We have to be ready, that's all," Rose went on. "So let everything go, and listen. I want you to get something for me out of the bottom of my closet. It's in a round hat box, under an old fur hat. Way back in the back."

She watched Henrietta shoulder her way past the dresses on a rod and begin to set out boxes. Boxes of shoes came first: Delman, Amalfi, Bally, I. Miller. Beside them, Henrietta placed a pair of high-heeled black boots. The tops, lightly dusted with mold, flopped over on the floor. There were dated silver sandals, boudoir pillows rewrapped in gift wrappings, purses stuffed with paper to help hold their shapes, and a large pasteboard box labeled "Letters." Finally, Henrietta brought out the hat box and crushed mink hat. Under the hat was a jewelry case of red Chinese brocade.

"She doesn't know about this," Rose said, untying the cord that held the rolled-up case together. From a pocket-like compartment, she took a charm bracelet heavy with charms, gave it a quick look, and laid it on the bed beside her.

Next came a pair of Victorian earrings of thin yellow-gold. She held them up briefly, shook the fancy dangles.

"Mama wore these in the Seminary," she said, and put them down by the bracelet.

When she took out a round baby locket, she paused. "Ah!" She looked at the dented tooth marks, turned the locket over in her hand, tried to remember what was in it. She would open it later and see, she decided, and laid it down by the earrings.

Last she brought out a ring box of faded morocco. Inside, against a background of what was once white satin, a large square sapphire caught the morning light. The stone, of deep but brilliant blue, was surrounded with diamonds like a frame. When it wouldn't go on the ring finger of her arthritic right hand, a hard push got it over the one on her left. On her hand, with its splotches like bruises and navy-blue veins, she looked at the ring and sighed.

"A man not my husband gave me this, years ago." She held out her hand for Henrietta to see. "I never wore it, wasn't supposed to have it; but he said it was the color of my eyes. . . . He wanted me to marry him, leave Allen."

Henrietta sat like a listening child. "You didn't love him?"

"Oh, yes." Rose looked at her. "I love him today, in his grave. But he was married already, with a wife and three children. And I had my own little family. Our paths didn't cross until too late, that's all."

She took off the ring and slipped it back in its slot. Silence fell like an intermission. Overhead, the sound of a plane grew loud, then faded.

"Wear your ring now," said Henrietta.

"No, I want you to give it to Catherine to sell. It could help, a little." She snapped the box shut. "You can tell her I don't know where it came from. Just say I can't remember."

When Henrietta came back with Rose's noon meal, she was smiling. She put down the tray, adjusted Rose's pillows, and set the tray on her lap. Under a metal warming top, beside a slice of ham, was a bowl of collard greens, dark and shiny from the salt pork cooked in them, not too much but not too little for flavor. There was an ear of boiled corn, a crisp brown cornstick, two spring onions, and a small cruet of hot pepper sauce. A sprig of fresh mint bobbed about on top of a glass of iced tea.

Rose looked at the tray. How many times had she sat down to a meal such as this at her own table? From his place at the head, Allen had served the plates. From the foot, she had seen to seconds, refills, and bread hot enough to melt butter on contact. For this she had rung a silver bell to the right of her plate. And always, as her mother had taught her, she'd tried to make mealtimes pleasant. "Shoot somebody later," her mother had said.

Looking back, she'd done a few things right, Rose thought. She'd stood by Allen till the end and hadn't faltered. She'd watched him go down year after year, no matter what they did or didn't do, and had braced him up as best she could. Though he couldn't speak at the last, his eyes had lit up when she came into the room. It hadn't all been dancing.

"Thank you, Henrietta," she said. "I don't know *when* I've had any collards."

"Give you strength," said Henrietta.

Rose ate collards, cornbread, everything, including a piece of pound cake rich with butter and eggs for dessert. When Henrietta came back for the tray, Rose asked her to sit.

"How long before I 'goes' again, do you think?" she asked.

Henrietta was slow to answer. "Can't nobody tell about that," she said.

"What will become of you?"

"I be taking care of somebody right on. I don't have no trouble finding jobs."

They sat in silence, looking out the window.

"You never told me what you want in this world," Rose said at last. "I'd like to know before we part."

"What I want?" Henrietta frowned. "My mama told me to don't want *nothing,* just take what God send and be thankful." She stood up and took the tray. "Sometime He send a little satisfaction along. I be looking out for that."

Rose propped up on an elbow. "That's what you've been to me," she cried, staring at Henrietta with wide naked eyes. "A satisfaction!" She opened her mouth to say more, but something closed in her throat.

On the tray, dishes began to slide and Henrietta had to stop them. "Nap time," she said quickly, with everything back in place.

Rose watched her leave the room, heard her rubber soles squeak down the hall. The kitchen door swung open and shut.

Rose made her way to the edge of the bed. Careful not to lose her balance, she opened the drawer to the table beside it and took out the jewelry case there.

Inside the locket there was nothing. No picture, baby hair, nothing. As it lay on her palm, she could hear again a fat girl sobbing, bubbles on her braces. "Leave me alone, Mama! You don't care about me. All you want is for me to be alive." And later, the same girl, older and calmer but the same. "Why can't you understand, Mama? I don't want to wear your wedding dress. If Jesus came down and made it fit me, I still wouldn't wear it."

Briefly, Rose looked over the charms on the bracelet. One of her father's cuff links; a gold cross from her grandmother Rose —Rose Lanier St. Clair, she was, a model of virtue but plain; a round disc engraved in old-fashioned script—Rose Pardue, Black Belt Cotton Queen, 1917; an 18K number "1."

Carefully, she put it all back in the drawer.

Stretched out at last, flat on her back except for her head on a pillow, she turned her face toward the window and thought of the blank from which she'd so far returned. A long shudder possessed her. She fought it off with a full deep breath, which she let out by degrees, and fixed her mind on the ring, the furniture, and a possible happy ending. The ring could save the furniture, Catherine could somehow forgive her, then she could forgive herself, and so on.

She didn't hear the doorbell when the antique dealer came, nor Henrietta hurry down the hall to let him in. When, on their way to the parlor, Henrietta looked in before closing the door, Rose was asleep. Pale, thin, neatly covered by the bedspread, she was almost like a wrinkle on the big Pardue bed, something a hand could smooth out.

BIOGRAPHICAL NOTES
STORIES FROM PREVIOUS VOLUMES

BIOGRAPHICAL NOTES

Rick Bass was born and raised in Texas. After college in Utah, he worked for some years in Mississippi as a geologist, and now makes his home in Montana. He has recently published two collections—one of short stories, *The Watch* (Norton, 1989), and one of nonfiction pieces, *Oil Notes* (Houghton Mifflin/Seymour Lawrence, 1989).

Madison Smartt Bell is the author of a collection of short stories, *Zero db*, and five novels, most recently, *Soldier's Joy*. Born and raised in Tennessee, he now lives in Maryland, where he teaches at Goucher College, along with his wife, the poet Elizabeth Spires.

James Gordon Bennett "was born jaundiced and an Army brat" at Ft. Bragg, North Carolina. He attended Johns Hopkins and Stanford, and teaches in the writing program at Louisiana State University in Baton Rouge. His stories have appeared in many magazines and literary quarterlies including *The Antioch Review*, *Quarterly West*, *Western Humanities Review*, and *The Yale Review*.

Larry Brown was born in Oxford, Mississippi, and has worked as a firefighter there for more than fifteen years. His first story collection, *Facing the Music*, was published in 1988 by Algonquin and his first novel, *Dirty Work* is just out, also from Algonquin.

Mary Ward Brown has lived all her life in Alabama. Her collection of short stories, *Tongues of Flame*, received the PEN/Hemingway award in 1987. One of her stories is included in *The Human Experience, Contemporary Soviet and American Fiction and Poetry*, published simultaneously by Alfred A. Knopf in New York and Khudozhestvennya Literatura, a leading publishing house in Moscow, this year.

Kelly Cherry, who teaches at the University of Wisconsin-Madison, was born in Louisiana, spent her early childhood in Ithaca, New York, and

moved to Virginia when she was nine. She has published four novels—
The Lost Traveller's Dream, In the Wink of an Eye, Augusta Played, and
Sick and Full of Burning—and three volumes of poetry. She has received
fellowships from the National Endowment for the Arts and the Wiscon-
sin Arts Board. She was recently a fellow at the Virginia Center for the
Creative Arts.

David Huddle, from Ivanhoe, Virginia, now lives in Burlington, Vermont, and teaches at the University of Vermont and the Bread Loaf
School of English. He is the author of *Paper Boy* and *Only the Little Bone*
and most recently of *Stopping by Home* and *The High Spirits: Stories of Men
and Women.*

Sandy Huss teaches fiction writing in the MFA Creative Writing Program at the University of Alabama at Tuscaloosa. Her stories have appeared in *TriQuarterly, River Styx,* and *Rusty Edge.*

Frank Manley was raised in Atlanta, Georgia, and teaches at Emory
University. He and his wife, Carolyn Holliday, have two children, Evelyn
and Mary, and spend as much time as they can on an old farm in the
mountains of north Georgia. *Within the Ribbons,* a collection of nine of
his short stories, is published this year by North Point Press.

Bobbie Ann Mason grew up on a farm in western Kentucky. After college and graduate school, she spent most of the 1970s teaching journalism
before turning full-time to fiction writing in 1979. Her most recent book
is a collection of stories called *Love Life* (Harper & Row, 1989). She lives
now in Pennsylvania.

Lewis Nordan is the author of two collections of short fiction, *The All-
Girl Football Team* and *Welcome to the Arrow-Catcher Fair,* both recently
released by Vintage Contemporaries, Random House. He is a native of
Itta Bena, Mississippi, and currently teaches at the University of Pitts-
burgh.

Kurt Rheinheimer, a Baltimore native, has lived for the past 14 years in
Roanoke, Virginia, where he serves as editor of *Blue Ridge Country* maga-
zine. His fiction has appeared in many magazines, including *Redbook,
Playgirl, Michigan Quarterly Review, StoryQuarterly,* and *Memphis.*

Mark Richard was born in Lake Charles, Louisiana, and grew up in
Texas, Virginia, and North Carolina. His stories have appeared in *Esquire,
Shenandoah, The Quarterly, Antaeus, Grand Street,* and other magazines.
His first collection, *The Ice at the Bottom of the World,* is published this
year by Alfred A. Knopf, Inc.

Annette Sanford is a native of Cuero, Texas, and now lives with her husband, Lukey, in Ganado, Texas, where she taught high school English for twenty-five years before becoming a full-time writer. Her first collection of short stories, *Lasting Attachments*, is published this year by SMU Press, Dallas.

Paula Sharp's first novel, *The Woman Who Was Not All There* (Harper & Row), about a single woman raising four children in Durham, North Carolina, received the 1988 Joe Savago New Voice Award. She is a translator of Latin American short fiction, and of Antonio Skarmeta's novel, *The Insurrection* (Ediciones del Norte). She works in Manhattan as a public defender.

Shannon Ravenel, the editor, was born and raised in the Carolinas—Charlotte, Camden, and Charleston. After graduating from Hollins College, she went to work in publishing. For the last dozen years, she has served as Series Editor of *The Best American Short Stories* series and, for the last seven, as Senior Editor of Algonquin Books of Chapel Hill. She lives in St. Louis with her husband, Dale Purves, and their two daughters.

STORIES FROM PREVIOUS VOLUMES

1986

BRIDGING, by Max Apple (*The Atlantic*)

TRIPTYCH 2, by Madison Smartt Bell (*The Crescent Review*)

TONGUES OF FLAME, by Mary Ward Brown (*Prairie Schooner*)

COMMUNION, by Suzanne Brown (*The Southern Review*)

THE CONVICT, by James Lee Burke (*Kenyon Review*)

AIR, by Ron Carlson (*Carolina Quarterly*)

SAYS VELMA, by Doug Crowell (*Mississippi Review*)

MARTHA JEAN, by Leon V. Driskell (*Prairie Schooner*)

THE WORLD RECORD HOLDER, by Elizabeth Harris (*Southwest Review*)

SOMETHING GOOD FOR GINNIE, by Mary Hood (*The Georgia Review*)

SUMMER OF THE MAGIC SHOW, by David Huddle (*Grand Street*)

HOLDING ON, by Gloria Norris (*The Sewanee Review*)

UMPIRE, by Kurt Rheinheimer (*Quarterly Review*)

DELIVERY, by W. A. Smith (*FM Five*)

SOMETHING TO LOSE, by Wallace Whatley (*The Southern Review*)

WALLWORK, by Luke Whisnant (*New Mexico Humanities Review*)

CHICKEN SIMON, by Sylvia Wilkinson (*The Chattahoochee Review*)

1987

DEPENDENTS, by James Gordon Bennett (*The Virginia Quarterly*)

EDWARD AND JILL, by Robert Boswell (*The Georgia Review*)

PETER THE ROCK, by Rosanne Coggeshall (*The Southern Review*)

HEROIC MEASURES/ VITAL SIGNS, by John William Corrington (*The Southern Review*)

MAGNOLIA, by Vicki Covington (*The New Yorker*)

DRESSED LIKE SUMMER LEAVES, by Andre Dubus (*The Sewanee Review*)

AFTER MOORE, by Mary Hood
(*The Georgia Review*)
VINCRISTINE, by Trudy Lewis
(*The Greensboro Review*)
SUGAR, THE EUNUCHS,
AND BIG G. B., by Lewis
Nordan (*The Southern Review*)
THE PURE IN HEART, by
Peggy Payne (*The Crescent Review*)
WHERE PELHAM FELL, by
Bob Shacochis (*Esquire*)
LIFE ON THE MOON, by Lee
Smith (*Redbook*)
HEART, by Marly Swick (*Playgirl*)
LADY OF SPAIN, by Robert
Taylor, Jr. (*The Hudson Review*)
ACROSS FROM THE
MOTOHEADS, by Luke
Whisnant (*Grand Street*)

1988

GEORGE BAILEY
FISHING, by Ellen Akins
(*Southwest Review*)
THE WATCH, by Rick Bass (*The Quarterly*)
THE MAN WHO KNEW
BELLE STARR, by Richard
Bausch (*The Atlantic*)

FACING THE MUSIC, by
Larry Brown (*Mississippi Review*)
BELONGING, by Pam Durban
(*The Indiana Review*)
GAME FARM, by John Rolfe
Gardiner (*The New Yorker*)
GAS, by Jim Hall (*The Georgia Review*)
METROPOLITAN, by Charlotte
Holmes (*Grand Street*)
LIKE THE OLD WOLF IN
ALL THOSE WOLF
STORIES, by Nanci Kincaid
(*St. Andrews Review*)
ROSE-JOHNNY, by Barbara
Kingsolver (*The Virginia Quarterly Review*)
HALF-MEASURES, by Trudy
Lewis (*Carolina Quarterly*)
FIRST UNION BLUES, by Jill
McCorkle (*Southern Magazine*)
HAPPINESS OF THE
GARDEN VARIETY, by
Mark Richard (*Shenandoah*)
THE CRUMB, by Sunny Rogers
(*The Quarterly*)
LIMITED ACCESS, by Annette
Sanford (*The Ohio Review*)
VOICE, by Eve Shelnutt (*The Chariton Review*)